Logans Lethal Lessons

By Grant Heming

Grant Heming

I am dedicating this story to all the friends, family, and close neighbors who continue to inspire me to be the best version of myself. I also want to specifically mention the names of many of the characters in this story including Jacob, Dare, Karoline, Jared, Kamren, Armando, Payton, Jarret, Lindsey, Gracie, Jason, Jim, Dylan, Chloe, Mom, Dad, and many more.

Grant Heming

This book is a work of fiction. All of the characters, incidents, settings, are purely fiction, except for the few references of public figures and other incidents, are imaginary. Any resemblance to actual resemblance to any realistic events, works, or businesses is purely coincidental.

No part of this book may be reproduced in any form or by any electronic or mechanical means, including information storage and retrieval systems, without permission from the author, except for the use of brief quotations in a book review.

"Nothing is easier than denouncing the evildoer. Nothing is more difficult than understanding him."- Fyodor Dostoyevsky.

Grant Heming

Logans Lethal Lessons

Table of Contents

Chapter 1
Ozone Mist- 11

Chapter 2
Jessica's Birthday- 29

Chapter 3
Overdosed- 49

Chapter 4
Joe Walker- 63

Chapter 5
The Witness- 87

Chapter 6
What just happened?- 96

Chapter 7
Jason Clark- 109

Chapter 8

The Pig Farm- 130

Chapter 9

Seeing Things Differently- 147

Chapter 10

I'm Moving Out- 165

Chapter 11

We can't- 179

Chapter 12

Last Day of School- 195

Chapter 13

What am I doing?- 211

Chapter 14

I'm going to finish this- 227

Chapter 15

A War on Drugs- 246

Chapter 16

House Hunting- 266

Chapter 17

Mister Mist- 282

Chapter 18

New Beginnings- 293

Grant Heming

Chapter 1

Ozone Mist

One of the harshest rules in life is the fact that every day people are forced into making choices in life. Some of these choices have very little thought or need for it. Sometimes people are forced into making difficult decisions that may continue to weigh on them until the end of their days, things they wish they could undo, but can't.

Regardless of whatever choices we make in our lives, one thing is for certain; everyone will be forced to live with the choices and decisions that they've made during their time on Earth. but they will also be forced to live with the consequences. For example, right now, I'm being forced to live with the repercussions of choosing my best friend, Jacob Breland, as my teammate on our two-person team in our pool game inside the game room at Eastcliff State College.

Our game-room offered a variety of different activities including video games, board, and card games, ping-pong sets, even air hockey, but the one activity I think my friends and I find most enjoyable when we're stressed over our classes or whatever else life had to offer us was a good-old fashioned game of eight-ball pool, at least when we had the free time.

Normally, Jacob served as a worthy rival when he and I played against each other one-on-one, but truth be told, that's because we both equally sucked at it. Don't get me wrong, every now and then we both have days where we are focused enough to actually put effort and slaughter the other. Frankly, it's actually a rare thing for the both of us to be teamed up together when we play on teams. The first time was freshman year, back when Jacob and I first met our friend Andrew Wallace, or as we commonly know him as Andy and Jessica Kennedy, who is now my girlfriend.

On the days that we got out of class early, the four of us would come down here and team-up to fight off the others. Admittedly, Jessica could easily beat Jacob and I when we would play cut-throat (or a three-person game) and Andy could beat all three of us, which is why it was fun when I was on his team.

But as time goes on, so do the great pool players such as Andy, who graduated last year and Jessica, Jacob, and I were about to do the same within the coming weeks. We all have our final exams coming up next week as we all have had to prepare for the fact that we're all about to enter the next chapter of our lives, which is more or less disturbing than the thought that one test has the ability to determine whether or not we graduate.

After finishing up our classes for the day, Jacob and I met up and decided to hangout in the game-room and do a little one-on-one. Unfortunately, there were only so many sets and tables to do for a college campus with thousands of students. As we went inside to see who all was in there, we saw several of our friends, including Jarrett Weldon and Nathaniel Figgures.

Jarrett is actually one of my oldest friends. We've known each other since we were in elementary school. After he was held back one year, he eventually graduated from high school and followed me to the same college and, surprisingly, a similar field. I'm a criminal justice major with the intent on becoming a police officer and eventually becoming a crime scene investigator. Jarrett has plans to become a lawyer, more than likely a corporate attorney at a fancy law firm, but who knows for certain where we'll actually end up.

Nathaniel, on the other hand, is someone I met during my freshman year of college. We met right here in the game-room, one of the places he frequents when he wasn't in class. Nathaniel is an African American twenty-three-year-old who, like me, had a goatee, even if his was a slightly different style. He was studying to become an accountant and was on the verge of graduating with us. When he wasn't wearing fancy clothing for his classes, he almost always had on the same red jacket and a wide pair of glasses and remains one of the friendliest people you could ever meet.

"What's up, bro?" he asked setting aside his pool-stick as he saw the two of us walk in. He then greeted us both with a fist-bump.

"You know how it is, man. Finals week is upon us once again," I said. He sighed as his smile began to fade.

"Dude, I know. I got three on the same day!" he said, sounding very stressed.

"Jeez. That's rough," said Jacob, beginning to lean against the table as I began to lean against the wall.

"Well, look on the bright side. It'll be the last time we have to worry about finals, three of us at least. Sorry, Jarrett," I pointed out. I looked at Jarrett as he sat down with a smile, not even raising his hand as he extended his middle finger towards me.

"Are you ready for yours?" asked Jacob, looking back at Nathaniel.

"Bro, I got Advanced Accounting and Cost Accounting, but I'm not worried about that one. It's the Auditing and Attesting with the Accounting Info-systems that's got me stressed out," he stated as he picked his stick and shot the white cue ball at the yellow-striped number nine ball on the table.

The ball continued to bounce towards a bunch of other balls bunched together, knocking in only one of his intended targets in a hole. I admit that I tried to focus my attention on his sporting skills rather than trying to focus or understand whatever kind of accounting work he said he had to deal with. Either way, I sympathized with him. "What about you guys?"

"Well, I don't have one for interning. I can easily ace the Methods of Teaching and Assessment and Curriculum. The only one that's really going to be a challenge is Principles and Methods of Teaching," claimed Jacob.

"What about you, Logan?" he asked me before taking another shot, when I wasn't really paying attention.

"I got an essay in American Music, which is basically a guaranteed hundred, especially since I've already finished it. Spanish for Criminal Justice is easy and online. So, all I really have to worry about is Senior Capstone for Criminal Justice and Advanced Criminological Theory. The good news is that the theory exam will be about an hour and a half before the Capstone final, so I'll have some time to study before that one."

"Dang, it still sounds rough," said Nathaniel.

"Well, theory is just theory, so…" I started, before shrugging it off. "What about you Jarrett?"

The three of us looked towards where Jarrett was sitting. However, to our surprise, he looked as though he was only seconds away from falling asleep.

"Dude, I think he's out," said Jacob with half a grin on his face, still looking somewhat surprised.

"Whatever, who wants to take his place?" asked Nathaniel.

"I don't care," said Jacob, looking at me.

"I got an idea," said Nathaniel, going over to Jarrett, who was still relaxing before grabbing his pool stick. "Why don't you guys, just take turns? That way, when I whoop both of you guys, it'll be like a double victory."

"Alright," I said as I took his stick and started shooting. Jacob and I started to take turns, but as we continued to shoot, we found that we were both losing by three balls. Jacob grabbed the stick from me, starting to look more determined. Despite the determination all over his face, he accidentally shot the cue ball towards the door we had just passed through.

"Easy there, compadre," I told him as Nathaniel started looking startled.

"Oh, you should talk," Jacob said. "At least I've never shot it on another table."

"Here he goes again," I mumbled under my breath.

"What?" asked Nathaniel.

"Okay, so check this out, man. It was the beginning of our second-year here. We come in here, to this same table playing against each other," started Jacob, looking and pointing towards the table adjacent to ours next to me. "...Logan shoots the cue ball off this table onto that one when two other guys are playing, without even touching any of the balls on the table and sinking it into their corner pocket."

"For real?" asked Nathaniel, looking quite mind-blown. I did everything I could to keep myself from laughing. I couldn't find it to face him and simply nodded. "That's crazy."

After a few more shots and a couple of close comebacks, I'm ashamed to confess that Nathaniel had defeated both of us by a single ball lead.

"Alright. Congrats, big man," I said as I patted him on the back and handed Jacob my stick.

"What about you, Jarrett. Want to get beat again?" asked Nathaniel as we saw Jacob was completely unconscious.

"He's out," said Jacob. Nathaniel and I walked over to him. I kicked Jarrett's leg as a way to wake him up, but he seemed unresponsive.

"Jarrett," I called out as I slapped his arm, realizing he still wasn't waking up and starting to become a little concerned for our friend.

"Dude, come on," said Nathaniel, beginning to slap his face rather hard.

I felt my heart begin to race as I wasn't sure what was actually going on with our friend. Jacob began to look a little concerned as we continued our attempts to wake up Jarrett. After a heated slap to his face courtesy of my right hand, Jarrett finally began to open his eyes and relief began to shower over the three of us, as well as the others in the game room, who also began to look concerned.

"What? What's going on?" asked Jarrett, acting like he'd just woken up from a several-day long nap.

"We were trying to get your attention and thought you were dead, man," claimed Jacob. Jarrett scratched the back of his head as he saw everyone staring at him. He scoffed.

"Nah, man. I'm good," he stated with a smile on his face. We continued to stare at him for another moment, as I began to notice that his eyes were abnormally red.

"What's with your eyes?" I asked as I stared at his eyes. On a normal day, his eyes were as blue as the sky, but today those blue eyes looked bloodshot.

I think it would've been easy to make a few assumptions based on

Jarrett's behavior and eyes, but this seemed a little darker than your average stoner. Jacob walked over and sighed.

"You're doing Ozone, aren't you?" Jacob asked. Jarrett looked quite startled by Jacob's accusation, even though I really didn't understand what he meant. Jarrett quickly reverted back into his cool and chilled state of mind.

"Nah, man. I don't do that stuff. You know me," he claimed. I looked over to Jacob, who didn't look too amused or convinced by his friend.

"Oh my God, dude," said Nathaniel, listening and realizing that he'd apparently been getting involved with Ozone the whole time he'd been with us. "Dude, you can't be doing that shit, bro."

"You're lying," accused Jacob as Jarrett continued to lie back in the chair as we surrounded him.

"I'm telling you, bro. I'm good," Jarrett claimed, trying to play-off both of Jacob and Nathaniel's concerns as if they were no big deal. I had never heard of this "Ozone," but if it was making Jarrett behave this way, I knew that it couldn't be good.

"You're not good. Your eyes are freaking red. They look like popped blood vessels. We seriously just thought you had overdosed a minute ago," Nathaniel claimed.

"Come on. You're over-exaggerating, man," Jarrett said, beginning to sound like he was under the influence of something.

"We were really concerned, man," I told him, trying to convince him of the apparent seriousness of the matter. He glanced over to me, looking confused, even though he still had a smile on his face.

"Exagger…Ager…Ager the badger," he started to say, before he started laughing, as if someone had told him the funniest joke he'd ever heard. I admit that if I wasn't as concerned as I was, I may have found his state of mind quite amusing.

"How the hell are you going to be a lawyer if you're as high as fucking Willie Nelson at Woodstock?" asked Jacob. Jarrett looked at us, knowing he didn't have any answers, and it was becoming more and more clear that he wasn't in any real position to be able to give any kind of clear or concise answer. Jacob then glanced over at Nathaniel. "Did you give it to him?"

"Hey, you know I never touch that kind of shit," he immediately defending himself as Jacob looking at me.

"Don't look at me. All I'm going on is the context clues of your conversation," I said, as Jacob looked disappointed at our mutual friend.

"Who gave you the Ozone?" asked Jacob as Jarrett went back to his dumbfounded look. Jacob sighed.

"Can you do me a solid and keep an eye on him for a little bit?" he asked Nathaniel. He nodded as he signaled me that it was time to leave. "We'll be back for him in a few minutes."

"Where are we going?" I asked, wondering how I managed to fit into his grand plan.

"Well, we're going to go find Krista so I can explain to her why we're going to have Jarrett in the back of my car while he's whacked out on drugs on our way home because it's clear that he's in no shape to drive," Jacob stated as I looked back at Jarrett. He was right, that much was obvious. Jarrett had no business driving home while under the influence. After we left the game room, there wasn't a word said between the two of us as we continued walking. I saw how frustrated Jacob looked, which for him was a very rare look indeed.

"Hey, what the hell was he on?" I finally asked him.

Without giving even a single glance my way, he answered, "It's called Ozone Mist."

"I've never heard of Ozone Mist," I said, as he looked at me quite shocked.

"What? Really?" Jacob asked as he stopped walking.

"Really," I told him.

"I'm surprised, especially considering that you're the one who's going into law enforcement. It's like the new drug nowadays. It's been in the news a lot," Jacob explained, as he raised an eyebrow.

"Well, you know that I don't like to watch that shit," I reminded him.

"Yeah, but that is the garbage that's been giving the cops hell. People use that shit as a new form of release. It's supposedly really addictive," he continued to explain. I found it rather interesting that he knew so much about the drug before an actual criminologist.

"You seem to know a lot about it," I pointed out.

"Yeah. Well, after I caught some bums outside my work that nearly overdosed, I read something about it on the internet," Jacob explained.

"Is it dangerous?" I asked. "I mean, obviously most illegal drugs are considered bad, but…"

"Compared to the average drug, it's supposed to affect everyone differently and it depends on how much you use."

"Like alcohol?" I asked.

"Sort of. I mean, it's kind of hard to explain," he said as he began to scratch the back of his head, trying to think of the right words to explain.

"Try, if you don't mind," I insisted, as he began to look uneasy.

"Well, my understanding of the concept is that it depends on your state of mind once you've taken it. Like, when you're stressed out, it's harder for it to take effect. The more you take, the more you become addicted, and after doing it again and again, that's when people are more likely to use too much," Jacob claimed.

"How? Are they just trying to make the next fix better than the last?" I asked.

"Well, they call it 'Ozone Mist' because once you've taken the actual pill, you leave it in your mouth and let it dissolve. The aroma, or mist, of the drug is how it fucks you up. You can smoke it, you can just enjoy it inside your head, but it'll mess you up all the same."

"But you said in there that Jarrett had used it before, right?" I inferred. Jacob continued to look rather uneasy as he nodded for confirmation.

"I caught him with it once. He said he was planning on quitting, but you saw how fucked up he was in the game room. There's no way he's off the stuff," Jacob claimed.

"Do you think he's going to be okay?" I asked.

"Oh, him? He'll hopefully be alright as long as someone keeps an eye on him. The problem is what happens when someone isn't looking out for him. I mean, the way you saw him acting, that's normal for those who partake of the Mist, but if he accidentally takes too much, he's going to…" started Jacob as he slid his finger across his throat to indicate that our friend was at a serious risk of dying.

"Well, obviously, we can't just force him to go to rehab," I told him.

"Well, his family and his girlfriend probably don't even know that he's using. I've had my suspicions, but I wasn't sure until I found it on him. He's been smart about hiding it so far," Jacob informed me.

"Yeah, but if he uses too much, they'll be forced to figure it out the hard way," I couldn't help but think out loud, hoping it wouldn't come to that.

"Yeah, I know. That's why I'm going to drop him off at his house and try to convince him to get help over the summer when he sobers up," Jacob told me.

"Do you think you'll be able to get through to him? I mean, he's always been a stubborn son of a bitch," I reminded him. Jacob sighed again.

"I don't know, but I hope so," said Jacob as the two of us approached, our beloved girlfriends, Jessica Kennedy and Krista Bridges. The two ladies waved at us as he began to lean over to whisper something to me privately. "Logan, please tell me you didn't forget what today is."

"It's Tuesday," I told him, as Jacob started looking quite concerned. I began to smile as I patted him on the back. "I'm kidding. Yes, I know what today is."

"Hey," greeted Krista as she gave Jacob a hug. Even though it was clear that Jacob wasn't in a very good mood at that moment, he responded to her loving gesture with a similar one in return, with an attempted smile on his face.

"Hi," I said to Jessica as I couldn't help but grin and kiss her on the cheek. "Happy Birthday."

"Thank you, baby," she said.

"Hey, Jess. Happy Birthday," said Jacob, who looked like he was trying to fake his happy face a little harder because it was Jessica's birthday. He hugged her, but I think it was painfully clear that something was amiss with him.

"Thanks, Jake. What are you guys up to?" Jessica asked.

"Well, we were actually on our way to find you guys," I said as I patted Jacob on the back.

"Yeah? It looks like we found you first," said Krista, smirking.

"That is debatable, especially considering we walked up to you," I pointed out.

"Or maybe we just wanted you to think that," Jessica continued to pointlessly argue, much to my own amusement.

"Unless we just wanted you to think what you thought we had thought and I'm going to stop before this goes any further," I said as I let out a small chuckle.

"That's probably the smartest thing you've ever done," claimed Jacob to me as he turned to Jessica. "So, do you have any special plans for your big day?"

"Yeah. My family, Logan, and I are going out to dinner tonight at Heaven's Harmony," she answered.

"Oh, fancy," Jacob said with a smile.

"You guys are more than welcome to come if you want. Logan's buying," Jessica claimed as she patted me on the back. I sighed and looked down in shame at the thought of how fast Jessica would soon have me bankrupt.

"Oh, I wish we could, but I have to work tonight," said Jacob, as Krista began shaking her head, indicating she had the same problem. Jacob began looking at her, less than thrilled, subliminally trying to tell her that they had to go. "But we will be thinking of you tonight."

"Okay," Jessica responded.

"Well, I need to borrow Krista for a little while, but I hope you two have fun and I hope you enjoy the rest of your birthday," stated Jacob.

"Thank you," Jessica responded with a smile, giving him a grateful hug.

"I'll see you later. Have fun tonight," stated Krista as the two began walking away, and Jessica lost part of her smile as she looked at me.

"Thanks, see ya!" said Jess as the two of them continued on their way.

"So, how's your day going?" I asked her.

"It's going alright. The lecture in ecotoxicology was boring as hell, but the research lab was fun with the turtles. So, all in all, it's been pretty good," Jessica responded.

"That's good because I promise I'm going to do everything I can to make the rest of the day nothing short of great. Look at me. We're going to go the whole nine yards with this! You got it," I said, sounding so ridiculously stern that I knew it would be impossible to actually be taken seriously.

"Thanks, Logan," she said as she began laughing. We began holding hands as we took the long half-mile walk to our cars.

"So, Jacob seemed to be in a cheerful mood, today," stated Jessica sarcastically. I sighed.

"Yeah, don't take it personally. He's having a rough day," I explained.

"I could tell, but I've never seen him so calm or down. It was kind of like almost like a scary quiet, for him. Usually Krista and I end up begging for one or both of you to shut up. What's wrong with him? Or is it something you shouldn't talk about?" Jessica asked, sounding concerned. Although I didn't know if it was my business to actually mention Jarrett's problem, I figured that Jessica would at least serve as another helping hand should we force Jarrett into an intervention.

"Well, no. It's nothing like that. It's just that one of our friends, a guy I've known since we were little...well, you know my friend Jarrett, right?" I asked.

"Yeah," she answered.

"Well, we were all hanging out and he just passed out, like out of nowhere, and when he woke up he was acting weird. Apparently, he's been doing some sort of new drug, and it's not the first time that he's done it, either," I told her. She raised an eyebrow as she began to look rather concerned.

"It's not that Mist stuff, is it?" she asked. I stood frozen for a moment as I was confused by the fact that she also knew more about it than I did. It seemed as though everyone knew about this Ozone Mist except me. Had I really just failed to notice it on the news, or had I somehow found myself living under a rock for a while without even realizing it?

"How could you possibly know that?" I asked her. She stopped and looked at me as she put her hand on my cheek, giving me a sympathetic smile.

"Well, for starters, I'm smart, baby," she pointed out as she gently patted my cheek. It was a point that I couldn't disagree with. "I also work at a pharmacy, remember? Not to mention that it has been in the news and on the internet for a couple of months."

"Well, apparently I haven't been paying any attention considering I hadn't heard of it until just a few minutes ago," I told her.

"Well, according to Daddy, that shit has been creating a real problem," Jessica claimed.

"Your father is working on the case?" I asked, sounding more interested.

"Yeah, Daddy's been trying to put a stop to Ozone Mist for a while. Dozens of people have already overdosed on it, with no sign of stopping anytime soon. He's been working a bunch of nights and it's really been stressing him out," she told me.

"That sucks. Do you know if he's going to be able to make it to dinner, tonight?" I asked.

"He said this morning that he was going to try, but it wouldn't be the first birthday that he's missed," she said, looking rather disappointed. Given that I just promised I'd try to make her birthday perfect, I felt like I was off to a bit of a rough start.

"Well, I'm sure he's always tried to be there," I told her. I knew her father. He could be stern and dedicated to his work, but I also knew that he worked as hard as he did because he wanted to keep his hometown safe for his family.

"Oh, I know. If he isn't, he'll find a way to make it up to me. He always has, same with Dalton, Nicky's, or Mom's," she explained, bringing half her smile back. A step in the right direction, but I knew she deserved better from her boyfriend.

"Well, if he isn't there. I promise I'll make it twice as fun…one for him and one for me," I assured her.

"I don't really think that's how it works, but who said you were even invited?" she asked as she tried to keep herself from giggling.

"Well, I would hope that I would be invited," I informed her.

"Nope, sorry. You didn't make the cut," she claimed, acting like she had been breaking awkward bad news my way. I knew she was joking, but I knew even on her birthday, I wasn't going to let her win this game.

"Well, that's too bad, especially after I went out of my way to get you such a nice gift," I told her.

"What?" she asked, looking rather interested.

"Well, it doesn't matter if I'm not invited, does it?" I pointed out, looking up as if I were pouting.

"I didn't mean it," she said rather quickly, almost to the point where I almost started to laugh.

"Nope, you've done made me mad," I said as I crossed my arms, looking at her; acting still frustrated.

"Fine, then pitch a fit about it," she stated as though she wasn't going to let me get the upper hand in the kind of mind games we were playing with each other.

"I will," I informed her as I couldn't help but let out half a grin. It was only a second afterwards that we both ended up laughing. As we continued walking and talking, one of my former professors began making her way towards the two of us. I was hoping that she would continue to walk past us, hoping to avoid a conversation. Unfortunately, I wasn't that lucky.

"Hello, Logan," said Professor Sampson, who stopped to speak with me.

"Hi, professor. How's it going?" I asked, trying to fake a smile, feeling it was the only thing to say.

"Alright. How about you?" she asked.

"Fine. Thank you," I said, doing everything I could to ensure that the conversation would stay short. Despite my best efforts to ensure that Jessica and I kept walking, Jessica completely stopped in order to have a friendly conversation with the professor.

"Are you both ready for your finals?" she asked.

"Yep," I mumbled, still trying to a fake smile. Jessica nodded as well.

"Good. Just think, you both only have a few more days of college," Sampson stated.

"Mm-hmm. We're counting down the days," Jessica stated with a smile.

"Well, best of luck to both of you," she said with a smile.

"Thank you," I said as she continued to walk past the two of us. I then wrapped my arm around Jessica as we continued on our own way.

"Ugh. I hate that lady," I whispered as we walked past her.

"Why? What did she ever do to you?" she asked with half a smile, looking back at me.

"That's my English professor from last semester," I explained as I couldn't help but glance back at the professor.

"I take it you have no intention of recommending her to any future students, then?" Jessica assumed.

"Not likely. She was a hardcore bitch," I told her.

"How?" she asked, seemingly shocked by my statement for whatever reason.

"Well, she was just usually stuck-up and rude," I told her.

"Well, she seemed polite, but I could definitely see it," said Jessica, looking back at the professor's dress and heels. Even the way she was walking indicated she was a high-maintenance bitch.

"Let me put it to you this way, she was so bad that one of my friends dropped her class after a week. Part of me just wanted to hit her upside the head with a baseball bat, but only part of me."

"That seems a little extreme, doesn't it? Maybe just a little bit?" she asked, looking a tiny bit disturbed.

"Oh, relax. It's not like I've ever had any real desire to harm her. Okay, at least not enough to leave any kind of permanent damage," I stated with a smile.

"Good. You're not smart enough to get away with murder, baby. I don't care how many law classes you've taken," Jessica stated with a smile.

"Thanks for the confidence, but I suppose you're right," I tried to say convincingly. I tried even harder to appreciate the irony of her statement.

"Besides, I don't know what I would do if you were caught doing something that awful," she stated as she began to lean on my arm as we continued walking.

"Well, fortunately, you'll never have to find out," I told her with a smile. Especially considering the fact that I've already gotten away with taking the life of a human being, and on more than one occasion.

Chapter 2

Jessica's Birthday

Now, I know what you're probably thinking. This guy was involved in a murder? He seems like such a nice guy. In what kind of world could he possibly have it in himself to take the life of anybody. Unfortunately, the answer is this world. Although, in my defense, the situation was a little more complicated than that.

My name is Logan Mills. I am from a small town in the northern part of Georgia called Rockgate. I also attend Eastcliff State College, which is roughly thirty miles from home. After four years of hard work and dedication, I am only a few pesky final exams away from graduating with a Bachelor's degree with some of my closest friends. Ironically, my degree is in Criminal Justice.

But I'm sure that you're not really interested in little old me, especially when murder has somehow found its way into the mix. I always wanted to use what I've learned in my college classes to make the world a better place because all I've ever really wanted to do was help people. Unfortunately, life is a little bit more complicated than that. Almost six months ago, I wanted to use my specific skill set to try to help bring in a serial killer roaming the streets of Rockgate called the Boulevard Butcher. At least that's what the media and police called him. The Butcher had brutally slain his victims and dumped their dead bodies on the side of the road, like a cigarette butt or a common piece of trash.

For weeks, the Butcher's spree continued on, and the local and state police had been stumped. In one of my classes, I was told to report on the killer based on what the authorities already knew, or suspected at least. I used this information and found out that the reason the killer couldn't be stopped was because the police were looking for more than one killer, they just didn't know it. This was a group of killers who were smart enough to alibi themselves.

After I stumbled on the group in the middle of a murder, they chased me down the streets. I barely managed to get away from them. Despite my best efforts, one of them, a man named Ryan Bailey, found me and attacked me. As he did everything he could to kill me, I managed to overpower Bailey and stabbed him with his own knife, in self-defense.

In a moment of sheer panic, I ran away and decided to let his associates clean-up the mess for me. The stress and guilt over just thinking about what I'd done was almost too much to bear. After that horrible night, I did everything I could think of to try to forget everything that had happened, even resulting in some less than wise choices and distractions to ease myself of the guilt, never expecting what was to come next.

The very next night, two homicide detectives, one of whom was Jessica's father, Detective David Kennedy, who had helped me with my original research on the Butcher arrived at my doorstep and told me my father had become the Butcher's latest victim. I figured the Butchers must've seen my father and thought he was the one who interrupted their murder, killed Bailey, and decided to take his life in retaliation.

Consumed with so much anger and guilt, I decided to end the Boulevard Butchers in my own way, once and for all. I hunted down the head of the group, a man by the name of Arthur Phillips. After he confessed to being the one who killed the majority of victims, including my father, I thought about all the lives he'd taken and how many people he'd hurt. I also thought of how many people he would hurt until he was stopped. I found something deep and dark within myself and finished it. I admit that it was an overwhelming, bittersweet feeling that still continues to haunt me.

The other murderer in the group was a man named Mason Thomas. I decided that it would be more appropriate for Thomas to go to prison for his crimes and the crimes of the group than to take his life. Unfortunately, both Bailey and Phillips have gone down in history as poor and innocent victims, I suppose serving up Thomas as the only killer was better than nothing, especially when my life was also on the line.

Since then, I've tried to put my ghosts to bed and move on with my life by doing what my father would've wanted…for me to try to make the world a better place. As for my guilt and shame in the knowledge of my past dark deeds, I've learned to simply live with them. It still hurts like hell from time to time, but I allow myself to endure it as my own personal penance. Although there are times when those feelings of regret begin to overwhelm me, I manage to cope with feeling regret or remorse over what I'd done by thinking about the pain that Phillips and Bailey had inflicted on their victims and the families of their victims, including my own. I then begin to think about how many people I have saved from a similar fate, and the burden becomes easier to carry.

I mean, how many more people would've been found on the side of the street butchered if I hadn't gotten involved in the first place? One? Ten? Fifty? Fortunately, like how many licks does it take to the center of a tootsie pop, the world will never likely know that answer. From a certain point-of-view, I'm sure I could argue that I did make the world a better place, not to make excuses or defend my dark actions, but just to end their reign of terror.

After all the excitement with Arthur Phillips and his cronies, I have tried to focus more on my studies in order to graduate with my friends within the next couple of weeks. I have just recently applied to the summer police academy in Rockgate and continued to build on a healthy relationship with my girlfriend, Jessica Kennedy, hoping that with her love and support, I may be able to bury the darker parts of my life, for good.

But as she mentioned earlier, tonight was her birthday dinner, and I had every intention of ensuring that it was as special as she deserved. After departing from her at school, I went home to relax before it was time to meet her family. As the afternoon quickly turned into early evening, I knew I'd soon have to get ready.

I knew we were going to a fancier place than anywhere I was really used to dining and thought it best to dress the part. I decided to wear one of my nicer buttoned short-sleeved shirts with a nice clean pair of jeans. I made sure to make sure that my hair was appropriately clean and combed.

After getting ready, I made my way to the restaurant, incidentally getting there a few minutes early and found myself waiting for Jessica and her family to arrive. I waited in my car and listened to one of my CD's and got out to greet them when I saw their vehicle pull into the parking lot of the restaurant. Jessica smiled when she saw me.

"Hey, baby," I told her as I kissed her on her cheek. As she walked past me, I saw her mother with her children getting out of the car. I held the door for them as we made our way into the restaurant.

"Ladies," I said as I greeted them inside.

"Thank you," said her mother with a smile as her daughter walked behind her.

"Since when are you such a gentleman?" asked Jessica's sister, Nicky, with a smile on her face and a raised eyebrow.

"Honestly, about thirty-four minutes ago, give or take a few seconds," I told her as she walked in the restaurant as I heard her scoff. Following the ladies came Jessica's brother, Dalton, accompanied by his girlfriend Andrea.

"Ladies," I repeated, as they approached me. Andrea walked through first as Dalton walked past, returning my courtesy with a grateful smile and his middle finger extended my way until he was inside. As we made our way inside, I realized that their father wasn't there and figured he wouldn't likely be joining us for dinner based on Jessica's previous assumptions. I decided not to mention that observation, knowing it could be considered a sore subject for them.

"Yeah, you can shut the door, man. Dad probably isn't coming," remarked Dalton, looking disappointed. I only thought of the irony of how I barely even had time to process my thought before it was brought up.

"He did say that he was going to try to make it," interrupted Jessica, trying her best to defend their father. I didn't know if it was denial, but I figured she was entitled to as much on her birthday.

"He's said that, before," pointed out Dalton.

"That's enough, you two," said Mrs. Kennedy.

"So, Logan? How does it feel…knowing you're about to from graduate college?" Dalton asked me as we were being taken to our table.

"Well, it's a little overwhelming to be completely honest," I said. I took a deep breath as I thought of everything that'd happened over the past four years. All the people I'd met, all the memories made; to think that this huge part of my life was coming to an end just seemed so unreal.

"Not that you'd know," interrupted Nicky.

"Why is everyone picking on me all of a sudden?" asked Dalton.

"It's Jessica's birthday. She said it was okay," claimed Nicky. Dalton looked confused as Andrea made her way back to his side.

"It's okay, baby. I won't let them bully too much," she stated.

"Thank you," he replied, with a grin on his face.

"…without me," she finished. His grin quickly faded. He simply stood frozen for a moment as I patted him on the back. I don't know if he could tell, but I had a hard time not laughing at him.

"I think you've found your soulmate," I said, as he scoffed. The waitress finally showed us to our table. A large round table with eight chairs underneath. I was given the honor of sitting next to the birthday girl, who sat next to her sister. Dalton sat in between me and Andrea, with an empty chair next to Mrs. Kennedy and another next to Andrea.

It wasn't long before the waitress came to take our drink orders. Before she had the opportunity to finish, Jessica's father, David, walked in as though he was rushing. He made his way to our table. It was clear that he'd come straight from work because he was wearing his normal white shirt and tie that he would wear at the Rockgate Police Station, where he worked as a detective, primarily on homicides.

"Sorry, I'm late," he said, as bumped into the waitress, making his way to the seat, directly across from mine and Jessica's. "Oh, I'm so sorry."

The waitress ignored it and smiled, but I could tell it was a practiced smile, as he sat down in front of her and ordered the exact same thing that his wife had, without even glancing at the menu or asking what she'd gotten. As the waitress walked away, David walked to the other side of the table and hugged Jessica and kissed her forehead.

"I am so sorry that I am late. Traffic was crazy," he said, looking rather apologetic.

"At least you're here," she said with a smile as he turned to me.

"Logan, it's nice to see you," he said as he shook my hand with a tight grip.

"You too, sir," I said, as I returned the gesture with a smile, before he sat back down next to his wife.

As far as the average relationship between a boyfriend and the girlfriend's father, I'd like to think that David and I get along better than most. For the most part, he's always seemed to approve of my relationship with Jessica. He's also given me advice when it was needed regarding possible future careers in law enforcement, from time to time.

The only real problem was that, because he truly was good at his job, I'd always been afraid of the possibility that one day he would put the pieces together of what really happened in the Boulevard Butcher case. He had already confessed his suspicions about the timing of the case's conclusion immediately after my interest in it.

Fortunately, I was careful enough not to leave any type of evidence and was able to spin a narrative that was convincing enough for him to not investigate the case any further after catching Mason Thomas. It's been six months and aside from a single brief comment of coincidence before Thanksgiving dinner, he hasn't said another word about the case. Ensuring, that for the most part, I should be in the clear.

"So, how was your day?" Mrs. Kennedy asked her husband.

"Oh," he started as he sighed. "It was alright. I mean, there haven't been any deaths reported today. We took down another Ozone dealer, but he didn't really have much to seize and had no available information we could use to find out who's been cooking up this garbage."

"At least it's another pill-pusher off the streets," I pointed out, hoping to look on the bright side. He looked across the table at me as he nodded, agreeing with my comment. It wasn't a thought positive enough to make him smile, though.

Everyone at the table sat silent as David continued to speak about the troubles that the surrounding communities had been suffering with regard to the new drug epidemic and the stress and challenges he and his colleagues had been facing at work. Jessica looked at me for a moment as he was talking. Although, there was no actual conversation on the subject, I could tell she was questioning whether or not she should mention my friend Jarrett's addiction. David then shook his head for a moment, attracting everyone's attention.

"I'm sorry. I shouldn't be talking about my work at the dinner table. Let alone today," David said as he looked to Jessica. "So, how has your big day been so far?"

"It's been okay for the most part," she said as I looked at her, wondering what exactly she was going to say regarding our ill friend. "The research lab was fun, but other than that, there wasn't much."

"It's going to be like that more and more the older you get, kiddo. You mark my words," said her father as I looked at her. She looked back at me with a slight disappointment in herself for not saying anything about Jarrett. I decided to pat her gently on the back, both of us unsure if it was really our place to say anything about the matter, let alone to a police officer, even if it was her father. The food arrived shortly after our conversation. The dinner that was served looked delicious, almost as mouth-watering as the smell when it was sat down in front of us. The steak that was placed in front of me had clearly been charred and well done to perfection as it sat beside a warm, fluffy baked potato with a small scoop of butter on top to give it a little flavor.

Jessica decided to go with a surf-n-turf like her father and mother. The plate looked delectable as well, as it had a smaller steak on their plates; with several pieces of sizzling grilled shrimp on the side. It looked rather appetizing until I saw them begin to eat and noticed the steak was only cooked medium as I saw the slightly pink center as it was being cut. Personally, I had nothing against a steak that was cooked differently, but I personally prefer mine to be completely cooked.

Apparently, the beef wasn't big with Dalton and his girlfriend. Dalton had a large plate of ribs completely covered in barbecue sauce. Andrea, on the other hand, decided to order fish that I later learned was in fact Salmon. It was an interesting take on salmon, considering the only experience I'd had with it was from a small red can growing up.

The plate that was sitting in front of Nicky was different than everyone else at the table, as she only had a large bowl of salad with a tiny scoop of Thousand Island dressing on the very edge of the plate. Personally, I'm not as big a fan of salad, at least not enough to order it as my entrée, but I can appreciate the giant smile on her face as it was placed in front of her.

After roughly half an hour of dining, talking, and enjoying a delicious mouth-watering steak, the check was paid and dinner was over and we all made our way out of the restaurant stuffed and content with our food and service. As we walked out the door, everyone stood outside for a moment continuing their discussions before leaving their own separate ways.

"Oh my god. That was so good," stated Dalton as he began holding his stomach as if he were a pregnant woman.

"How can you even tell? You ate your ribs faster than anyone I've ever seen," I retorted.

"I was starving," he replied. "I hadn't eaten all day."

"Well, you still got some sauce on your face," pointed out Jessica, walking next to me.

Andrea looked at the small stain under the right side of her boyfriend's lip and used her finger to wipe it off. He laughed as he watched her lick the sauce off her finger; giving him a special kind of expression that suggested that she was enjoying it. Based on the way they were looking at each other, we quickly decided it would probably be best to leave the two of them alone for whatever plans they more than likely had for the rest of their evening. Although I wasn't an official investigator yet, I suspected they were about to enjoy their own special kind of dessert together.

"Well, you guys have a good night," I told them.

"Goodnight, buddy," he told me as we walked over to him and shook my hand. He then walked over to Jessica and hugged her. "Happy Birthday!"

"Thanks Dalton," she said as Andrea walked over and gave both of us an equally warming hug.

"Happy Birthday," Andrea said as she hugged Jessica.

"Thank you. We enjoyed having you with us," Jessica said as the two of them left in his truck.

"So, are you happy we came here for your birthday?" I asked her. She looked at me completely disgusted as she held her stomach.

"Yes…and no. I'm disgustingly full. Ugh! I feel like I'm about to burst. You need to carry me to the car," she told me as she began leaning on me.

"I have a better idea," I told her what I had in mind. The two of us made our way over to her family car as her parents and sister waited for her to hurry up. I decided to tell Jessica that I wasn't finished with her yet because I had a special birthday surprise for her.

"Hey, is it alright if Logan gives me a ride? He says he has a last-minute surprise," asked Jessica as her mother looked at her husband, who looked at her with acceptance.

"Of course, it's okay. Just remember that you both still have school in the morning," stated Mrs. Kennedy.

"But if the surprise leads to us becoming grandparents, don't bother bringing her home," stated her father. I admit that I found it funny, but I did my best to not laugh. It was difficult.

Jessica looked only slightly amused as she rolled her eyes as we walked away from them. Although, I didn't see what exactly happened next, I heard a large smacking sound coming from the direction of Jessica's parents' truck. I heard David begin to laugh as we made our way to my car. I could see Mrs. Kennedy looking less than amused by her husband's attempt at humor.

"So, where are we going?" she asked as I started the car.

"If I tell you, now, it wouldn't be a surprise, would it?" I responded as I pulled out of the parking lot and began driving.

"Maybe…maybe not. Either way, I can act surprised when we get there," she said with a low-key grin.

"Nice try, honey, but we've had a good thing going for us. What kind of boyfriend would I be if you had to start 'faking it' on your birthday?" I told her as she began laughing and less than gently smacked my arm as I tried to hold my own laughter in a gesture I'm sure she'd learned from her mother. "You set me up for that comment. I'm sorry."

"Well, who said tonight is when I started faking it?" she asked as I sighed, knowing I had been defeated in our brief battle of wits.

"Oh, shit. Now, that was cold," I told her, still wearing an amused smile.

"You started it," she said, giggling, as we began to make our way back to my house. As we got out of the car, she began walking towards my front door. I began walking towards the street. She looked at me as I signaled for her.

"Come on," I insisted.

"Where are we going?" she asked.

"I thought we could just go for a walk for a minute, you know? It's a nice night. The sun is just beginning to set. Come on, we can walk off our dinner," I insisted, as she began to walk beside me. We walked down several streets and eventually made our way to Rockgate Park, where we made our way towards a small wooden bench by an old oak tree.

"Well, I guess this place is as good as any," I said as we sat down.

"Well, what's the surprise?"

"Well, it's not really a surprise as much as it is your birthday present," I stated.

"Okay," she said. I began to pull it out of a shirt pocket.

"Wait. Close your eyes," I requested. She gave me an irritated look for a moment as I gave her my own stern, insistent expression that would last until she did as I asked. I was only a second away from pulling out my gift. I heard a very loud, unpleasant sound coming from behind us.

"Hey!" shouted a loud voice.

We both immediately opened our eyes and looked over to see a man wearing a large brown coat and a beanie, even in the seventy-degree weather of late April, yelling at something. At first, we thought he was yelling for someone and realized that he was just clearly under the influence of something.

Every time we heard him yelling, I could feel an unsettling feeling in the back of my neck, like my sixth sense for danger had been activated. I wasn't sure what a crazed dumbass like that might try to do.

He immediately began thrashing and moving in a way that made you think he was actually dancing as he began picking up random litter in the park. At first, we did our best to try to ignore the unsettling junkie, until I noticed that he was beginning to charge towards the two of us, like he was in a marathon.

I did everything I could to not scare Jessica, who was facing away from him as I began to prepare myself for anything. As he got closer and closer, he quickly charged past the two of us and picked up another piece of random litter that laid only a few feet away from our feet. As he picked it up, she began to hold me a little tighter as he began to dash back to where he was originally picking up trash.

"Tell you what. Why don't we choose a different place, for this?" I suggested, still feeling rather creeped out by the environment. She seemed a little too startled to actually answer me. Instead of actually speaking, she merely nodded as we made our way away from the eco-friendly creeper that clearly needed dance lessons.

As we made our way a decent distance away from the park creeper, we found ourselves a slightly more pleasant bench with a better view of the playground without any people to interrupt or louse up anymore of our preferably private moments.

I stared at the bench as I saw an advertisement on the bench with a guy smiling behind a large building. I looked at it and read 'Adams Apartments and Homes. Call me: Jordan Adams, at 706-555-0810 and I'll find you your new home.' I then turned back to Jessica, who still seemed a little shaken from the local creep.

"Well, that was something," I said as we sat down, trying to ease the tension.

"I know. You never know what people like that could do," Jessica stated.

"He was probably on something," I told her.

"Probably Ozone," she theorized.

"I thought that stuff was like pot, supposed to make you just baked, not raving like that lunatic. I mean, that's what Jarrett was like earlier," I told her in confusion.

"Well, according to Daddy, everyone can be affected differently. Some are barely affected by it, some are affected by becoming a raving lunatic like that possible crackhead, and some end up like potheads, completely chilled and comfortable," she explained.

"That's a little disturbing," I said, at the thought that people would willingly choose to take a drug without knowing how it would affect them.

"No, what's a little disturbing is the fact that an overdose is so easy because the drug is based on specific biology and people still take the chance without any regard for their own well-being," she said, sounding rather strained by the subject, just like her father had at dinner.

"Well, contrary to popular belief, there is an idiot problem in this country," I pointed out, once again, hoping to ease the tension with humor.

"Well, that's beside the point. Daddy has had to deal with over two dozen overdoses this month, including a woman who was found overdosed with her baby sitting next to his dead mother while the father was at work," she stated. It was a rather unsettling idea to put in someone's head.

"Oh, shit," I uttered.

"There's also been like a dozen people that have been hospitalized after nearly overdosing on it. I just hope that Jarrett stops before it's too late," she stated, looking more worried than strained.

"Alright. Well, enough about death and drugs, it's your birthday and you still have one last gift," I reminded her.

"Alright," she said.

"Close your eyes," I insisted again. She rolled her eyes and sighed and eventually saw things my way, deciding to finally comply with my request. This time, without interruption, I pulled out a small necklace from my shirt pocket with a small heart dangling from the end of the chain as I whispered softly in her ear. "Okay…look."

She opened her eyes as she began to feel it in her hand and looked at the heart. She then noticed that it had both of our names engraved on the edges of the front. She turned around back at me and gave me a big hug.

"Oh my god," she said as she took it from me to get a better look.

"For your birthday, I thought it was only right that I should give you my heart in a way that looked good on you," I said with a grin. "Turn it on the back."

"I love you," she read from the back of the heart as she looked back at me.

"Put it on me," she insisted, with excitement. She turned her back to me as I gently placed the necklace around Jessica's neck. She turned back around at me and looked down.

"What's it made of?" she asked.

"It's silver. Or at least that's what the guy who engraved it told me," I told her.

"I don't care. I love it!" she said in excitement as she kissed me. "I love you so much."

"I love you too. I hope you've enjoyed your birthday," I told her, ecstatic to see Jessica so happy on her birthday.

"I have but this just made it so much better," she said as she continued to examine her new necklace and leaned closer towards me as we watched the sun continue to set until it was dark. It wasn't long after that we walked back towards my house and I took her home.

"Hey, there's something I want to talk to you about," she asked before we actually got into my car.

"What's up?" I asked as I opened the door to my side.

"Did you know that Jacob and Krista are moving in together?" she asked. For a moment, I stood frozen, coming to grips with what I was being told. Although I admit that part of it was from the shock of knowing that our friends were taking such a huge step in their relationship, my new feeling of discomfort was because I knew where she was about to go with it.

"Really?" I asked, doing my best to sound surprised.

"Yep. She told me that before you guys walked up earlier," she claimed.

"Wow. That's kind of crazy. Then again, it's really not. I mean, it's them," I mentioned.

"They love each other," pointed out Jessica.

"Yes, they do," I stated.

"And it got me thinking…about us," she added. And here it was, just what I was expecting.

"How?" I asked as if I didn't already know where she was going with this conversation.

"I want us to move in together," she stated, clearly with no cause for confusion. I looked down and sighed because I wasn't really sure how to respond. It was a lot to process all of a sudden, especially since this is actually the first time we've actually talked or even thought about it. "Well?"

"Well, what?" I asked. "You want an answer, now?"

"No. Well, I mean…" she said.

"Look, I love you. That's not in question. It's just…" I started as I sighed again, not really sure what exactly I was going to say next.

"You need some time to think?" she assumed, taking the words right out of my mouth.

"Well, yes. I mean, it's a big step. There are so many things to consider when doing this. I mean, have you completely thought it through?" I asked.

"It was just an idea. Forget it," she said as she began to lower her head in disappointment as I pulled her head back up.

"Hey, I swear to you that there is nothing I would like more than to wake up next to you every single day of my life, but this is a very big decision. You have to consider places, rent and bills. It's just a lot to consider," I explained.

"Well, when Krista was talking about it, we started looking at places, and I found an apartment on the edge of Eastcliff. She actually got her and Jacob's new place from this guy from all the ads around town and Krista suggested him for us," she said as she pointed at the guy who was sitting right in between us painted on the park bench.

"Jordan Adams Apartments and Homes?" I asked as she nodded. "So…you already have a place in mind?"

"It's a nice place," she added.

"How much is rent?" I asked, raising an eyebrow.

"Krista and I already had a look around there for her and Jacob, but found one she liked better," she stated.

"Jess, how much are we talking about?" I asked.

"Okay, it's eight seventy-five a month with expenses," I began to nod my head as the number began to roll around my head for a moment as I scratched my head trying to process her request.

"You do remember that I am currently unemployed, right?" I stated.

"Yes, but I also know that we're about to graduate and you're about to go to a police academy, which you get paid for, and that's on top of the salary I make at the pharmacy," she pointed out.

"A policeman's salary," I noted. "Look, how about this. I promise to think about it."

"That's all I want," she claimed. I knew she meant that was all she wanted for the moment, but I knew that this conversation was far from over.

"Alright, let's get you home," I said as I started the car and took her back home. I began to think about her request. Moving in together? Sharing a bed and an apartment every single day and night in the hopes of building a home. As much as that idea gave me a sense of peace all the way to my soul, I knew that moving in together would be easier said than done.

There were a lot of things to consider changing when moving addresses. We both had to consider prices and places with preferably nice neighborhoods or streets, even if she seemed to have a handle on that department. Once we found a place we agreed on, we would have to pack up all of our belongings, pick out settings for the place, paint, and all sorts of other things.

We also had to consider the fact that this was going to be, without a doubt, one of the busiest and most important moments of our lives, and she's choosing to bring this all up when we needed to be focused on graduating college and I needed to be focused on becoming a police officer. As much as I hated the idea of disappointing Jessica, it just seemed to be rather inconvenient timing on her part to start this type of thinking.

On the other hand, I also knew that there would never really be a convenient time for something as complex as this, and I knew that if I was going to do something like this, I would want it to be with Jessica. I knew that I loved her and I knew that she felt the same way. So, maybe moving in together wasn't as crazy as I first thought.

I wonder what our families would say, though. I know that her family already had a little experience with this when Dalton moved in together with Andrea in Birminghill, but I have a feeling that my family would have stronger issue with the idea. My mother has been the only person that I have lived with since my father…died, six months ago.

She's always been a little overprotective, and that was before Dad passed. I can't imagine this conversation going over easily given the recent circumstances, for either of us. Just as well, I didn't like the idea of her living alone. As much as I loved Jessica, I couldn't simply give her the answer she was looking for as easily or as quickly as she more than likely wanted.

The entire ride over to her house, we didn't say much to each other as I was just processing, analyzing, and considering as many aspects and variables of the situation as I could think of. After I watched her get out of my car and head back inside her house, I took a deep breath, trying to prevent a headache from everything that was going through my head.

I sat in my car in silent peace for only a moment. The peace would've lasted longer if not for an unexpected interruption caused by my phone beginning to ring. I looked to see that Jacob was calling me, more than likely to give me an update on our addict of a friend.

"Hello," I said as I answered the phone.

"Hey," answered Jacob.

"What's up, buddy?" I asked.

"Uh, well…there's something I want to talk about…or rather, something I think you need to know," claimed Jacob, not sounding like his normal cheerful self.

"Alright," I stated.

"It's about Jarrett," he added.

"Is he finally going to rehab to get some help?" I asked.

"Well, no. Not exactly," Jacob stated, sounding rather uneasy.

"Okay, then what is it? Don't keep me in suspense. What's going on?" I asked him.

"Logan, Jarrett is dead," he told me, and an overwhelming feeling of shock began to hit me like a bolt of lightning.

Chapter 3

Overdosed

My phone dropped from my hand and into my lap as I heard this rather distressing news. I knew I had heard the words correctly, but I couldn't believe any of them. Jarrett Weldon, one of my oldest friends, was dead. No. That couldn't be. There had to be some sort of mistake.

"What the hell are you talking about, man?" I asked Jacob, trying to come to grips with what I was being told. "Jarrett isn't dead. He can't be."

"They found him overdosed in an alley a couple hours ago near his house," stated Jacob, speaking in a low tone, sounding upset himself.

"I can't believe it," I told him as I began to hold one of my hands against my leaning head. This sudden shock just seemed so unreal. "We just spoke to him earlier. You took him home, I mean…what happened?"

"I don't know, man. I took him home after school. He got out of my car. I helped him into his house and left him on his sofa. A few hours later, I got a call from Krista, who had just spoken to Sarah, saying he's dead," Jacob told me. I sighed.

"That is just fucking nuts, man. Do they know how he died yet?" I asked.

"Well, his family is wants to keep it under wraps for obvious reasons. I wouldn't be surprised if he overdosed on Ozone Mist. I thought about calling his girlfriend, Sarah, for more information, but she was having trouble just talking to Krista. I know that you've known him longer than I have, and I wanted to make sure that you knew," he told me, still rather put-off by this startling information.

"Yeah. I appreciate you calling to inform me. If you do hear anything else, let me know," I requested.

"Will do. I'll see you later, man," he said as he hung up the phone. I put my phone down in my pocket and sat in my car in silence for several minutes as I tried to come to grips with this devastating news. As I made my way home, all I could think about was how he had always been a loyal friend and how we used to be closer when we were younger. Now, he is just…gone. It just didn't seem real.

It wasn't long after I got home that I went to bed, unable to actually sleep. I spent the rest of the night in silence, thinking that I had just lost one of my oldest friends.

The next day was pretty hard as well. I ended up talking with several of our old friends from high school about what had happened to Jarrett, old friends that I hadn't spoken to since graduation. As more details were unveiled over the course of the next few days, I learned Jarrett's visitation and funeral arrangements were being held at the same funeral home that my father had been taken to, only six months earlier.

After talking with Jarrett's girlfriend, Sarah Bethune, myself, I learned that Jarrett's family wanted to have me as one of his pallbearers. As hard as I knew it would be to be forced to help bury him, I felt honored that they wanted me to help and accepted the position with a heavy heart.

In the morning of the Jarrett's funeral, Jacob, Jessica, Krista, and I all went together. As we got out of the car, I stood silent for a moment as I looked at the building, I saw Jarrett's father standing outside, talking with someone who looked like him and his late son. I froze as I couldn't help but remember how I had the same expression of pain that he had on his face when my father died and the knowledge that he'd just lost someone he loved so very much.

"Are you okay?" asked Jessica softly, looking at me with concern as I stared at the funeral home's entrance.

"Yeah," I answered as I barely nodded. "I just didn't think I would have to be back here so soon."

Jessica took my hand and began to hold it as she continued to look at me. Jacob then patted me on the back as he shrugged, signaling that we should go ahead and go inside. The four of us slowly made our way towards the doorway as I shook Jarrett's father's hand.

"Hey, Logan," Mr. Weldon greeted me, trying his best to fake a smile.

"Hey," I responded, not really sure of what to say to him, knowing that there really wasn't anything I could say that would likely make him feel any better. "I'm so sorry about Jarrett."

"Thank you for coming. I know Jarrett would've appreciated you guys coming," he told the four of us.

"Of course," stated Jacob, who shook his hand next with a sympathetic expression on his face.

"Well, Jarrett's room is down the hall on the left," he told us as I patted him on the back before we made our way inside. Even without his father's directions, it wasn't hard to figure out that it was Jarrett's room, especially when we saw his name on a small sign right above the door. As we made our way inside, we saw several people standing in the main room where Jarrett was. The main room was connected to another smaller room.

When we walked over, we immediately recognized our friend, Marcus Reed, who was talking with someone I assumed to be another co-worker of his and Jacobs, as I had seen them before at their sports store. Although I didn't know his name, he did have blonde hair that was only slightly longer than Jacobs. As soon as Marcus saw us walking in, he came up to us and greeted us. I think he was also trying to fake a smile, only succeeding slightly better than Mr. Weldon or the rest of us.

"What's up, buddy?" he asked Jacob, quieter and calmer than he normally would be, likely due to the circumstances of where we were, not to mention why we were unfortunately there.

"Hey, man," greeted Jacob, softly trying to put on a fake smile himself as he shook his hand. Jacob then looked over to his other co-worker that Marcus had been talking to and waved. "Hey, Tommy."

"Hey, Jake," Tom greeted as well.

Marcus then looked over to me. "Hey, buddy. It's good to see you."

"You too, bud," I told him as I also put on a fake smile. "I just wish it was under better circumstances."

"Yeah, I know," he said softly as Krista hugged him. I turned and saw a small pamphlet sitting next to the entrance that had a picture of Jarrett on the cover of it with the words "In loving memory" above his picture and, at the bottom, his name with the date he was born and the date he died. Inside was a bible verse, specifically Matthew 11:28, "Come to me, all you who are weary and burdened, and I will give you rest." On the right side of the pamphlet were more specific details regarding his funeral arrangements, including details of pallbearers who included Jacob, Marcus, and myself, along with a few other names I didn't recognize, likely those who were closer to Jarrett's family.

I signed the visitation log for Jessica and myself as Krista did the same thing for Jacob and herself. He continued to talk with his co-workers. After we all were signed in, Jess and I walked into the main room, where dozens of people stood, including Sarah Bethune and Jarrett's mother, both of whom I could tell were having trouble not breaking down and making a scene.

As we got closer to the casket, I saw many different types and colors of flowers, next to a large portrait of Jarrett, next to his casket, which had a small line of people walking by to pay their respects to the deceased. We made our way towards the end of the line behind of an older guy that was partially bald and who was wearing really strong cologne.

After several minutes in the line, we had finally made our way to the front of the line where Jarrett laid in his casket with his eyes shut and wearing a nice suit. As I got closer, I realized that his face was completely shaved rather than the small amount of scruff he usually carried on his face. As I saw him lying there, so completely lifeless, the only thing I could bring myself to do was sigh as I patted the edge of his casket, knowing he'd be soon be shut in this small box and lowered into the ground forever.

"Hey," I heard Jessica utter as I continued looking at Jarrett. I immediately reacted and realized that she was talking to Sarah, who had walked over to speak with us.

"Hi, guys," she said, putting on another fake smile that I could easily guess, she'd been forced to give a lot the past few days, before giving both Jess and I a hug, "Thank you guys for coming. I know Jarrett would've appreciated it."

"We are so sorry for your loss," Jessica said as I stood there, seeing Mrs. Weldon begin to walk over.

"Hi, Logan. Hi, Jessica," she greeted as she gave us both a hug. Based on her makeup, I could tell that she had been crying more than Sarah had, but it could've just been the differences in makeup.

She couldn't bring herself to even fake a smile, not that I could really blame her.

"I'm so sorry about Jarrett. If you guys need anything at all, we're here for you," I told them. The truth was that I knew saying that wasn't going to really bring anybody any peace. I mean, there really wasn't much that I or Jessica or anybody else coming to say goodbye to Jarrett could really do about it. I don't really know why I said it, I suppose it is the only thing that people can think to say when trying to comfort someone going through a hardship as horrible as this.

"Thank you," stated Mrs. Weldon, as they began to walk over to the next person in the line. As I looked back at Jarrett one last time, Jessica pulled me away so the line could continue to move along.

"Are you okay?" she asked me again.

"Yeah. It's just hard to believe, you know. I mean, Jacob and I were just talking to him in the game room a few days ago. Now…" I started just staring at the large portrait of him.

"I know, but…" she started, before looking to make sure that no one else could hear what she was about to say as she began to whisper, "…but that's what drug abuse will do to you."

"I get that, but what I don't understand is that he was in bad shape when Jacob took him home. How did he end up overdosed in an alley?" I asked her as we continued to make our way into the other room, where a video that included pictures of Jarrett with his family and friends was rolling. We took a seat next to Jacob, Marcus, and Krista as the video played.

"Hey," I said, as we sat back down. I saw that the photo on the screen was a photo of him from when he was younger, from when I knew him best. It quickly changed to a more recent picture of him and Sarah holding each other on the beach together. It was a nice photo where they both looked happy together. The next photo was of him with Jacob and me along with a few other people. The picture was of decent quality, but I quickly recognized the setting at the college. I think it may have even been his freshman year of college, as it was his first time in the game room and we all posed with our pool sticks in our hand.

"You remember when we took that photo?" asked Jacob, smiling.

"Yeah, me and Andy took care of you and Jarrett," I said, still keeping my focus on the video as a real grin appeared on my face.

"You guys cheated," he accused as we continued to watch the video. After another few minutes, everyone was asked to gather together in a large room to pray for Jarrett one more time before the funeral service began. Afterwards, they asked everyone to make their way to the actual service in the church as they began to close Jarrett's casket.

As pallbearers, Jacob, Marcus, and I were all asked to sit specifically behind the family when we go into the church as were the other pallbearers. Jessica and Krista got on the row of seats behind us, but we sat right behind Jarrett's parents and Sarah. The service was nice. The church was completely full as people who wanted to come say goodbye to Jarrett.

It was hard to hear everyone get emotional and try to hold in their emotions. I heard Sarah sniffle a lot, especially during the first and final songs of the service. The truth was that I felt emotional about the whole situation myself, but tried to hold back my own personal emotions over losing my friend. I looked next to me to see that although Marcus was looking sad, he wasn't really getting emotional over what was happening, I did see a tear go down Jacob's face. He was much closer to Jarrett than I was nowadays, so for him I'm guessing it was harder to have to say goodbye to his friend than it was for me.

I grabbed a tissue from the box that was placed in-between us and gave it to him. I didn't look at him as I gave it to him, to make sure he didn't think I would be judging him. He took it at first, looking as if I had insulted him, but decided to blow his nose as I patted him on the back. The service continued in between songs as both Jacob and someone else I really didn't recognize, but could tell was a family friend, stood up and told funny and serious stories about Jarrett throughout his life.

At the end of the service, everyone began to make their way to the actual cemetery, the pallbearers got up, picked up the casket, and made our way to the hearse. After putting Jarrett in the hearse, I saw Sarah, her parents and Mr. and Mrs. Weldon get into the funeral car designated for the family. I met back up with Jacob as we made our way back to his car to follow the family to the cemetery.

As I was about to make my way towards Jacob's car, I noticed that someone was standing outside the door wearing a pair of sunglasses and curly blonde hair, but was one of the few people not wearing a suit or any real type of fancy clothing. The guy was wearing a regular black shirt and a pair of dark jeans, talking with another guy who was dressed more appropriately for a funeral. I don't remember seeing him inside the large crowd for the visitation, but what really threw me off was the fact that I could see him giving the other man a small brown bag. I really didn't have time to get a long look, but I could definitely swear he was holding a bag.

"Come on, man. We can't fall behind," stated Jacob. I realized that the others were already buckled in the car and I jumped in last, buckling myself up as Jacob began to drive out of the parking lot to follow the other cars. I tried to get another look at the man with the sunglasses, but he quickly went around the building before I could do anything else.

Somehow, we still managed to be one of the first few cars at the cemetery. The sad truth was it was a beautiful day to be outside for any other reason. After waiting several minutes for everyone to gather around Jarrett's final resting place, we all watched as the priest said his final words and his family and loved ones said their final goodbyes before laying my old friend in the ground forevermore.

As the preacher continued to speak for Jarrett, I looked over and noticed that several graves away, the same guy at the funeral home wasn't so much paying attention to the funeral as much as he was talking to what appeared to be a gardener or another possible service person from the funeral home. I couldn't help but get a weird feeling from the guy who would come for the funeral visitation and funeral, but not pay any attention to what was being said.

As we all began to disband after it was over, I wanted to know what that guy was doing and found myself walking over towards him. The closer I got to him, the sooner I saw both of his pockets were bulging full of something I wasn't entirely sure of. When I got closer, both he and the gardener looked up at me. The gardener immediately looked startled and began to quickly walk away from me, as if he didn't want to be recognized. I did notice he also had a small brown bag in his hand; that's when I began to piece together what exactly he was doing.

"How's it going?" I asked him.

"It's going alright, I guess," the man responded.

"You a friend of the family?" I asked, pointing back at the funeral service.

"No. Me and the kid have known each other for a while. It's a real shame what happened to him," the man claimed.

"Yeah. It is. You did hear how it happened, right?" I asked him.

"You know. I didn't even ask," he responded, as he finally glanced over to face me.

"I heard it was an overdose," I told him. He froze, before taking a deep breath.

"Seriously. Oh, man. That's crazy," he told me.

"I'm just saying. It may not be the best time or place to be selling drugs," I told him as he started looking at me as startled as his previous customer did, before I walked into the picture. The truth was that I didn't have any idea if I was right, but based on the amount of suspicious behavior, I thought it was an educated guess.

"I don't know what you're talking about," he replied, sounding insulted by the accusation.

"Relax, man. Do I look like a cop to you?" I stated. "Were you Jarret's supplier?"

"I ain't got no drugs, man and I never gave them to him. Fuck off," he said with hostility, taking off his sunglasses. If he was telling the truth, he wasn't very convincing.

"What's going on, here?" asked Jacob, walking up behind me as the man started walking beside me.

"Hey, Breland. It's been a while," said the man.

"Not long enough, Walker," responded Jacob, who began to look at me. "What are you guys talking about?"

"Not much. I was just talking to this guy about how he knew, Jarrett," I answered. Jacob began to look quite frustrated, which is the second time this week I've seen him irritated. I was really quite shocked when I noticed Jacob's hand beginning to form a fist. However, Jacob knew Walker. Although I wasn't sure how, the one thing that was clear was the fact that he was ready to hit him.

"Well, we need to go, now, and really, Joe? You're going to conduct your business, here?" he asked, trying to pull me away.

"I don't know what you are talking about. I'm only here to say goodbye to a really nice guy. Now, if you'll excuse me," Walker responded, before walking back to his car.

"How do you know that guy?" I asked Jacob, still looking frustrated.

"His name is Joe Walker. He came into our store every now and then trying to offer and sell people drugs. It used to be harmless stuff like Marijuana, then cocaine, but more recently, he's been trying to push Ozone," Jacob told me. I glanced back over to Walker, who looked as though he was leaving.

"You never...?" I asked him, wondering if he had ever accepted one of Walker's offers.

"Do I look like someone who does that shit?" he asked in a rhetorical sense. "That shit will mess you up. You saw what happened to Jarrett."

"So that was his supplier?" I asked, looking back to see Walker getting into his own vehicle. Although I knew the answer already, I was truly curious to know how much Jacob knew.

"Well, Jarrett never told me who he had gotten the drugs from, but if I had to guess. I'd say it's a safe bet that it was him. Now, why the hell he would show his face here, I couldn't tell you," he responded. "So, what were you doing talking to him?"

"I saw him at the funeral home before we left, acting shady. A minute ago, I saw him here passing along a bag that I figured had to be illegal," I informed him.

"Take my word, man. You don't want to get involved with a creep like Walker. Rumor has it that he has been suspected of killing people," Jacob added. I then stopped and looked at him, confused.

"If he killed someone, then why isn't he rotting in prison, right now?" I asked.

"Well, I really don't know the details, but from what I heard, he was suspected of killing this guy who ended up dead after getting into a fight with him. The police said it was an overdose but…" Jacob began to say.

"Let me guess, the guy that overdosed didn't really use drugs," I said.

"That's what I heard."

"Well, where did you hear all this?" I asked him.

"Uh…from another co-worker of ours who had dealt with him before," he responded, as we both continued back to the truck and went home. The whole way home, nobody really said anything. I think everybody was just reeling from the service. Me…I was focused on what Jacob had told me about Joe Walker.

When I got home from the service, I decided to do my own research on Mr. Joe Walker. I decided to look him up on social media, only to find several guys named Joe or Joseph Walker who lived near Rockgate and Birminghill, none of whom I could tell were the man I saw selling drugs today. The more I thought about it, the farther stretch I figured it would be for someone who had spent the last several years in prison would have many people to connect to on social media, anyways.

I decided to look him up online and found several more hits. I thought more about the man's appearance and realized that he looked like he was probably in his late twenties to early thirties, which narrowed down my list to several likely people. I then decided to look up his name with the word drugs and found an article talking about a man named Joseph Walker who pleaded guilty to heroin possession several years ago.

I then looked up and found his name in an article a few months older involving the story that Jacob had told me about. Apparently, in December 2013, Rhett Green was found dead in the street overdosed on cocaine, and Walker had been arrested for selling the drugs that caused his death, but police were unable to prove that it was Walker since their only previous contact between Walker and Green was when they were both arrested at a bar a few days earlier after having a few too many drinks.

After sitting in front of my computer, it wasn't long before I realized that the articles told me nothing about him that I didn't already know. As I sat there, I then began to wonder why I was even looking Joe Walker up to begin with. I mean, Walker was a scumbag, but that didn't mean he was necessarily involved with Green's death or Jarrett's. I mean, if the police were unable to prove his guilt, maybe that's because he was truly innocent in the incident, but then again, what are the odds that someone you don't like ends up dead in your method of expertise and you didn't know about it? Still…why was I getting involved?

Maybe because if he was involved with someone's death, he should have to pay for it. And if he sold Jarrett the drugs that ended his life, then he should have to answer for the harm that he's helped cause. I clicked off the article since I knew that it wasn't really going to get me anywhere. Realizing it wasn't going to make me feel better about what happened to Jarrett, I decided to go for a drive in my car.

After driving a few minutes, I ended up passing by the alley where Jarrett was found dead and thought about how Rhett Green had also been found in the street. Although that could have just been a coincidence, but what if it wasn't? What if Rhett Green had been made to look like an overdose and left in the street. What if Jarrett had been made to look like an overdose?! That was a very disturbing thought to cross my mind.

I knew the scene of his death wouldn't likely tell me anything about his death and decided to simply keep driving. I then continued to drive and eventually pulled onto the street where Jarrett's family lived. I stopped and parked for a moment on the other side of the street and could see Mr. and Mrs. Weldon, holding each other and crying through the window, devastated over the loss of their only child, who would never get another chance at life.

The worst part about all of this was that I actually knew everything that was going through their minds. The pain of losing someone you love, someone who has been taken from you too soon. Whether or not Walker had anything to do with his actual death, Jarrett had been taken. Unfortunately, the police didn't seem to have the means or the stomach to seek out justice the same way that I did for my father. If for no other reason than to ensure they have a sense of peace, maybe I should try to find the answers…my own way.

Chapter 4

Joe Walker

What am I even doing…considering doing *that* again? What the fuck is wrong with me? It wasn't bad enough that I was involved in two deaths already? Even if both of the people I killed had victims of their own and would've no doubt continued to kill until they were stopped by someone else…no. No, I can't consider doing anything like that again. I just can't.

It was nothing short of a miracle when I managed not to get caught the first two times, and there was always a chance that could always come back to haunt me, especially when one of their accomplices, Mason Thomas, was sitting in a jail cell right now, waiting for his case to go to trial in a few months. No. I still couldn't even consider it. What I did was horrible and should never be spoken of, to anyone.

If I'm going to even consider finding justice for Jarrett, I needed to do it the way that I'm supposed to, through the confines of the law. The real question I needed to consider was if Jarrett's death was, ruled an accidental overdose, how could I force the police to continue working on his case? Would Jessica's father be willing to help me out? I decided to turn around and head over to the local police station, hoping that David was working today's shift.

After parking my car, I made my way inside. After several months of coming to visit David every now and then, certain officers, including David's partner, Detective Russo, and luckily, the desk sergeant, had gotten used to seeing me around. In certain ways, David had become like my mentor when it came to my interest in the field of criminal investigation. After making my way to his desk in the middle of the station, I looked around to see that David wasn't anywhere to be found. I stood in front of his desk for a moment and was soon approached by Detective Russo.

"How's it going, Logan?" he asked as I sat down in the chair in front of David's desk for a moment. He didn't seem to be in a good mood, but I figured he was trying to be polite.

"Not much. I just wanted to see if uh…Detective Kennedy was here or not," I answered.

"Yeah, he's here. He's in the boss' office, right now. He should be out soon, though," Russo claimed.

"Alright. I'll just wait here, then. Thanks," I said. Russo continued to stare at me for a moment before walking over to his own desk. I sat there for only a moment. I began to stare at David's computer. I knew that the police system would more than likely have information on Joe Walker, especially with a record like his. I then thought that if I could get enough on Walker, I may be able to find something that could help put him away.

I began to look around as casually as possible to make sure that no one was paying attention to me. It was clear that everyone in sight was working hard on their own work or talking without care, certainly not enough to pay attention to little old Logan, whose only goal was to help ensure that another bad guy was off the streets. I knew that I would have to act fast and took a quick breath, knowing how tricky it would be to break the law in the middle of a police station. I figured if anyone else asked, I could just say that I was waiting for David, and wanted to check my email or something.

A moment or two later, I decided to act and decided to jump. The moment I got up from the chair to jump behind David's desk, I bumped into someone who I immediately realized was David himself.

"Hey, Logan," he greeted, looking slightly shocked to see me.

"Hey!" I said, surprised to see him appear in front of me so quickly. "Hi. How's it going?"

"It's going alright. I'm kind of surprised to see you here. I thought you and Jessica had to attend a funeral or something," he stated.

"Yeah, our friend Jarrett. He died of an overdose on Ozone Mist," I told him. David looked up at me and sighed.

"I'm sorry to hear that. The truth is that we've had multiple cases just like his come in this week alone. Lieutenant Pierce has been busting my balls trying to find the source of the shit, but we can't seem to get anything useful."

"So, the investigation isn't going well?" I asked.

"Hell, no. Obviously, I'm not supposed to talk about an on-going investigation, but we've had dozens of cases coming in from other departments like Eastcliff, Birminghill, Goldmarsh, and the state departments. They're talking about sending the DEA down here to assist, but..." started David, who frankly looked too exhausted to finish his thought.

"Well, that's actually why I'm here. I think I actually found out the name of Jarrett's dealer who was at the service. A guy named Joe Walker," I told him. I figured that maybe I should go back to my original idea of getting David to help me out rather than going back to my darker methods of breaking the law that I'm planning on protecting soon.

"Joe Walker? The name does sound familiar," stated David, who began to log into his system. After a moment of him typing on his computer, I decided to casually walk behind his desk to see him pull up the final summary on Walker's criminal history. This time, I could see Walker's eyes clearly rather than the sunglasses from earlier in his mugshot.

"Yeah. Joseph Reese Walker. Yeah, I remember this guy. We suspected him of killing his girlfriend a few years back, but we could never get anything to stick," stated David, beginning to look disgusted at his screen.

"Wait, what?" I asked.

"Yeah, like roughly ten years ago, back when I was just starting out in homicide. My first partner and I found the body of a woman named Morgan Turner, who had been found to have ingested several different kinds of drugs. We had found her suicide note, but there was something kind of odd about the whole thing. I could just feel it, you know," David told me. I knew the exact feeling he was talking about because it was the same feeling I had with Jarrett's body being found in the alley.

"Yeah. I think I understand that feeling," I told him as he looked back at me.

"Well, we also suspected him in another guy's death a few years ago, but there still wasn't enough evidence until we got him on the drug charges. Are you telling me that this guy is selling Ozone, now?" he asked.

"Well, I can't prove it. I did see him selling something shady at the service, though," I answered.

"Selling drugs at a funeral service, that sick fucking…" David began to say. He didn't finish the sentence, he only sighed as he continued to read Walker's record. I began to look closer at Walker's file on the computer to try to find an address. Instead of finding his home address, I learned that Walker had a longer criminal history than I thought, all the way back to his teen years.

Apparently, when he was seventeen, Walker was arrested for possession of marijuana, as Jacob said. It also included the fact that Walker had also served four years after being arrested in 2014 for possession of heroin. I saw his personal information, including his height, weight, and date of birth, but there were no signs to indicate where his current place of residence was. Before I could continue to look at his page, David clicked off the screen before I could find what I was looking for.

"Well, I do appreciate you giving me this information on Walker. If we're lucky, we'll be able to use this lead to finally put this piece of garbage away for good."

"My pleasure," I responded. "But how are you going to get him on practically nothing?"

"Nothing? You just gave me a suspect that could crack my case wide open. Walker is on parole, so we can go visit his last known address, and even if he's not there, I may be able to catch him continuing his business at the cemetery. It's that kind of lead that can help you land a job here. My question is, if we couldn't find anyone connected to Ozone, how did you?"

"Uh…a friend of mine and Jarrett's recognized him as Jarrett's dealer at the service," I claimed.

"Well, if you'll excuse me, I'm going to go follow the lead. Thanks, Logan. I owe you one," he said, beginning to walk away from his desk. As I made my way back to my car. I began to think about what Jacob had told me, about Walker selling his drugs around his store.

I then began to wonder why I hadn't told David about Walker's business outside Jarrett and Jacob's sports store? And why was I so determined to see Walker finished. Was it because, deep-down, I continued to believe that something still wasn't right or because I believed he was the one who killed Jarrett? After sitting in my car for another few minutes, I saw David and his partner begin to make their own way outside, knowing that they were most likely going to go to Walker's home to question him.

I took a deep-breath and decided to follow them out of the parking lot. I kept my distance from their car to ensure that they didn't think that they were being followed. As I continued driving, I continued to ask myself why I was doing this. The only answer I could find was that I wanted to ensure that Walker paid for his crimes and maybe get some closure for Jarrett's family.

After several minutes of driving, we made our way to the shadier parts of Rockgate and finally made it to an apartment complex. The building looked rundown, and frankly dirty, a friendly environment for Rockgate's finest that I assumed that one or more officers were more than likely familiar with. Call it an educated guess. I parked at a gas station across the street as the detective's pulled up front of the apartment building.

Minutes after they went upstairs to Walker's apartment, David and Russo came back down. They didn't seem too happy with what they had accomplished, I could see it on their faces. They sat there for a minute before making their own way back to the station. Now, I knew where Walker lived, but I didn't know which room was his or if he was even still here. Detective's Kennedy and Russo were now going to be looking for Walker. In all likelihood, they'll end up tracking him down, arrest him for his drug crimes, and give him a plea deal to turn over some bigger asshole and putting him right back on the street to do it again.

I know I'm wanting to go into law enforcement to make a difference, but if they couldn't prove Walker killed before, how would they this time? Maybe…maybe I should get involved. It's not that I wanted to break the law or even kill again, I just didn't want someone like Walker to have the chance to hurt anyone else, whether or not he was actually a direct murderer.

I then had another idea, I should ambush Walker, scare him until he admitted what he'd done, I could leave him for the police to deal with as they saw fit, and if he didn't, I put the fear of God and justice into him until he came clean about his illegal activities. Although I have faith in the criminal justice system. The problem was that sometimes, the system was just not strong enough to protect the people that it was sworn to protect. At least, not until it's too late. How many people would have to die because of some scumbag like Walker, trying to make a quick buck?

At least I knew where to start, at his apartment. I thought it would likely be a bad idea to go into the same building just minutes after the police, but I thought the appropriate thing to do would be to come back later. I decided to go home and check up on my own family for the rest of the night, knowing how tired I was. The problem was that despite the fact that I was surrounded by loved ones who cared about me, I couldn't really focus on anything else, not my mother, not my friends, not Jessica, not my homework, or any other graduation necessities.

The only thing I could think about was how there was a possible serial murderer out there at the moment, probably pushing drugs. He was out there and if he didn't actually hurt someone himself, he was potentially leading people to their deaths, creating an environment of temptation that some, unfortunately, were not strong enough to resist by themselves. It didn't take a detective to know that Walker was a scumbag, guilty of who knew how many crimes, I just wanted to make sure he would be stopped before he got the chance to hurt someone else.

The next day, I went back to the shady apartment building when I thought Walker would be least likely to be there, in the early afternoon, which seemed to be his known hours of service. I didn't think it was likely I'd be recognized, but I decided to wear a cap and jacket to try to disguise myself, just in case any of Rockgate's finest decided to check out Joe's apartment or in case they were still watching for Joe.

I walked to the front desk, where an older woman was reading a magazine and smoking a cigarette. I stood there for a moment to try to get her attention and eventually coughed. I'm pretty sure she saw me walk up but was hoping I would go away after a moment or two of being unnoticed.

"Can I help you?" she asked, sounding less than thrilled that I was interrupting her.

"Yeah. I was looking for a friend of mine that I'm pretty sure lives here…a Joe Walker," I stated.

"You're too late," she responded immediately, without even blinking.

"What do you mean?" I asked.

"I mean, Walker lives up in Room three-o-six, but he hasn't been home in days and the cops just came by yesterday looking for him, so more than likely he's back in jail, by now," she claimed.

"Oh, okay. Just out of curiosity, do you remember the last time you saw him?" I asked her. She began to look really annoyed by my questions and tapped the butt of her cigarette into her ashtray.

"A few days ago. I don't know…maybe Tuesday," she said.

"Thanks," I said as she went back to her magazine, paying little to no attention to me. I realized immediately that Tuesday night was the night that Jarrett died. I've never been one to believe in coincidences, but if I had been involved with someone's death. Actually, I suppose I should say when I was in fact involved with someone's death, I didn't want to go home only to be found out. I hid what I did and went back to my normal schedule.

Jacob did say that he liked to hang around their sports store, so I figured that would be a good place to look for him or within the surrounding areas. As I turned around to leave, I saw the exit, and I saw the elevator next to the staircase. I stood in the middle, looking back to make sure the lady at the desk wasn't paying any attention. I decided to take the staircase to check out Walker's residence.

After several flights of stairs, I finally made it to the third floor and found Walker's apartment on the other side of the hall. I jiggled the door handle to learn that the door was locked. I knew that, based on the information the manager had given me that he would likely be out for a while, so I decided to take the less ethical approach and let myself in. Fortunately, all it took was a little skill and a sturdy paperclip, both of which I just so happened to have on me.

The truth was that, as I made my way into Walker's apartment, I truly wasn't sure what exactly I was going to find. I knew that I was trying to find something that could likely tie Walker to one of the deaths he'd been involved with or maybe proof of a case the police couldn't manage to connect him to.

The inside of Walker's apartment looked run down just like the outside. The first thing I noticed when I went inside was the paint looking as if it was starting to peel. I noticed the cracks inside that likely haven't been dealt with since I've been alive. There was a large brown couch in front of a large television sitting in front of it, roughly fifty inches or so. It was clear that Joe had a decent income from his drug operations, but clearly not enough to try to impress someone with it.

There were many clothes lying on the floor, many of which were so filthy that you could smell them. There was also a Styrofoam plate sitting on the counter. I walked over to his kitchen and began peeking through his shelves, hoping to find something to help me. I then heard a small thud and froze. I couldn't imagine Walker being back here yet, but the woman downstairs did say he'd been gone for a while.

I heard another thud and realized that whatever it was, it was coming from the person who lived next door. I wasn't quite sure what was causing all the commotion in a place like this. There was really no telling, from someone jumping up and down to someone hitting the floor unconscious or dead. I then heard another thud as I heard a woman yell from the wall.

"Oh, yeah. Oh, fuck!" she screamed as the pacing of the thuds began to increase. I stepped away from the wall in disgust, as I had no desire to listen to Walker's neighbors having intercourse any longer.

Assuming, just assuming, that I decided to involve myself in this situation any further, I couldn't bring illegally obtained evidence back to the Rockgate Police Department. That would be more complex than my life could handle, not to mention if someone caught me in here. I decided to keep my visit brief and quickly made my way towards Walker's bedroom, hoping I would be able to find what I sought there.

Walker's bedroom wasn't much tidier than the rest of his apartment. There were two empty beer bottles on his nightstand. The truth was that there was no telling whether or not I was going to find anything even remotely incriminating here. As I stood in the middle of the bedroom, I decided to take a breather and think. If I was guilty of something that I didn't want anyone else to know about and was proud enough to do it again, where would I hide the evidence that connected me to it?

Nevertheless, I began looking in his drawers in his nightstand and began to search his closet. I then decided to lift up Walker's mattress and finally found what I was looking for. I found a journal that belonged to Walker that contained a log of many, if not all, of his business transactions over the past few months.

As I continued to read from his journal, I discovered that this journal described the past few years of his life, right about the time he went to prison on his heroin charges. It included details about his relationship with Morgan Turner a few years earlier and how she turned into a narc for the authorities after being caught with cocaine in exchange for testimony linking Walker to the heroin rings back in the day. It also detailed how he found out, and how hurt he was over her betrayal. It described how he ended their relationship by dealing with her, but there was no damning evidence that linked him to her death or words to suggest what he did to her.

The book also detailed how startled he was when connected to the death of Rhett Green, before being sent to prison, stating he was happy to be caught only on the drug charges. Based on the way it was written, it sounded like Walker was guilty of more than selling drugs, but there still wasn't enough to prove that he was actually involved with anybody's death, including Greens or Turners.

I began to skim through the book. I found well over a dozen different stories, who were actually clients that he could keep track of. Although I knew that I was more than likely safe from being found in Walker's apartment, I figured that I should probably finish reading his journal through the pictures on my phone. I pulled out my phone and began taking pictures of the remaining pages, and putting them back where I found it.

After realizing that there wasn't much left to check in this rat-hole of an apartment, I decided to lock the door behind me as I left. When I went back downstairs, I checked first before I could be seen, and saw that the manager was still sitting at her desk reading her magazine, where she was when I left her earlier. I then made as little sound as possible before making my way to the door.

The only sounds I heard her make were her coughs coming from smoking. After making it out of the building without being noticed, I walked back to my car, which was parked on the other side of the street. After I got to my car and drove off, I went home and decided to write down all the names that I had found in Walker's book.

I went back to my normal weekend routine of spending time with my family and friends and spent some time studying for my upcoming final exams. When I had free time, though, I began to research the names. I will admit that a few of the names were more difficult to identify as it included multiple individuals with the more common names and were near the same area. Fortunately, the majority of names were easy to research.

After crossing every name off my list, I learned a few interesting facts about individuals on the list as roughly half of the names have been or are currently incarcerated due to crimes related to drugs. I also found some information interesting as thirteen of those names have been found overdosed on drugs. Two of those thirteen overdoses had been talking to Walker about getting help when he came around pushing his pills.

A third deceased former client of Walker's, named Bobby Hamilton, had been found dead a week after being released from jail for drug possession. It seems that Joe thought it was kind of suspicious the next time he came around looking to score Ozone asking Joe questions he didn't like. However, when the police found Hamilton dead, they could never successfully connect it to Walker.

After finishing my research, I came to the conclusion that there were a lot of suspicious circumstances regarding Joe Walker. It seemed pretty clear to me that he was a criminal and he was completely guilty of drug crimes. Although there was no definite proof, I do believe that Walker was more than just connected to many of these deaths, if not all of them. I think that Walker has been getting away with far worse crimes than the police realize, and he has been doing so for a very long time.

It made me sick to my stomach to think that someone like Walker was walking and working out there, somewhere with the police unable to stop him. The situation reminded me of the very similar situation I found myself in several months ago when dealing with the men terrorizing Rockgate as the Boulevard Butchers.

The police were unable to stop Arthur Phillips and his crew, but I could. Whether or not it was truly right or wrong, they were stopped, and people were safe from the Butcher's knife, forever without being caught. Maybe…this one time, I could intervene in the situation like I did before. Wait a second. What was I thinking? I can't. No matter how many people Walker may have already killed. I then looked back at the list that included dozens of names and saw how all the people on that list were victims of their own drug abuse, not to mention potentially one of the future overdoses.

Just for the record, if I were to even consider doing something like that again, ever! I have to do it like I did before, but I haven't proven beyond any doubt that Walker was guilty of killing anyone, no matter how suspicious the situation truly was. I needed to protect my identity in the event that I didn't get the answers I wanted and I came to realize that maybe Walker wasn't actually guilty of murder after all.

It was an overwhelming thought, to even think about doing that again. It made my hands shake just thinking of having total control over another human being. This situation is different than last time. Last time, I knew without a doubt that Arthur Phillips and his crew (with the exception of Brian Mitchell) were guilty of killing my father and the others, before I began to hunt them down, but with Walker, things were different.

I haven't personally seen him kill anyone, and I didn't have definitive proof of his guilt, but I think that there might be enough circumstantial factors for me to have my own personal interrogation with Walker. If I am seriously considering doing something like…this again, I have to take a few extra precautions that I didn't take last time. Last time, I didn't care if Phillips saw my face because I knew I was going to finish him off. I had no immediate plans to kill Joe Walker. I did, however, want to see him off the streets. If I wasn't going to finish him off, I would need a way to conceal my identity.

I figured an old-fashioned ski mask might as well do the job. I would also need the right tools for the job. Fortunately, my method with Phillips worked well last time, and I still had the gloves I had gotten from my last little dark endeavor. I did know that I would need a location that would be isolated enough for Joe and me to not be disturbed, along with the necessary tools I'd need to preside over his interrogation.

I decided to pay a visit to the grocery store I used to work at, where I picked up the supplies I knew I'd likely need. I tried to think of every step I took the last time I was about to do something like this. If Walker really was guilty of killing anyone, I'd need to scare him into confessing to the police, if for no other reason than his own safety, from me. Seeing as how I knew his type of work, he could potentially be armed and I knew that since I'd gotten rid of the knife I had used on Arthur Phillips months ago, that I would likely need a new knife, just in case I needed to threaten him or cut my losses. It doesn't hurt to be prepared.

After picking up an instrument that I thought would best be suited for my endeavors, I went to another aisle and decided to get a few rolls of duck-tape to ensure that Walker wouldn't be able to try anything that I would find less than desirable. I did decide to pick up a few groceries that I knew mom would more than likely need and appreciate while I was there. After saying hello to some of my old coworkers, paying, and leaving, I went home to put up the groceries before planning my attack on Walker.

I knew that the first thing I would need to do would be to find him. Apparently, he'd been laying low since Jarrett's death. He hasn't been back to his apartment, but he has been working on his drugs. I can't imagine him working twenty-four hours straight for this many days and thought he may be celebrating his work or hiding out in case someone wanted to talk to him about his illicit activities. Either way, it didn't matter.

I knew it would be pointless to look or wait for him at his home. I had to think of a place that the police wouldn't think to look for Walker. Fortunately, I think my subconscious already gave me the answer to that when I decided not to tell David about Walker's connection to Jarrett. Seeing as how Walker liked to spend time outside Jacob's sports store.

I decided to take a short trip by there to see if Walker had decided to come to work around the sports store. Granted, it was a long shot, but I figured it was better than having no hunch at all. I decided to put my cap back on, in the hopes that I wouldn't be recognized. I looked around to see if Walker was anywhere to be found. I went inside and saw my friend Marcus working, but I didn't see any sign of Walker. I then decided to have a look around the building and saw nothing back there but a large dumpster. I looked down and sighed in disappointment, knowing that Walker wasn't here, and nearly jumped as I heard a familiar voice behind me.

"Logan?" I heard the voice say. I turned around to see my best friend, Jacob Breland, in his work uniform. Nothing too fancy, just a polo shirt, a pair of khaki pants, and a lanyard holding his badge with his name on it.

"Hey, buddy. How's it going?" I asked him.

"It's going alright. What are you doing back here?" he asked me.

"I…uh…saw you walk back here and thought I would surprise you, but apparently you got the drop on me," I lied with a smile.

"Really? Why are you lying to me?" he asked me with a stern face as he crossed his arms.

"What do you mean?" I asked in confusion.

"Logan, I just followed you back here. I saw you sneaking around in your red cap, which I've never seen you wear a cap in the ten years we've known each other," he told me.

"Well, I thought about giving it a try. Apparently, it's not working for me, so if you'll excuse me," I said as I tried to get away from Jacob, before he started to catch onto me.

"Don't lie to me, man. I already know why you're here," said Jacob.

"I somehow doubt that, man," I told him.

"You're looking for Joe Walker, right?" he stated. I found it somewhat chilling to think that Jacob may very well know that much of why I was here. It was rather unsettling to be reminded that Jacob was, in fact, smarter than I normally gave him credit for.

"Wha...you mean the drug guy from the funeral? No. Why would I?" I asked him, looking confused by his accusation.

"You're looking to score drugs, aren't you?" he asked, looking uneasy.

"You think that I'm here to…" I started, thinking of how relieved I was for him to think I was wanting to get high, in comparison to the reality of the situation.

"Don't deny it. Jarrett had the same look of determination on his face that you had when I saw you walk back here. Walker hasn't been around here in days, man. What would Jessica say if she saw you like this, right now?" he asked me.

I thought long and hard as I thought about what Jessica might actually have to say about all this, about what I've done and what I was planning to do. I also thought about what would happen if someone else got addicted to Walker's drugs, but I knew that nothing would be helpful if I didn't find him, first.

"Jacob. I promise you that I have no desire to get high on drugs," I assured him.

"Then why would you be back here?" he asked. I stood there for a moment as I had to think of an excuse that would stop his questions regarding my private business. It took me a moment to figure out a decent story. I then sighed as I walked closer to him and began to answer his question.

"Look, if you must know, I went to Jessica's dad with the info you gave me about Walker and now I'm trying to help find him. I'm not supposed to tell anyone, so I need you to stop asking questions, okay? But maybe you can help us. I know you talked to him, but do you have any idea of where he could be hiding out or…?" I started.

"Come here," he told me as we walked back to the front of the building. He then pointed towards a restaurant on the other side of the street. "You see that guy outside the Taco Bell."

"Yeah? What about it?"

"I've seen him and Walker do business. I don't know if he's one of Walker's customers or suppliers, but I have seen them talking together. Maybe he can help you out," Jacob suggested.

"Okay, thanks buddy," I said, as I decided to walk over and have a small chat with Walker's associate. It made sense that Walker wouldn't come back around the store after what happened to Jarrett, just like he wouldn't go back to his home in case someone wanted to ask him questions he would feel less than comfortable with.

Walker's supposed friend was skinny. He had a bit of a buzz cut that supplied little noticeable hair while wearing a filthy brown jacket. As a matter of fact, Walker's associate looked quite similar to the eco-friendly creeper Jessica and I had crossed paths with in the park on her birthday. The only difference, aside from slight facial differences and a long hairy beard, was the fact that he didn't seem too concerned about protecting the environment. Unlike Walker, this guy gave the image you would expect from a drug dealer, or user, and smelled like one as I could smell him from ten feet away.

"Pardon me," I said as I approached him. It took him a moment to notice I was there. It seemed clear he was under the influence of something.

"Hi. Can I help you?" he quickly spat out.

"I was told that if I wanted to know where to find Joe Walker, that you may be able to help me out," I claimed.

"Me? No. I don't know who that is," he stated as he began to scratch his arm while slightly shaking.

"Well, a friend of mine told me that he saw you talking to him a few days ago. Apparently, you two know each other."

"I talk with a lot of guys," he claimed, looking annoyed.

"Well, this guy likes to sell Ozone at the sports store down the street, has blond curly hair, ringing any bells?" I asked. He began to look as if I had startled him.

"Blondie?" He answered as he began to nod, as he began to really shake. "Yeah, I know him. Blondie is a scary guy. He caught me coming by here a couple of times. I told him…I told him that I didn't want trouble, I just wanted a taste, but he didn't want to sell to me. Can you believe that, as long as I've known him?"

"Do you have any idea where I can find Blondie?" I asked, trying to be polite.

"He won't want to see you. Blondie…he wouldn't want…" he started.

I got closer to him and gave him a very specific look, a look to make sure my new friend know that despite his warnings, I was still very determined to locate Joe Walker.

"I need to know where he is," I told him intently. It took him a couple of minutes to understand the situation that he was in, but once I persuaded the junkie to focus on my questions, he told me about another place that Walker liked to hang around when he was less focused on selling his supply rather than enjoying it, a drug house a few blocks away from his apartment.

As I made my way over to the address that the addict gave me, I noticed the place that I was driving to was on the street as the abandoned Green-star factory where Arthur Phillips died. The truth was that it wasn't a memory I was excited to relive, but it was kind of poetic that I should end up this close to the building I killed Phillips in when I was planning on abducting Walker. Maybe it was the universe's way of telling me that I was doing the right thing, but where I should take Walker to somewhere that I can ensure our private conversation stayed private.

I parked outside of the building and saw that it was a large, skinny, two-level house that smelled as bad as it looked from the outside, with all the paint fading off the front of the building and garbage out front. Unfortunately, it fits right in with this neighborhood. I sat out in my car for a moment as I put my gloves on and thought about how I was going to subdue Walker, assuming he was inside with all the others.

I knew that no one was around the area and decided to put on my mask and put on a hoodie to blend in with those who liked to hang around places like this. I also decided to keep a weapon just in case I needed it. When I made my way to the door, I realized that it was locked as I tried to walk in. It was a large door, and I knew how hard it would likely be to try to knock it down and thought I should use the old-fashioned method of knocking on the door.

After a brief moment of waiting, I saw the door handle begin to turn and saw that the person answering was none other than Joe Walker himself, looking much worse than he did at the funeral. I watched as his eye widened when he saw me and my mask and tried to react. I knew I had to act quickly and pulled him from the doorway and threw him to the ground outside.

Walker laid on the ground for a moment, clearly under the influence, himself. He tried to get back up and pull out a gun while on his knees. I grabbed his arm as he tried to point his gun at me and pulled it away before he could fire a single shot. I then threw him back to the ground, before hitting him with the butt of his own weapon, before unloading it and throwing it away. The last thing I needed to worry about was someone as high as Walker, finding and deciding to play with a loaded weapon.

Once I had Walker lying on the ground, I decided to go back and shut the door, before I dragged his unconscious body over to my car. I taped his legs and hands together before putting him in the trunk of my car. I took off my mask for a moment and saw the Green-star factory from a distance, practically calling to me and telling me that I needed to deal with Walker there.

It was beginning to get dark as I took Walker back to the factory. As I opened it back up, I noticed that the place smelled and looked the exact same, even after six months had passed. After seeing a small amount of Phillips' blood still on the ground next to the table, the memories of what I did with Phillips began to flood my memory. The memories of our brawl on the factory floor from the point I managed to subdue him, from his confession, to the point that I was filled with such anger and hatred for him that I finished him off, once and for all.

I began to breathe in the knowledge of what I knew was about to happen; with the realization that there was no turning back at this point. I then went back to my car to put my mask back on before dragging the still unconscious Joe Walker to the table that Arthur

Phillips had died on. I taped him down the exact same way I taped down Phillips and stood over him for a moment to really come to terms with what I was about to do. After hovering over Walker for a few minutes, I knew that I wanted my answers and decided that it was time to get him.

"Rise and Shine, Joe," I stated, as I began to smack him awake. It took a few minutes since he was really out of it. "Hey!"

As Joe began to come around, he looked up at me and looked as if he wanted to jump. He then looked around and saw that he was bound to a table. He then began to try to wiggle and struggle on the table as I watched. It was like seeing a fly, desperately trying to free itself after getting tangled in a spider's web.

"What? What the fuck is this?" he asked.

"This…is your reckoning, Joe. It's time for you to come clean," I informed him.

"Who the fuck are you?" he asked me. I decided to take a step closer to him so he could see my eyes and know how serious I was.

"Let's just say, I'm a concerned citizen who has been keeping tabs on you and knows about all the shit you've been up to, from the early days of marijuana to heroin dealing, and now Ozone Mist," I stated.

"Look, man. I'm just a pill-pusher. It's just a job, man. It was just business," he claimed in desperation.

"Then why do it, Joe? Why kill those people?" I asked.

"What are you talking about? I haven't killed anyone," he claimed.

"Rhett Green, you were connected to his death at a bar fight, and was found dead, overdosed on heroin, right before you went to prison. Morgan Turner, that was your ex, right? She was going to testify against you and she was found dead before she got the chance, maybe even Jarrett Weldon," I continued to accuse, admittedly becoming angrier by the minute.

"You're out of your fucking mind!" he interrupted, as I decided to up my game a little bit and show him my knife so he would start taking me a little bit more seriously.

"No more lies. I'm going to ask you again…how many people, Joe?" I asked him. He finally stopped struggling for a moment as he began to look up at my face.

"Okay, look. I didn't have a choice. I had to kill them. All of them," he claimed.

"How many?" I asked. He was hesitant to answer my question. I then began to cut his arm, just enough to pressure him into answering my question.

"Five! Okay, five!" he shouted back in pain.

"Give me names, Joe. I saw at your place that you know all your clients," I ordered.

"I know you," he said, as I turned around.

"Excuse me?"

"I recognize you now. You're that guy talking to me at the funeral the other day, aren't you?" he asked. I sighed as I realized that there was no longer any reason to wear the mask, which made things more complicated as to how I could simply let him go when he'd seen who I was.

"Well, now that you've seen me for who I am, the least you can do is return the favor. Why did you kill them, Joe? Was it because they were planning on getting clean, no more business, some even choosing to turn against you in court. You certainly couldn't allow that, and you decided to do something about it, right?" I asked. I saw as a tear began to run down his eye. I found it interesting how he could show any tears after confessing to being involved with the deaths of five people.

"Look, the drug trade...it's a total secret. They all knew about my business. If I didn't kill them, they were going to turn me in. That's what happened last time, I can't afford another strike. It was them or me!"

"So, you fill them up with your drugs and leave them in the street like trash?" I asked him.

"Look, I'm sorry. I'm sorry. Please, you have to understand. I didn't have a choice," he claimed.

"See, but that's just it. You did. You did have a choice. You didn't have to get involved with the drug trade. You certainly didn't have to sell anything, and you didn't have to kill anybody."

"You wouldn't understand. I did what I had to do," he told me. I looked down on him with a complete feeling of disgust at how little he cared for others and killed all those people just because he was afraid they would testify against him. The idea of turning Walker over to the authorities began to fade as I saw this pathetic man lying in front of him.

"You know what, I'm starting to believe you. You just did what you had to do," I stated as I began to tighten the knife in my hand. Joe began to look less scared as he began to nod. I looked at him with a slight look of compassion, as he truly believed he had no choice. Unfortunately, I knew that this was a situation that Walker would find himself in again and again. As I thought about the fact that he was not only involved with my friend's death and knew who I was, I thought it would just be simpler for everyone to just get rid of him, once and for all. "Just like I'm doing what I have to."

Joe's eyes began to widen as I raised my knife in front of his face. He only had time to let out a single brief scream before the knife in my hand had done its job in a single blow as Joe Walker lay dead in front of me. I took a deep breath as I began to realize that I once again found myself in a position of having blood on my hands.

I began to handle Joe when I heard a noise coming from behind me. I froze for a moment, as I thought it might just be my imagination. Unfortunately, I realized my imagination was actually a most horrifying reality as the door of the factory quickly turned into a bright light as I turned around to see Detective David Kennedy walking towards me with a gun pointing towards me. I sighed as I turned around.

"Logan?" he asked, as he looked at me with an expression of complete shock.

Chapter 5

The Witness

The day that I've been afraid of for the past six months of my life, the day my darkness became exposed for what it was and I lost everything I've spent the last twenty-one years of my life trying to build for myself, was finally here. My heart began to race as I knew how bad the situation looked as I stood over Joe Walker's dead body. I couldn't believe I had let myself be caught up in this situation, especially after only moments of killing Walker. How the hell did I let this happen?

"Freeze!" I heard him yell, the moment I tried to walk closer to him.

"David. It's me," I told him as he looked at me in such shock over what he was seeing.

"Logan? What the fuck?" he asked, beginning to sound confused.

"Look, I can explain this," I tried to tell him as he began to walk closer to me.

"Get away from the body, Logan!" he ordered. I took a step back as David slowly approached Joe Walker's body while keeping his weapon pointed towards me. After making his way over to the body, David took a minute to see that it was in fact Joe Walker's body, that was currently bleeding out on the floor.

"What are you doing here, David?" I asked him, wondering why the hell he was even near the factory and not somewhere else…anywhere else.

"I followed that tip you gave us on Walker. It led us to a source who knew about a drug house down the block. After finding nothing, I heard someone yelling. Next thing I know, I find you standing over the guy I'm looking for. What the hell happened, Logan?" he asked me, looking slightly horrified at the body. I stood paralyzed as I sincerely tried to think of an answer that could explain what happened that would least likely result in my spending the rest of my life in prison. Unfortunately, my talent for telling convincing lies was nowhere to be found.

"I…I tried to follow up another lead to find Walker, for you," I started to tell him, as I began to make something up as I went along, "I found out about the house down the street from here and found Walker half-crazed on drugs. He tried to attack me," I claimed.

"And?" he asked.

"I guess I just snapped," I told him, unable to think of anything else to say. The sad truth was that I was at one point planning on giving Walker over to the authorities, but as I heard him confess, it was the sincere truth. I just snapped.

"What do you mean, you just snapped? He's taped to the fucking counter, Logan!" he yelled back at me.

"I can…" I started as I began to get closer to him.

"I said freeze!" he repeated. "Let me see your hands!"

"David," I said, trying to calm him down as I continued to hold my hands in the air.

"I said let me see your fucking hands, Logan!" he repeated, before I had the chance to raise my hands completely in the air. He slowly began to walk over to me as he began to pat me down. He then walked behind me as I heard a small cackling as he pulled something from the side of his belt. The next thing I felt was a small metal cuff beginning to tighten around my wrist.

"Let's go," he stated after tightening the other cuff around my other wrist, filling me with a strong feeling of dread. I couldn't believe that this was the way my life ended. The day that I lose my family. What was my mother going to do without me after just losing my father only six months ago? Oh, man. What a kick my fellow classmates were going to get knowing that I committed the acts we'd spent four years studying?

"You have the right to remain silent. Anything you say can and will be used against you in a court of law. You have the right to an attorney. If you cannot afford an attorney, one will be provided for you. Do you understand your rights?" he stated, knowing my Miranda rights.

"Wait!" I said. "Please, listen to me."

"Logan, do you understand your rights?" he asked me, looking at me in complete disappointment and disgust. I didn't really know what to say at that point, knowing just how cooked my goose was as that point. I looked down in shame and nodded.

"Get in the car, Logan," he told me as he pushed me inside. The back of the car was far from comfortable, as the cuffs pushed against my wrists with very little room to move around.

"David, just let me explain," I tried to explain.

"You just did, Logan. You told me you just snapped. That's what they all say," said David.

"You said you owed me one, remember?" I asked him.

"That was to help me out with a lead…on Walker, not to help you cover up his murder!" clarified David.

"Come on. This will destroy Jessica. Please, I'm all my mother has left," I pleaded.

"Then let me ask you this, man. Why the fuck didn't you think about them before sticking that knife into Joe Walker?" he asked.

"I did," I said softly as I leaned my head against the wall in the back of David's car.

"And?"

"…and I thought about the family members of the people that Walker had confessed to killing before you showed up, including Rhett Green, Morgan Turner, and Jarrett Weldon," I stated.

"So, they were murdered?" he asked as he froze to listen to what I had to say.

"They weren't the only ones," I added. Walker confessed to being involved in the deaths of five people, including those three. Victims that the police hadn't even linked him to."

"That doesn't mean you get to play judge, jury, and executioner. That's why we have an impartial system in place. That is why there are laws to help put bad guys like him behind bars, not in the ground."

"Walker already faced a judge and a jury, after killing before. He still managed to get back on the streets to push pills and kill people that could potentially bring him down. Just let me ask you something. Aren't you tired of scumbags and killers like Walker running around out there on the streets? Assuming you manage to arrest them, they cut deals, probation, some get off on technicalities. So, what is the point of having these systems and people like you to serve them, if they fail to protect the people they're supposed to protect?" I asked him as I sighed. I looked back up in my seat to see David still listening. "Look, I'm not saying what I did was right and I didn't enjoy it, but Walker was a killer and I am sure that if I hadn't stopped him, he would've done it again. He's evil, man."

"If killing people is just as evil, then what do you call what you just did in there?" David asked me. I sighed again.

"A necessary evil," I responded. David finally turned back around and looked at me, before he sighed.

"Shit," he uttered, before he got out of the car. He then walked around and opened the door of the side of the cop car that I was sitting in, before looking down at me. "Get out."

I must admit, I was more than slightly confused that my words had managed to get through to him, but I knew that I should do what David said before he decided to change his mind. I immediately jumped out of the police car and confronted him.

"Turn around," he ordered. I did as I was told as he began to unlock the handcuffs around my wrist and put them back on his belt. I really didn't know what to say because I really didn't want to jinx this gift that I was being given, as I knew that it could be taken away just as easily as he was giving it.

"Thank you," I softly said.

"Shut up," he told me, looking at me as if he really wanted to punch me in the face. I must admit, in any normal situation, I would be used to it, but right now, I just wanted to do what I was told in the hopes that it wouldn't end with me being locked up forever. He stood frozen for a moment as I stood next to him, just glad to be out of his handcuffs. I really didn't want to say anything else, but I knew that eventually, if anyone else saw us standing outside the factory and found out what was going on, we would both be in hot water.

"I really don't want to ruin this if you're letting me go, but why are you helping me?" I asked. He stared at me for a brief moment and sighed.

"We can talk about that later. Right now, we have to do something with him," he stated before we both looked back at the warehouse where Joe Walker's body was still lying and dripping blood on the floor.

"What do we do?" I asked in my rather dumbfounded state. Although I knew what I'd done in the past, I had other murderers take the rap for my previous crimes, but getting rid of a body where no one would be able to find it wasn't something I knew. Burying it somewhere was always a risk. I really didn't have any immediate connections to acid either.

"You're the one who brought him here to kill him. Are you telling me that you can't think of something?" he asked, beginning to sound distressed and frustrated.

"Well, clearly things have become a little more complicated and I'm in too much shock right now to remember!" I told him as I felt my heart still racing from the fact that I was almost arrested by the guy who was about to help me cover up Walker's murder.

"Okay. Calm down," he told me, beginning to look aggravated. He sighed. "Now, just take a deep breath. You're going to do exactly what I say, understand?"

"Fine," I told him.

"Come on," he insisted. We then went back into the factory and watched as the blood continued to drop onto the factory floor. "Cut him loose. I'll be right back"

I used the same knife I had just used to end Walker to cut his corpse free of the tape. David began to look around the factory, although I wasn't entirely sure why. I waited on him for a moment, just hoping that this night wouldn't end with me being arrested for murder. A few minutes later, David walked back over towards me, dragging a large roll of carpet on the ground.

"Where did you find that?" I asked, shocked at what exactly he had.

"We're in an old carpet factory, genius. It would help to have something to wrap the body in so it doesn't bleed in my car," he stated as he began to lay down the carpet on the floor; next to the table. He then signaled me over to help me place Walker on the carpet. No easy task, moving the bleeding, dead body of an easily two-hundred-pound man.

After gently placing Walker on the carpet, we began to roll it back up with him in the middle, another challenging task, I might add. By the time we finished, everything except Walker's feet was wrapped inside the carpet.

"Okay. Now, help me get him over to my car," he ordered. I questioned whether we should, as Walker's ankles remained obvious as they were sticking out of the carpet.

"What about...um..." I started as I pointed to Walker's ankles. David sighed as he looked frustrated.

"We'll worry about it, later. Come on," he insisted as we began to drag the carpet over. I then noticed that he was beginning to bleed through the carpet a small amount, but by the time we made it to David's car. It seemed to have stopped bleeding through. "Help me get him in the trunk."

It took a couple of minutes since David's car had a small trunk. It's like the car companies didn't consider the idea that people may want to store a body in the back of them or something...how inconsiderate of some people. After struggling with Walker's remains, we finally managed to cram the carpet inside.

"What now?" I asked as he shut the trunk door and looked at me.

"Now, we have to clean up the mess you made in there," he said, as he pointed back towards the factory. When we went inside, we both saw the table surrounded by a small pool of blood with bloody tape hanging from the end of the table. After we both came by the table, David walked over to a closet, where he found a mop and bleach. While he began to help clean up the blood on the floor, I began to peel the tape I had used to bind Walker down off it. It kind of made me sick to think of how warm it still was and how the smell of metal from the blood made me sick to my stomach to the point where it almost made me gag.

"Really?" asked David, when he saw me cough. "Don't even think about puking, that'd be something else we have to clean up."

"I have a weak stomach," I told him, which was normally the case, believe it or not.

"So, you could kill Joe Walker with no problems. Now, you're telling me that you have too weak a stomach to handle his remains?" he said as he went back to cleaning up the floor until he saw the tape in my hand. "Go get a trash bag. They're in the closet over there, where I found the mop."

I walked over to the closet and grabbed several white trash bags from a small roll. I began to put all the tape in a single bag. Fortunately, you'd never be able to tell from the outside of the bag that the tape was just used to assist a murder.

After several minutes of David cleaning the floors, the factory floor looked cleaner than it did when I first came inside six months ago. David and I put the supplies back in the closet. Although, he did remove the mop-head that had blood on it and put it in the same bag as the bloody tape.

"I got the body. You get the trash," he stated as I walked back outside and put the trash in the back of my own trunk.

"What are you going to do with him?" I asked him, when I walked back over to his car. David stared at the back of his car, continuing to look at me with aggravation.

"Why don't you just let me worry about that?" he suggested, before pointing back towards the road. "Why don't you just go on home?"

"I'm...I'm not just going to leave you when you're carrying my mess in the back of your car," I told him, sounding shocked that he would just tell me to go.

"There's nothing more you can do with Walker. Don't worry. I know how to make him disappear, somewhere no one will find him," he told me. I stared at him for a moment with an unsettling feeling in the back of my spine.

"How?" I asked.

"Go home, Logan," he repeated, I began to walk past him, before he grabbed my arm. "I think I don't need to tell you this, but obviously, I think it would be best if we kept what happened here tonight between us."

I nodded to him before he let me go. I then walked back to my car and drove off as I saw David staring at me while I was doing it. I did notice that he went back to focusing on Walker's corpse.

I must admit that this was not the way I expected this night to go. I mean, the plan was to use my coercion of Walker to get his confession and secretly give it to the police. Why did I do it again? And why did David help me? He's been an officer of the law for years. He put himself at risk by letting me go, not to mention his family. If anyone was to ever find out what we had just done, we would both lose everything and everyone we care about. I couldn't help but wonder, what the hell just happened?

Chapter 6

What just happened?

As I began to make my way home from my ordeal with Jessica's father and Joe Walker, I found myself wondering what exactly had just occurred between us. I mean, he caught me, dead to rights, standing over my victim. Instead of doing his job and arresting me for killing Walker. He decided not only to let me go, but even helped me cover up Walker's death. Why?

There was also something else that he'd said that confused me. He'd said that he knew exactly what he was going to do with Walker's body, when I didn't even have an official plan to dispose of him. How would he know how to dispose of a body at the top of his head? Could there be more to Detective David Kennedy than initially meets the eye?

After I made it home that night, I found myself still somewhat in a state of shock. The truth was that I really didn't know what was going to happen. I mean, David was still a cop and he had the body of my victim in his trunk. The only question was, if he really was planning on turning me in and arresting me, why help me out or act like he was going to?

What if he accidentally let slip what had happened, or worse…what if someone found out what we did, or found David disposing of Walker's body? What if Jessica found out? None of this made sense and the possibilities began to give me a headache. I really didn't know how this situation would play out. The thought that I could still be arrested for what I had done was a thought that gave me a deep amount of anxiety that made my head ache and my stomach turn.

When I walked into my home, I found my mother waiting for me. The truth was that I really wasn't sure what I was going to say to her or if I could even bring myself to say anything.

"Where have you been?" she asked.

"I...uh, I was out," I told her as I tried to avoid her, hoping she wouldn't notice how agitated I was feeling. As I made my way into the kitchen to get a drink, I felt a slight sense of dread when I heard her begin to follow me in the room to speak with me.

"Where were you?" she asked. I slowly drank from my bottle, hoping to think of a better answer before I stopped. "I was out with friends. We were studying for one of our finals coming up."

"I called you three times and you never picked up," she stated. I looked back on my phone and saw that she had indeed attempted to get ahold of me several times, including three missed phone calls, one text, and a voicemail. The truth of the matter was that I never felt my phone even vibrate once. The only thing I could feel for the last hour or so was my own heart pounding.

"I'm sorry," I told her. "I didn't even notice it. I've just been so busy."

"Well, that's fine, but when I try to get ahold of you, I need you to pick up so I don't have to worry about you all night," she requested.

"Okay," I said as I took another drink, still trying to avoid contact as I began to look away from her.

"Hey," she said as she kept trying to face me. "Are you okay?"

"Yeah. Why?" I asked as I put down my drink and finally managed to face her, hoping to get this conversation over with as soon as I could.

"Well, you just seem off," she stated. I shrugged as if I really didn't know what she was talking about as she continued to stare at me.

"Sorry. I really don't know what to tell you," I claimed.

"Seriously, are you alright? Did something happen?" she asked. There was a very small part of me that wanted to tell her exactly what had happened, like when I was little and had a bad day, hoping she could make everything all right. The rest of me never wanted her to find out what her husband had done or what he was realizing that he was capable of doing.

"Not really," I responded.

"I'm just worried about you," she said.

"I'm sorry, but I really don't know what to tell you. Maybe, I'm just stressed about my finals," I told her.

"Everything is going to be alright. You can do it. You always do, and it's the last time you'll have to worry about it."

"I know. Look, it's been a long day and I think I'm about to go to bed," I told her.

"Have you eaten anything?" she asked. My stomach still felt uneased after everything that had occurred and what may still happen regarding Walker and David. The thought of eating at the moment was almost as appealing as eating a hot dog while suffering from the world's worst hangover.

"Yeah," I lied, before hugging her. "Sleep tight."

"Okay, love you," she told me.

"Love you too," I responded, as I went back to my room. As I walked into my room and shut the door. I stood frozen for a moment as I found myself feeling the overwhelming feelings of anxiety and fear as I remained uncertain of what had just happened and terrified of what would happen next. I've never really been a fan of uncertainty and things beyond my own control.

It was a feeling that filled my entire body with dread. The exact same feeling of dread I felt after I…came into conflict with Ryan Bailey and the other Boulevard Butchers last year. The problem is that this time, I've actually been caught in the middle of one of my "dealings." I soon ended up taking off my clothes and getting into my bed, trying to find a way to rest, only to spend the entire night rolling uncomfortably in my sheets the entire night. I simply stared into the pitch-black darkness of my room and went over everything that David and I did with Joe Walker in my head. Over and over, I tried to think of it one action at a time. I then began to wonder what David meant when he said that he was going to take care of everything.

The problem that made me so uneasy was the fact that I had just committed a murder and I willingly let a homicide detective take the body. He had everything that tied me to the crime. Even if he had a moment of weakness by letting me go, he could've decided to change his mind and turn me into his superiors. It would be over, then. My life, my future, my family and friends, my everything, and I was just laying here waiting and praying that David would still be willing to save my life.

Although it was a good sign that he did decide to let me go home scot-free, what if there was something that both he and I missed? What if he was caught disposing of Joe Walker's bloody corpse? Even if he did like me enough to cover for me, he would certainly be done for. There would be no reason for him to protect me. What about Jessica? What would happen if her father was found in possession of a dead body covering for me? What would happen to her family if something happened to David because of me? It would destroy her.

Even if everything really was alright and we managed not to leave behind any evidence or proof of what we did and no one began to ask questions regarding Walker's disappearance, what would become of me and David? I mean, he was a decorated member of the Rockgate Police Department, he was the father of the love of my life. Would we just keep this as our dirty little secret, something that we both just got mixed up with and decide to never speak of again?

I mean, he had me. I just didn't really understand why he would let me go. The questions and suspense that kept me awake the rest of the night nearly made me sick to my stomach, to the point where I got up once just to go to the bathroom when I felt like I was going to be sick.

When I got up the next morning, I woke up with the hope that everything that had happened with Joe Walker was nothing more than a most horrible nightmare. I just hoped that everything would stay normal and I never even went into town yesterday, that Walker was still alive, maybe even Jarrett, and maybe even my dad was still alive. I just hoped that my life was going fine and I had nothing to worry about other than my finals and I had never been caught taking a human life. As I lay in bed for another moment, I realized that all of my concerns were not only real, they were overwhelmingly terrifying.

I didn't want to go to school. I knew that I would have to face Jess. What if David had said something or let something slip to his family or said something to her about me that made her start asking questions that I wasn't ready to answer. Jess is the last person in the world I would ever want to be caught up in the middle of my dark endeavors. I knew that it wouldn't be much longer before we both graduated and figured that if there was something I had to deal with, I might as well face it rather than continue to lie there wondering about maybes or what ifs.

I decided to push through my fears, worries, and concerns and face the day head-on, no matter what type of complications or challenges I knew the day was going to likely bring. I resumed my normal routine and thought that maybe, just maybe, everything was going to be alright and that I was going to be alright, too. I went online and saw many news articles, but nothing related to Joe Walker, David, or myself, which gave me a small sense of peace.

As I made my way over to the school, I was unable to activate my led-foot and engage in my average speedy driving, once I got on the interstate. I know it was highly unlike myself, but needless to say, I had a lot on my mind. Luckily, traffic wasn't too bad. With the exception of a car choosing to honk its horn at me for choosing to actually drive the speed limit. At least, until the driver found a chance to go around me. I paid the drive no mind though, I was too busy preparing that me end could still be near.

Murder, after all, was a serious offense that most cops tended to take seriously and wouldn't likely be willing to look the other way for. So, why had David? For me? The guy who had intercourse with his child? Possible, but I couldn't help but think there was more to that story. Even assuming that David had his reasons for protecting me, if he had decided to turn me in, I would've already heard something on the news or gotten a knock on the door from the police wanting to arrest me or at least question me by now, wouldn't I?

After I arrived at school, I knew the first thing I had to do before anything else was to find Jessica. I figured the worst part would be facing her, to see if her father may have given any hint or said anything about me or what'd happened the previous night. I knew where our friends liked to hang out before class and arrived earlier than normal in the hopes that I could figure some of this mess out.

As I made my way over to the student center where I figured she would be, I began to slow down as I realized that if she did know something that I rather she not, what would I say? What would I say if her father did say something about me, not being the man she thinks I am. How could I explain that to her? How could I be with her if she knew that I had a dark side that I could never tell her about?

As I faced the building, I realized that I didn't have the answers, which was becoming an annoying habit since I like to prepare myself for the tougher complications in life, but how could I prepare myself for this? Oh, you spoke with your father last night, Jessica? Oh, he said that? No, Jessica, I haven't killed anyone, not even a drug-dealing murderer who killed one of my closest friends. I can't imagine why your father would think that.

I took a deep breath as I made my way into the building. After a minute of looking around, I finally saw Jessica on the side of the room, sitting with our friends, talking. It made me sick to my stomach, thinking about what she may have even told our friends. It's bad enough that David knew about my darkness, but if Jessica knew and our friends knew, it would continue to spread like the common cold, except instead of a fever and a stuffy nose, ending with me in prison for murder. I took a deep breath and decided to walk up to them.

"Hey," I greeted them with a grin. She was standing looking aggravated with a slight hint of somewhere between disgust and anger. Although I wasn't entirely sure why she was giving me such a foul look, I knew that it more than likely wasn't going to be ending well for good ol' Logan. It also wasn't a good sign when I saw neither Jacob nor Krista smiling as I walked up to the group.

"I need to talk to you," she said sternly and very quickly. My heart began to beat faster as we began to walk away from Jacob and Krista, who began standing up as if they were about to leave.

"On that note, I think it's time to leave," stated Krista, looking to Jacob.

"I just walked over," I told them, as they began to grab their belongings.

"You're in trouble," Jacob stated mockingly before they began to walk away. The fact that he said it the way he did wasn't much of a relief considering the worst-case scenario would really end with me in the deepest trouble that I could imagine.

"Okay. That was weird," I told her as I watched them begin to walk away. Jessica was looking at me with her arms crossed and with what looked like disappointment on her face, something I never enjoy seeing, especially when I'm the reason. "What do you want to talk about?"

"Is there something you want to tell me about?" she asked me with a skeptical look. Although I knew it wasn't going to end well, I figured that plausible deniability and playing it cool would be the best play.

"N…no. Not at the top of my head," I answered. She didn't seem to appreciate that answer, as she began to look more irritated with me.

"Are you sure?" she asked. "Are you sure there isn't something that happened last night…with my dad?"

I began to feel that ultimate sense of dread as I knew that David had spoken to her about what happened. Even if I didn't know everything that has already been said, this was definitely swerving itself in a less than ideal direction.

Since I didn't know what her father had already told her about last night, I figured that I should still stick with my plan of denying it, at least until I knew what she knew.

"Why? Did he say anything?" I asked her, fearing her next

response, knowing that whatever she was about to say could dictate both of our entire lives.

"He told me that he caught you snooping around his investigation. He also told me that not only did you almost mess up his case against a local drug dealer, but he told me that you nearly put both of your lives at risk!" she stated, sounding angry. As much as I hated hearing her so upset with me, it was a relief to know that David hadn't told her anything else about last night.

"Yeah," I sighed as I turned my head, trying not to smile at the fact that I wasn't in nearly as bad a situation as I could've been. "Yeah. I fucked up, Jess. Did he give you any more details about…what happened?"

"More details? Yeah, he said that you were going off and acting like a vigilante, going around someone who was suspected in being involved in Jarrett's death! I mean, is that true?" she asked in disbelief.

"Yes," I said, telling her that absolute truth and nothing more. "I went to find Jarrett's drug dealer."

"What the hell were you thinking, baby?" she asked, looking more concerned than aggravated, which seemed to be a step in a better direction.

"I…I don't know. I mean, the more that I thought about what happened with Jarrett and the facts of his case. Things just seemed a little off with him doped up and being found on the street like that, so I went around asking questions. I saw Jarrett's dealer at the funeral and started looking into him," I told her.

"Why?" she asked as she sighed.

"I figured…that if he was involved with what happened to him then…maybe I could turn over what I had to your father and the police in the hopes it may lead them to whoever made the drug, so

Jarrett wouldn't have pointlessly died in vain," I said as I scratched my head. Jessica stared at me for a moment. It was hard to tell what exactly she was going to say, but instead of speaking, she leaned over and gave me a hug. Not really sure what to do with it, I simply decided to accept her gesture.

"I get it," she mumbled into my ear, before pulling away. "I get it. What happened to Jarrett was horrible. I get that you wouldn't want him to die in vain the way that he did, but Logan, you can't risk your own life just because Jarrett did. As much as I cared about and missed him, we have to accept that he made his own decisions. That means you can't go snooping around police investigations or interfering with daddy's work."

It was interesting to think that David didn't just rat me out the way he did, I find it even more interesting that he wouldn't have given any indication to Jessica about what I…what we did when he knew I'd be seeing her soon, especially if there was a small part of him that thought I could be dangerous.

"Just out of curiosity…what else did your father say to you on the matter or I guess I'm asking if he was upset or angry about?" I asked.

"Well, the truth is that he seemed kind of weird about it," she told me. "I mean, I think he just had a good day. The truth is that I've seen him get angrier over less, but he wasn't angry at all. In fact, that was the calmest I think I've seen him in months. Usually he's stressed out over his work, but…I don't know. It was like something changed." I really didn't know how to respond to that. Jessica's father had one of the most stressful jobs that I could think of. He may as well have thrown away his badge when he agreed to dispose of Joe Walker for me. Wouldn't covering up something like that and making him question his own morality make him even more stressed? I know this whole thing has stressed me out. It just didn't make sense.

"He also wanted me to tell you to come over tonight. He said that he wanted to further discuss seeing you last night, and if you still want a future working with him at the department. Look, you both mean the world to me, and all I want is for you two to get along," Jessica told me. I could tell she seemed rather distressed, but I also knew that this entire conversation could've been far worse.

"Hey, it'll be okay," I told her as I began to hold her hand and kissed her on the forehead. "We'll hash out everything we need to and put all of this behind us, I promise."

"Good. So, have you thought about what we talked about?" she asked. I froze for a second and tried to figure out what exactly she was talking about, and then I remembered that we had briefly talked about moving in together after graduation. The fact of the matter was that with everything that had been going on with Jarrett, then Walker, and now David, I hadn't once even thought about the idea of moving in with Jessica.

"Honestly…not much," I told her. "I mean, I know that we love each other and I know that we've…ya know…been intimate, but with everything that's been going on lately and with finals about to start. I just don't understand how you've had time to even think about stuff like that."

"Well, I understand that we both have a lot on our plates, right now, and I know that it probably isn't the best time to bring it up. The thing about it is that Krista was helping me pick out places, and there's a great little place, right outside of Birminghill. It's only a few miles away from both our homes and at a decent price. I want to try to make an appointment with that Adams real estate guy later to go check it out. I was wondering if you were interested in going to look at the place, before someone else decided to snatch it up."

"Okay…uh…I mean, if you want to show me the place later. I'll have a look," I said. She then began to smile as she began to get up. I grabbed my belongings too as I walked her to class. I realized that this was something serious that she was wanting for the both of us. I mean, our own home together. It was a big step for the both of us to take together.

We would both have to start paying for our own food, rent, and bills. Although she had a decent job, I was still unemployed since I'd left the store, figuring that a minimum wage job when I was only months away from jumping into my career in law enforcement would be a little ridiculous.

Not to mention all the packing and moving. If we needed furniture, we'd have to get that as well and leave our families. That I knew was going to be the hardest part of the decision, being forced to leave my mother. She'd just lost my father a few months ago, and now there was a chance that she could lose her son, if not to prison, then to Jessica. The idea of her being forced to live alone makes me sick to my stomach.

As I continued to think about everything that Jessica was asking me, in the back of my mind, I kept thinking to myself how I could even begin to make these plans and commitments to her when I had everything else on my plate. I mean, just because David didn't immediately turn me in or tell anyone didn't necessarily mean that he still couldn't. Although I figured that it was a good sign that he hadn't already, I knew that this entire ordeal was far from over.

Jessica also told me that he wanted to talk to me about what happened. What did that mean? Did that mean that he was okay with me killing Walker? For him, I suppose it would be just another scumbag dealer off the street, but David was still a cop. Could it be that he cared about me enough to simply let me off with a warning for committing a capital offense. I mean, that would certainly be ideal, but still makes the least amount of sense.

The worst part for me was the waiting…waiting to see David…the man who held my entire life in his hands. What if he decided to have a change of heart and began to feel guilt over what I did and the role he played in it? What if he wanted to do something about it? What if he already had? What if my life was already over and I was simply waiting to be arrested?

Chapter 7

Jason Clark

As I sat through my classes for the day, I began to practice and prepare myself for anything that David might want to talk about regarding...what had happened. From the possibility that he wanted to admit to his role in the situation or still wanted to cover the whole thing up, preferably the latter. I kept thinking about what would happen if he'd formed a group of his fellow officers together, waiting for me; hoping I would confess. The possibilities were endless, and that was what made me so nervous.

It also made me somewhat concerned to think about how the whole situation could lead him to get me to stay away from Jessica. As much as I cared about her, I'd lose her if I went to jail, but hopefully she wouldn't get mixed up in this mess that I'd created. The last thing I would want is for Jessica to ever learn about the darkness inside of me.

By the time my classes ended, I still wasn't really in the mood to eat much, but I realized that if today turned out to be my last day of freedom, I should enjoy my perks while I had them. I decided to stop by one of the local burger joints, called Betsy's Burgers, and ate a late lunch. After realizing I had gone almost an entire day without eating, my appetite came storming back like a flood, to the point I ended up getting another.

When I got home with a satisfying amount of food in my belly, I decided to relax in my own home until the afternoon turned to evening and I left to meet up with David to possibly surrender, or at the very least, figure out our next move. I continued to think about what would happen if I went over to speak with David, and I began to wonder if I should even go over there.

If it was a trap or some sort of sting, I would be arrested and my life would be over for sure. What if I were to just run away? What if I just left, packed my essentials, and made off? I went upstairs and even found my suitcase. I pulled it out as the notion of running seemed to work for me. Before I even began packing, though, I looked at the photo I kept of Jessica and me. We were so happy. We're still happy together. If I left like this, the police would start hunting me and harassing my friends and family, wondering about my whereabouts.

I couldn't put my mother or any of my friends and family through that, especially when I wasn't sure if my life was over, just yet. There was still a lot I didn't understand about the situation at hand, and I owed it, not only to all of the people I cared about, but I owed it to myself to figure things out…the right way. When I arrived at the Kennedy household, I slowly made my way up the driveway to see the family sitting in the living room. I saw that Jessica wasn't there and remembered that she was supposed to work tonight.

It was reassuring to know that if anything was to be said tonight, she wouldn't be around to witness it. Although it seemed like a reassuring sign to see that there were no other police cars sitting around the area that I could see, it felt like every step I took closer was another step closer to my doom. I knocked on the door to see Jessica's brother Dalton answer it.

"What's up, buddy?" he said as he looked at me. "You know, Jessie's not here. She's at work."

"Yeah. I know. I'm actually here to see your dad," I told him.

Dalton looked a little confused for a minute, but still invited me inside.

"Dad! Logan's here to see you!" he shouted as I saw Mrs. Kennedy sitting in the living room with Dalton.

"Hi, Logan. He'll be here in a minute. He's dealing with Nicky, right now," she stated as I began to hear shouting coming from upstairs.

"I said I don't want to talk about it!" I heard a female screaming. My incredible skills of deduction figured out that it was in fact Jessica's sister, Nicky. "Just leave me alone!"

"Fine!" I heard David yell as a door slammed very loudly. David then began to walk back down the stairs and stood frozen for a moment when he saw me.

"Hi," he said as I stood just as equally frozen for a moment, not really sure what to say when I really didn't have any idea what his next move was.

"He said he's here to see you," repeated Dalton, as David stared back at his family. Everyone stood quiet for another moment or two as Mrs. Kennedy began looking at the both of us.

"Is everything alright?" she asked as I looked at David. He glanced over to her for only a moment before he began to grin, whether it was a real one or not was beyond even my skills of deduction.

"Yes, everything is fine. I just asked Logan to come over this evening to talk to him for a minute. Say, Logan. Why don't we talk out here?" As he began pointing towards the doorway, it seemed sort of pointless to try to run at this point. He led me out the door as we both stood on the porch for a moment.

The fact of the matter was that I really didn't know what to say to David. I really didn't even know if I had a right to say anything to him after what I did. I mean, what do you do when someone helps you cover up a murder…thanks a lot? I stared at the driveway for a minute as David began to stand next to me. We stood there for a minute in silence, as I think we were both trying to think of an appropriate thing to say to each other.

"So…what was that about?" I asked, hoping to break the tension between us.

"Nicky has been acting wild the last couple of days," he responded, sounding rather annoyed.

"Maybe just teenage drama stuff," I suggested.

"You know, I didn't ask you to come over to talk about my kid's problems," he stated sternly. I sighed as I nodded. "You know what I wanted to talk to you about."

"Yeah," I softly said.

"You told me that you killed Walker in self-defense, that he tried to attack you and you fought him off," he stated as I nodded at him as he continued to stare at me. "I looked at Walker's body, Logan. He had no markings to indicate that he was in a struggle."

"I don't know what to tell you," I told him.

"You don't know what to tell me? How about you tell me the truth," he suggested. "I saw you, Logan. You had him completely immobilized. He was completely at your mercy. I saw that look on your face. You wanted to kill him. Now, I want you to tell me why. You owe me that much."

I stayed quiet for another moment, as I wasn't sure whether or not I was being recorded or not. I noticed that David didn't say anything.

"You remember my friend Jarrett who died?" I asked.

"Yeah. What about him?" he asked.

"I did my own research. I paid my own visit to Walker's apartment and found proof that he not only killed Jarrett, but was also involved with several other deaths that were made to look like overdoses," I answered.

"Why didn't you come to me with this?" he asked.

"My methods of obtaining the proof were less than legal, remember? Besides, I was only going based on a hunch. When I saw what he had done and how many people he'd done it to…he had to be stopped. You know, I'm right," I said as I realized that I was confessing to murder to a cop and sighed.

"The way that you had him bound, it was very neat and precise, even for a criminal justice student's first time committing murder, unless it wasn't," he stated.

"What are you talking about?" I asked him as it became more and more obvious that his suspicions of me were real and were finally coming back to haunt me.

"I let you go and even disposed of the body for you so don't bullshit me, right now. Have you ever done…something like that before last night?" he asked. I didn't see any real point in lying to him at this point, especially when he made very good points, as he already claimed that he wasn't going to arrest me. I knew my secrets regarding the Boulevard Butchers had been weighing on me for all of these months. If David truly sought to help me, then maybe it was finally time to tell him the truth.

"Yes," I confessed softly, as David nodded.

"Okay. How many?" he asked.

"Two…or maybe one and a half. The first time was an accident when he was trying to kill me," I claimed.

"Who?" he asked. I froze as I realized that I was finally coming clean about all of my debatably evil deeds.

"Logan!" he shouted, trying to regain my focus.

"Do you remember Arthur Phillips and Ryan Bailey, the guys who you suspected in the Boulevard Butcher investigation? Mason Thomas didn't kill them. After doing my own research, I found out they were all in on the killings together. They were all in on the Boulevard Butcher killings. That's how they were able to get away with it for so long. They alibied each other out on different nights and eventually began to get together to enjoy the killings together when they were sure they were covered," I told him.

"So, you killed Bailey and Phillips?" he asked.

"Bailey caught me investigating them, and he tried to kill me. I didn't mean for it to happen. It just did," I said, in all honesty.

"And Phillips?" he asked.

"He killed my father, remember?" I stated sternly, sounding less than remorseful as I said it, probably because when it came to him, I had no remorse for taking his life. "Was I supposed to just sit around and hope that one of them made a mistake…after killing who knew how many others?"

"Well…most people would say yes. That's exactly what you were supposed to do, and wait for us to do our job and catch them," David said.

"If I hadn't intervened, you never would've caught them, but you already know that, don't you?" I asked.

"I knew it was too easy, catching Mason Thomas the way that we did," he stated. "You left Thomas' DNA on the body for us to find, didn't you?"

"He was guilty of murder. It gave the victims closure, and the killings stopped. I figured it was as close to a happy ending as anyone could hope for. So...what now?"

"Now? Now, we're going to go for a ride," he said as we began to walk over to his truck.

"Where are we going?" I asked, terrified at what the answer would be.

"Well, first we're going to stop by Jessica's pharmacy for a minute."

My heart began to race as I heard that. I didn't know whether or not he was bringing me to Jessica to say goodbye to her before he arrested me or if he wanted me to tell her the truth of the matter. My hands began to shake at the thought that I'd have to lose her, but I realized that I didn't have much of a say in the matter. The two of us didn't say a word the entire ride over. David got out of the car as he signaled for me to do the same. I took a deep, slow breath before getting out and walked next to him.

"What are we doing here?" I asked, sounding more and more terrified.

"You'll see," he answered as we went through the front door. For some reason, that didn't fill me with any encouragement. Nonetheless, I followed David to the back where Jessica was working with one of her co-workers and smiled as she saw the two of us.

"Hey, snickerdoodle," said David, as Jessica turned over to see the both of us and smiled.

"Hi, daddy!" she said as she looked at me. "What are you guys doing here?"

"Well, I thought that tonight would be a good enough night to take Logan out on one of my late-night hunting trips," he stated.

She lost her smile and began to look at me with skepticism. "I'm just here to pick up my special sedatives for the trip."

I really didn't know what to say in the situation. He said that he was here to pick it up for a hunting trip, but what kind of hunting trip?

"For real?" she asked, giving the both of us an expression that suggested judgement. "As if it wasn't bad enough that you go out at night and kill defenseless animals, but now you've got to get him in on it, too?"

"Well, I figured that if I don't want this one to keep interfering with my work, I may as well take him under my wing. And if you two are going to continue to get closer and see each other, I should get to know him a little bit more. And after talking at the house, I learned that Logan knows a thing or two about hunting," he stated. I didn't find it reassuring for him to tell Jessica these certain details, it's like he was deliberately hanging a sign out in front of the both of us that gave her all but the truth about my deepest, darkest secrets.

"Well, at least this way, we can hunt without hurting the animals for long. Come on, please, baby?" he asked.

"Is he coming back?" she asked, as he glanced over in my direction, before turning back.

"More than likely, but I can't make any promises," David responded, sounding more sympathetic than I ever thought he would. She looked at the both of us as if we had both been making fun of her as she sternly slammed a brown bag on the counter.

"That'll be forty-seven-twenty-two," she said sounding upset. As David started paying for his sedatives, Jessica stared at me with sheer aggravation. I didn't really want to say anything as I knew that I was already in hot water with her as it was and I didn't want to make her upset with me any more than she already was.

"Would it make you feel better if I told you that we were only going after predators, that kill other innocent animals?" he asked as he ran his card.

"No. It really doesn't. You know, I hate it when you go hunting. Killing is wrong. Period," she stated. I took a moment to take in her words as I felt the irony that her own boyfriend was technically a murderer. Just another reason I hated irony. Jessica reluctantly handed her father the small brown bag.

"You should know that I'm very disappointed in you," she said, staring directly at me, before walking away from the both of us. It always hurt when I knew that Jess was mad at me, but for once I wasn't in much of a position to say anything to make her feel better.

"It's okay, Logan," David stated as he patted me on the shoulder. "She gets that way every time I come here to pick up this stuff. She'll get over it."

"Why? What is that?" I couldn't help but ask.

"It's just a few over-the-counter sedatives," he answered.

"So, you've come to get this type of stuff, before?" I asked as we made our way out of Jess' pharmacy.

"Yeah. I usually like to go night hunting in the woods every now and then," David answered.

"So, what does this have to do with…what we were talking about back at your house?" I asked him as I got into the passenger side of his car.

"You'll see…in time," he responded as he started the car. The answer he gave was still far from comforting. He said that he liked to go hunting…for animals, specifically predators. Could it be possible? Could Detective David Kennedy of the Rockgate Police Department actually have his own dirty little secrets? It would explain how he knew what to do with Walker's body. But Jessica's father…a killer?

If that was the case, did that mean that lethal Logan could very well be his next victim? Did he choose to spare me from getting arrested because he wanted me all to himself? That would certainly be an unexpected complication in his relationship with Jessica or mine if I managed to overpower him, should the situation come to that. I figured that if this was the road we were destined to take together, I may as well face it head-on.

"Are you going to kill me?" I asked as we made our way to a red light. He slowly looked over to me in a way that made him look rather creepy as the light glared directly on to the side of his face and he let out a small laugh.

"No. I wasn't planning to," he responded as the light began to change. We eventually drove another few minutes down to Birminghill, to one of the rougher neighborhoods. It's the kind of place that most people, in good sense, wouldn't occupy unless they were planning on committing felonies.

The fact that David was driving the both of us through this neighborhood wasn't making me feel any better about his overall plan or what role I was to play in his grand design.

"What are we doing here?" I asked when he stopped the car. He pulled his key from the ignition and picked up his bag of sedatives. He turned to me and stared at me with a slight look of uncertainty on his face.

"Stay in the car," he requested as he opened his car door. "I'll be back in a minute."

"What?" I asked as he went over to his back seat and grabbed what looked like a larger bag, but it was kind of hard to tell in the dark blackness of night.

"I have to grab something. Just hang on a minute," he requested before walking away from the car.

I wasn't entirely sure what he was planning on grabbing, but decided to entertain myself by flicking David's locked window switch, even if it didn't affect the window in the slightest. After several minutes of flicking the switch and listening only to the flickering, I began to look out the window to see only a single seemingly homeless person sleeping against a brick wall covered in graffiti, under the giant letters reading MAD SLUTZ in bright blue letters. For some reason or another, I didn't think the hobo seemed to mind the misspelled word. Aside from that single person, there was no one else in sight. No one at all.

David had taken the keys with him, so there was no way I could even listen to the radio. I pulled out my phone to see that we were in a dead zone, so there was no way for me to look at my social media. I was simply stuck in this dark, empty neighborhood, all by myself. In the back of my mind, I kept thinking that if I was in a horror film, it wouldn't be long before the psycho killer popped out and attacked me. An ironic analogy, I know, but even I couldn't help but feel discouraged by my surroundings, especially in this part of town.

After another moment of sitting in the car, I decided to take my seatbelt off and look around to see that there was still no sign of David anywhere in sight. After another moment or so, I began to wonder if something could've happened to him. What if he'd been jumped by a gang or something? I know that he requested that I stay in the car, but I figured that if something did happen to him, then he may need the backup. And if something were to happen to me, then at least I wouldn't have to worry about David arresting or killing me anymore.

I opened the door of the car and got out. I looked both ways to realize that there was still no sign of David anywhere. I decided to take a few steps away from the car to look down the next street where David was headed. I kept my eye on his car to make sure that no one got any bright ideas about taking it for a joy ride. I quickly took a peek down the street, only to see no sign of him or anyone else in sight and returned to my seat in the car, before something could happen the moment I reopened the passenger door.

"Logan," said David, popping up next to me, as I jumped. "I thought I told you to stay in the car."

"Sorry," I told him as I felt my heart begin to race. "You were gone for almost twenty minutes."

"I told you that I had to pick something up," he told me as I saw a very large brown bag, lying on the ground as he began to open his trunk again.

"What is that?" I asked as he stared at me again.

"Get back in the car," he ordered me as he began to pick up the package over his shoulder. I got back into the car as David began to stuff the large bag in the back of his trunk. He looked like he was struggling with it, but I really didn't want him to be aggravated with me anymore than I could've imagined, so I decided to simply follow his request.

After dealing with the bag, David returned to the driver's side, out of breath, and started the car again. After driving another half-hour down the parkway, we made our way to the border of Eastcliff and Rockgate, where we finally stopped in front of a large factory.

"What are we doing here?" I asked him as he got out of the car.

"Come on," he requested. I sat frozen for a moment, but decided to get out of the car to see David dragging his large package inside the factory. Unlike the Green-star factory in Rockgate, this building seemed to still be in operation, based on the condition the building was in and the large number of company trucks sitting outside, but why would he choose to take me to a factory that was still clearly in operation.

"Where are we?" I asked as he continued to struggle with his package. He then stopped and dropped the package as he began to stare at me.

"Here," he stated, ignoring my question. "You handle this."

I began to grab the bag and realized that whatever was inside was heavy, easily over a hundred pounds. There was no sign of movement inside the bag, so if it was a person or large animal, there was no sign of life. I then began to think. Was this Joe Walker? Did he hide him away to dispose of him? It wasn't the same bags we'd used last night, unless they were just in this larger and thicker bag. There was a small bad smell in the air around me, but I couldn't tell if it was coming from the bag or the area. The closer we got to the factory's main entrance, the more I began to suspect the smell wasn't coming from the bag, after all.

When we walked inside, I noticed that the lights were on, but no one aside from the two of us was there. I wasn't even sure if we had any real right to be there. The smell was really strong, though, and it wasn't pleasant, but I couldn't really say that it was horrible. After another moment or two of following David through the factory, I realized that the smell was raw dead meat.

"This is a meat packing factory, isn't it?" I asked.

"Yep," he responded. After another few minutes, we approached a large door. David opened it as I continued to drag the package through and realized that I was walking into a large meat locker as I saw large stocks of meat on hooks with instruments that seemed quite disturbing. David then closed the door behind us.

"What are we doing here?" I asked as I sat the package down beside me. David looked at the bag and then glanced over to me.

"Now, while I set everything up, I want you to go back to my car and get the file in the compartment on the passenger side door. Don't open it, just bring it," he told me as he handed me his keys. I did as he requested and walked out to his car and grabbed the file as he requested. I saw several papers sticking out, but really didn't want to pry, and simply returned to David as I locked the car back.

I walked back inside the meat locker as I saw David standing outside. This time he was wearing black gloves. I admit that I was beginning to feel more and more uncomfortable by the moment. Not to mention the fact that I still didn't understand why we were here.

"Thank you," he responded.

"So, now that we're here. Can you tell me what all this is about?" I asked. He looked at me with a slight gaze of disappointment.

"Haven't you figured it out, yet?" he asked as we walked back into the locker. The truth was that I wasn't entirely sure why we were there. At this point, I had a couple of working theories. The leading one that seemed to make sense the most was the idea that we were about to dispose of Joe Walker's body. "Well, come and see for yourself, then."

When we walked back inside together, I saw what appeared to be a human body hanging from one of the hooks. It was rather disturbing to see the body dangling and hanging. His hands were tied together as both of his arms were being hung from his arm-pits without actually being stabbed like the other packaged meat in the room. The body had a hood over its head, so I had no idea who it was, but I knew it couldn't be Walker, because this body seemed to be intact.

"David, what the fuck?!" I asked as I stared at him.

"Shh…be quiet," he hissed. "Come on."

After we walked back inside, I took every step with caution as

David and I walked closer towards our apparent detainee. I could see that there was no movement, but remained unsure as to whether or not the man in the hood was actually breathing or not.

"Is he...?" I began to ask as David walked closer to the two of us.

"No. He's not dead, not yet," answered David. I stared at him for a moment as I realized exactly why he had brought us all here.

"You brought me here to...to kill this guy?" I asked, shocked by the idea of him being involved in something so heinous. It was one thing to be involved in the cover-up of an intense crime of passion, but this was completely planned; premeditated murder.

"No," he responded. "I brought him here so we could kill him."

"We?" I asked. "David, no. No. I can't do this."

"Yes. Yes, you can," he insisted. "You've killed before, and more than once."

"That was...different," I tried to tell him. The fact of the matter was that it really wasn't so different. Although it was true that I killed Ryan Bailey and Joe Walker in a heated crime of passion. I did hunt Arthur Phillips down to get revenge for my father's murder, even if I hesitated. I had planned to kill him because I wanted him dead and to make sure he couldn't do it again. But that was personal, I...I really didn't even know what to make of this. "Besides, I didn't even know who this is."

"When I found you standing over Walker last night, I realized that he'd never be able to hurt anyone again, just like with the Boulevard Butchers. When the law failed to stop them, you didn't. You found your own proof, beyond any kind of doubt, and stopped them," said David. I looked back at the guy being strung up like a piece of meat, unsure of what to think.

"I don't..." I began to say. The only problem was that I really didn't know what to say.

"Look, I tell you what. Put this on," requested David as he handed me a ski mask. "We'll wake him up and I'll tell you what I have on him. If you don't think I have enough proof against him, he'll have no idea who we are and we'll let him go. If you do see things my way, we'll do what we came here to do. Fair?" suggested David.

I looked down at the mask and thought that if David believed in me enough to cover-up Joe Walker's death, it was only fair that I should be gracious enough to at least hear what he had on this guy. I did owe him, didn't I?

"Okay," I told him, as I reluctantly put on my mask. I watched David put on a similar mask as he took the hood off of the man's face. I saw that the man was unconscious. I did notice that he had light-brown hair that looked almost like a mixture of slight red, and mostly brown hair. He had a small amount of scruff around his chin and freckles on his cheeks.

David walked over to the man and put something around his face. It was hard for me to see what he had, but it wasn't but a moment later when I saw our captive's eyes begin to flutter. He began to look around and began to pull on his restraints as he began to realize what type of situation he was in.

"What the hell?" asked the man, as he fully began to wake up and began to panic as he realized his feet weren't even touching the ground. "Who are you? Why am I here?"

"You're here to pay for your crimes," answered David in a chilling voice, beginning to slowly pace around the man as he began to face me. "I want you to meet Jason Clark."

"Okay," I told him, as I saw the terrified expression on Clark's face. "Why am I meeting him?"

"The reason I brought us here is because you need to understand that people like this are everywhere. People that destroy the lives of others," David told me.

"I don't know what you're talking about, man. Please, just let me go," Clark pleaded.

"I don't know about this," I whispered in his ear. He looked slightly aggravated at me, before turning back to Clark with the same look, before walking over and picking up the file that I'd just retrieved from the car.

"You don't know what I'm talking about?" David asked as he began to open up the file and read it. "Jason Tyler Clark. Born April the twenty-ninth nineteen-ninety. You've been arrested twice for possession of marijuana and then served five years in prison for the involuntary manslaughter of Curtis Anderson. Apparently, you 'accidentally' hit him with your car while under the influence," David accused as Clark stopped struggling and looked down as he began to sniffle.

"Okay…yes. It was an accident. I didn't mean to hurt him. I know that I've made some mistakes in the past, but I'm different now!" Clark shouted as David began to sit the file down.

"Hey, look. He made a stupid mistake and paid for it. Look at him," I whispered. "I'm not going to hurt this guy over something unintentional."

"Is that what you think?" David asked as he looked back over to Clark.

"Tell my friend here what you've been up to since you got out of prison," requested David.

"I…I've been working as a stocker at the local Walmart," responded Clark.

"Oh…but you've been stocking more than just chips and toilet paper, haven't you, Jason?" retorted David, as Clark began to look slightly nervous. "I know for a fact that the moment you got out of prison, you went right back to the drug world."

"That's not true," insisted Clark.

"But Marijuana is what got you busted for wasn't it, and that's not the top thing on the street anymore is it? What is the new drug craze hitting the streets?" asked David, as he began to look back over to me as I began to see the point that David was trying to make.

"You're saying this guy is involved with the Ozone epidemic?" I asked as Clark began to look calmer.

"What is that?" asked Clark calmly, as if he had practiced that statement before. This was the moment I began to question whether or not this guy was really as innocent as he claimed to be.

"He's not just involved with it. He is one of the big time local sellers of Ozone," David stated. "He had several guys working for him throughout the streets. Want to guess the name of Clark's top seller?"

"Walker? You were Joe Walker's boss?" I asked as David began to nod as Clark continued to struggle in his chains.

"I don't know who that is," Clark claimed.

"I already spoke with Walker. He gave you up," stated David. "Now, you're going to tell us who the head of the operation is."

"I'm telling you, man…" Clark continued to plead.

"Shut up!" ordered David as he began to grab Clark by the throat. Clark tried to put on a bold look, but I could tell that he truly was beginning to experience fear. The truth was that I was beginning to feel a little unsettled myself, seeing David in this manner. The truth was that I myself have killed before, but this was a side of David that I would never have believed was there, had I not been forced to see it with my own two eyes. This didn't seem to be him trying to stop the Ozone epidemic, this was his rage, finally making an appearance out in the open in a way I'd never seen.

"David," I muttered out softly to where neither one of them likely heard me, or completely ignored me as he continued to stare at Clark as if he were the cat that just caught himself a mouse.

"Last chance," David ordered, as he pulled out a large knife. "What do you know?!"

"Okay...okay," cried Clark. "I'll...tell you whatever you want to know. Just please..." he began to whimper in his chains as David began to look calmer. David then sat the knife aside and released his grip on Clark.

"Who is creating the Ozone?" David calmly asked.

"I don't know his real name. I swear," stated Clark. "We always just call him...Mister Mist."

"You've got to do better than that, Jason," David stated as he began to pick up the knife again.

"Wait. I can give you description. He is a skinny white guy. I'd say he's in his late thirties. He has a small amount of facial scruff. He always wearing a fancy suit," Clark said.

"Okay. Now, it's time to clean the house," stated David as he handed me the knife. I didn't want to take it as he began to look at me with fierce determination.

I then looked over to Clark and knew that he was a criminal, but I wasn't sure if that meant that he deserved the same treatment as Arthur Phillips, not without asking him a few questions of my own.

"When was Walker dropping bodies? Did he do that by his own choice or did you tell him to?" I asked Clark.

"Whatever Joey did is on him. I didn't have to tell him to do anything," Clark responded. For some reason, I didn't believe him.

"So, you didn't put him up to killing any of his clients?" I asked.

"Even the ones who got caught and were desperate enough to answer any questions they had to get out of jail?"

"It makes sense," pointed out David. "If Walker was about to get sold out, Clark would be going down with him."

"What does it even matter what Joey did or what I said?" asked Clark in a different tone, changing from being riddled with fear to one filled with far more arrogance. "It doesn't matter. They didn't matter. They were just junkies, dying from their own addictions. Even if they were targeted, there will be another junkie dead in the gutter tomorrow, whether or not you…" continued Clark, as I started to become frustrated with his words and lack of interest in the lives of his victims. I began to think about all the evil this man had done, and before I knew it, I grabbed the knife that David had given me and slit Clark's throat in a single stroke.

Clark began to shake as blood began to splatter from his neck. It wasn't something that I enjoyed watching. A small amount of blood began to squirt onto me, but the rest of it flowed from his body. After a brief moment of watching Clark continue to bleed out onto the floor, he stopped twitching entirely as he began to give both David and I, nothing more than a cold dead stare as his body continued to hang from the hook. I couldn't help but look upon the body I'd created in horror.

"I'm sorry. I shouldn't have done that," I stated as David stood back up. He then took off his mask and took the knife away from my hand, which was shaking.

"It's okay," David told me. "He was guilty of a lot worse than just drug crimes. Trust me."

"You knew. Somehow, you knew I'd kill him," I told him as I pulled off my mask. "That's why you brought me here, isn't it?"

"Logan, I brought you here to prove a point. The world is filled with people just like Walker and Clark. They prey on innocent people and they won't stop unless someone stops them, and unfortunately, the police can only do so much to stop these guys," he told me as he sighed as we both gazed upon the work that we had both done.

"David...we just killed someone," I stated, just staring at the body as the blood began to slow down.

"I know. Now, come on. We need to clean up," he told me as I continued to stare at Jason Clark's dead body.

Chapter 8

The Pig Farm

I must admit that this was not the way I was expecting this evening to go. I mean, I've always thought of David as this hard-boiled, serious, and dedicated officer of the law. And yet, here we both were, standing in front of the man that we killed. It was only within a few minutes that the floor under Jason Clark had developed into a small puddle of red blood. The only thing that was left was the lifeless corpse hovering over the red puddle.

"Hey," said David, trying to get my attention. I turned around to see him beginning to move as he handed me the knife. "Go wash that off."

Although I was still rather shocked by everything that I'd done, I did as he asked and walked over to the sink on the far wall. I turned on the hose hovering over the sink and began to spray the thick substance off the knife. It took a moment to completely get off, but eventually I was willing to comply with the decent water pressure. After several minutes, I finished washing the knife until I could no longer see anything but a distorted reflection of myself.

I then looked down to see the red mess in the sink and proceeded to clean that as well. Fortunately, the sink was already stained with red animal blood, so it seemed unlikely that anyone would be able to tell the difference between the blood of an animal and a human by the time I finished cleaning up. As I continued to wash out the sink, I looked over to David, who was beginning to pull Clark down from his hook. As he sat Clark on the floor, Clark's face ended up staring directly towards me and the sink in a manner most unsettling. It was like his corpse was asking…why we had done this to him?

As I looked back at the sink, I found myself questioning David. Instead of wondering whether or not he was going to arrest me anymore, I found myself wondering, why did David do all of this? I mean, even if he was exactly right about the world being filled with bad people who preyed on the innocent. It just didn't make sense.

Could it be that after all of these years of working as a cop and seeing bad guys slip through the cracks in the system, David saw what I did and realized that the occasional act of what I considered a necessary evil wasn't as evil as most people would see it and decided that he wanted in? Or could the darkness that clouds the minds of many men also hold its own little candlelight within David's mind as well.

Whatever the reasoning behind this evening's events; after finishing cleaning the sink thoroughly, I walked back over to David as he placed Clark's body on the floor. We both stared at the body thoroughly. Although I couldn't really speak for David, I felt a sense of disgust, not only for what we had done to Clark, but for what Clark had done in his life. I knew that many say that two wrongs don't make a right, but at least Clark…nor Walker would have the chance to hurt anyone else…and I guess that there is some level of justice in that belief, right?

I looked at David, whose expression seemed to be leaning more towards a sense of determination. He began to get up and examine Clark from different angles. From left to right, from his head to his toes.

"What are you doing?" I asked as he continued his focus on Clark. David didn't even pass a glance in my direction.

"We need to get rid of the body," he stated.

"Yeah, I figured. What's your plan?" I asked.

"Well, I need you to go over there and hand me that large meat cleaver," he told me as I looked over to see multiple knives and sharp objects. I slowly walked over as I gazed upon them all. Many of them were heavily stained, through years of cutting through tender meats, such as steaks, pork, and chicken.

I carefully picked up the meat-cleaver. It was clearly one of the newer tools in the factory as it was so silvery/shiny that I could clearly see my reflection. I saw my face was filled with the uncertainty of all of this, but decided to do as I was requested and handed David the cleaver.

As I watched David begin to work on Clark's body, I must admit I was horrified at the amount of thought that David had put into this, but the truth was that I hadn't even considered doing something like this. I mean, even with as much thought and planning as I had put into killing Phillips and the other Butchers, I never went through with it. At least, nothing compared to this.

I know I've been involved with the occasional taking of a life, whether you wanted to consider them human or not, but I've never been involved with a dismemberment of this level. The only thing that I've ever come close to dismembering was a frog in seventh grade biology and even that wasn't anything like this.

It took longer than I thought it would, mainly because I couldn't bring myself to assist him in the dismemberment, just as he didn't assist me in the actual killing. By the time it was over, there was a large mess on the floor, and Jason Clark was in several pieces. It was far too gory to put into words, so I won't even try. The smell didn't help the situation. The air began to fill with the wretched odor of copper, just as it did with Arthur Phillips, only a lot stronger. It took every fiber of my being to prevent myself from throwing up my lunch.

The smell didn't seem to bother David in the least as he continued his work, maybe because he was used to it after working homicides for the city for years, or maybe he just didn't seem to mind. The fact that he didn't seem to mind the smell didn't make me feel any better about the situation he'd dragged me into. The amount of cold calculation that David was putting into this and as I thought that there were some killers out there that actually enjoyed this type of killing, the more it made me think about how truly sick some people are, present company excluded.

The floor was covered in a large pool of blood as different parts of Clark began to bleed out at the same time. I then looked over to see that Clark's clothing had been thrown over in a pile on the other side of the room. I stared at David, who began to stand up with a small amount of blood on his face. As he looked back at me, I must admit it was rather unsettling to see him this way. Part of me was tempted to confront him and ask him how doing something like this, something so brutal, seemed to be so easy for him.

Despite the gruesome situation I found myself in, I decided to keep my own opinions to myself, seeing as how I was technically the one who took Clark's life. Part of me began to wonder if David cut him up because it was the most convenient way to get rid of Clark, or at least what was left of Clark, or because he simply wanted to. Normally, I wouldn't even question him, but as I looked to David in that moment, I knew that it was becoming more and more obvious that I had no real idea who I was dealing with.

"What now?" I asked.

"Now, we are going to finish cleaning up," he stated. "Go get the garbage bags from the truck. They should be in the back seat on the passenger side."

I once again found myself running back to the truck to get supplies. As I made my way back to the truck, I unlocked it and saw a small orange box that said Hefty and grabbed it. As I relocked the car and made my way back inside, I began to make my way back towards the building as I saw a large bright light begin to shine over me.

The light made my heart jump as I realized that someone was there and was about to catch us in the middle of this heinous act. I jumped away from the light as soon as I could. As I got away from the light, it was only a moment later when the light turned itself off. It seemed a little odd until I realized that the factory had a censor light installed. It also seemed a little odd that they would install such a thing. I began to think and realized it must've been a security measure.

"Oh, shit," I thought aloud myself, as I realized that a place that would install a light to scare off intruders would no doubt be able to afford a security camera. My heart began to race as I ran back inside to David, who looked like he was waiting on me.

"David," I stated. "I think we may have a problem."

"What kind of problem?" he asked sternly as he jumped to his feet.

"This place has security," I told him, as he began to look less concerned than I did.

"Well, yeah. I figured as much," he stated. I began to look confused as he began to walk over to me. "Relax. I'll go find the security room and make sure they won't be able to find anything on us."

"Okay," I told him, beginning to feel a little better.

"While I go do that, why don't you start putting Mr. Clark in the garbage bags," he suggested. "One part per bag. The bigger parts, you may want to double up."

I nodded as he walked out of the room. I must admit, as I looked down at the disgusting mess, I had a hard time doing the task he requested, as the smell alone was almost too much to bear. I began to place Clark's remains in the bag as respectfully as I could, figuring that as the one who ended his life, he should at least be owed that much, even after all the evil he'd done during his life.

It became extremely difficult to try to fill the bags without making a mess all over myself. I then looked around and saw several used red aprons with stains on them and decided to borrow one as I finished the task at hand. When it was all said and done, Jason Clark had been separated into seven large black garbage bags, double bagged considering I think we could agree that we didn't want to take the chance of possible leaking bag. His clothes were also placed in a separate bag in the same way. It wasn't long after that David returned with a small disc in his hand.

"Is it done?" he asked as he saw me tying up the last bag.

"Yeah, he's in there. These are just his clothes," I said as I handed him the bag and looked at the disc. "That the security footage?"

"Not for long," he said as he placed it in his pocket and began to look over at the bags.

"What now?" I asked.

"Well, I'll start taking him back to my car. Seeing as how we don't want anyone to know we were here, I think you may want to finish cleaning up the mess," he said as he pointed towards a large silver box on the wall. I walked over and saw a large water hose inside. As David began playing his role, I began to hose down the floor. It was a larger mess than I anticipated and only spread as I shot the pool of blood with the water.

It seemed to agitate the smell, and not for the better. With a little time, the floor began to look like the original shade of red it was before we showed up. As I began to think of the poor people who work here during the day and make similar, probably slightly less gory messes, it made me have a whole new appreciation for our friendly neighborhood meat-packers.

After David had finished putting the trash bags in his truck, he decided to help me finish cleaning. He walked over by the hose box and got bleach to help make sure the floor was clean and began to scrub the floor to ensure it was spotless of any trace that we were ever. Hopefully, the spotless job we did on the place would make up for any possible health code violations we may have caused with our business.

After roughly an hour of cleaning up the place and cleaning Clark, we began to head out and went back to the car. As I got in the car and thought of the large bags containing an actual dead human being, my stomach wasn't really okay with the thought of everything we had just done.

"Where next?" I reluctantly asked as David began to start the car, somewhat afraid of what he was planning next.

"Well, now that he's dead. We have to get rid of the body and any evidence of the crime," he said.

"How are you planning to get rid of him?" I asked.

"The same way I got rid of Walker for you last night."

"So, what? Burying him? Acid? Burn the body?" I asked as he scoffed.

"Well, not exactly," he said. "You'll see when we get there."

I was really getting tired of him saying that to me. I stared at him for a moment as he started up his car. We made our way from Birminghill to Rockgate, all the way to the small town of Goldmarsh, roughly the same distance, but in the opposite direction.

The longer the two of us sat in the car with Clark lying in the back, the more unsettled I felt as I continued to fear the possibility of being pulled over, even if David was a fellow police officer. The idea of being caught in the middle of the act would certainly be a less than ideal way to end this seemingly endless day.

The entire drive down, we passed multiple police cars, which practically made my skin crawl. As we continued to drive, I nearly jumped out of my seat to see one of the Rocky County police cars lights begin to flash. As the light got closer, my heart began to pound faster and faster as David prepared to slow down our vehicle.

"Easy," he softly said. We slowed down our vehicle as the police car passed us to catch a red Honda in front of us. Although David seemed to be much calmer about the situation, I could tell that he was feeling as much relief as I was. We both continued down towards Goldmarsh. After getting off the interstate, we made our way towards an extremely country-type county.

There were very few actual houses in the area. After driving for five minutes around nothing but grassland, David pulled in front of a small yellow farmhouse located directly next to a much larger red barn.

"Where are we?" I asked. David looked at me for a moment before choosing to ignore my question.

"Get out," he responded, as he opened the door on his side. I decided to do the same as I made my way beside him.

It was hard to see where exactly we were going in the darkness of night, but I continued to follow David as we made our way over to a small pin by a barn. I also had to admit, the wretched odor of the farm was a major improvement compared to the smell of Clark's dead body at the meat locker.

"Alright, now. When he gets over here, I don't want you to say much. Remember, if anyone asks, we've been out hunting," David whispered to me.

"Yeah, I know that's what we told Jessica, but who are we…" I began to ask before I heard a door swing open.

"Hey, buddy," I heard David call out, seemingly to noone. I began to focus as I saw a dark silhouette beginning to walk from the farmhouse. As the man walked closer, I saw his face and saw that the man was older, or looked a little older than David. He had dark skin with a small amount of fuzz that almost made up a moustache, while wearing gloves and a plaid yellow shirt.

"How's it going, you ol' prick?" the farmer responded as he shook David's hand, before the farmer pulled David closer for a proper hug.

"Who are you calling old, ya dried up piece of dog-shit?" asked David as the two stared at each other and began to laugh as David patted him on the back.

"So, who's the kid?" asked the farmer, looking at me.

"This is Logan. He's Jessica's boyfriend until she meets a rich doctor," said David, as his friend laughed.

"Nice to meet you, Logan," said the farmer, taking off his glove to shake my hand.

"You too," I responded, faking another grin.

"Logan, this is Brandon Carter. He is one of my oldest friends and runs this farm. Every now and then we try to get together and go hunting," David explained. I stood frozen and began to wonder what exactly they meant by going to hunt. Did Carter know the truth? Surely not, especially if David didn't want me to speak much.

"Man, we ain't done that in years. What are you talking about?"

Carter pointed out. "So, now that the introductions are out of the way? What brings you both by here this fine evening?"

"Well, I just took Logan on his first hunting trip. We were in the area and I figured I'd feed your pigs something better than that shit you've been feeding them all these years," he said. I stood frozen as I realized the real reason we were here. David was planning on feeding Clark to Carter's pigs. I must admit, out of all the methods I've heard of getting rid of a body, I had to admit that it was efficient as long as we weren't getting caught, if not a little disturbing.

"Two nights in a row?" asked Carter, looking somewhat surprised. "You get the week off from the station or something?"

"Week off?" scoffed David. "I nearly missed my own daughter's birthday party."

"That's right. Last week was her birthday, wasn't it? Tell her that Uncle Brandon says hi," he stated. "Actually, you better tell her Logan. Something tells me you're more likely to see her sooner than this old fart."

"Again, with this? You're older than me, ya senile dildo," stated David as he continued to laugh. "Did you take the kid where we used to go hunting?"

"Uh...yeah," David responded with hesitation.

"What did you think of our secret spot?" asked Carter. David gave me a stern look, likely hoping I would keep my mouth shut before I said anything to cause alarm.

"It was nice," I claimed.

"He doesn't talk much, does he?" asked Carter, looking back at David.

"Yeah, he's just shy. He didn't know we were coming here. Plus, he's not really used to see the animal blood and gore that we're used to."

"So, do you guys go hunting often?" I asked. Carter looked over as David looked slightly aggravated as I opened my mouth again. I think he was just afraid that I might give away certain details of our evening as I continued talking.

"Well, we haven't been in…what? Two years?" asked Carter as David nodded.

"Yeah, I say that sounds about right, give or take a couple months," David said.

"What's the largest thing you've dealt with?" I asked as David.

"This," responded Carter, who pulled out his cell phone and showed the two of us a photo of the of the both of them, holding a deer. "Two hundred and thirteen pounds. Shot down by yours truly."

"Wow," I stated.

"Well, we're not going to be here long. The pigs are still up, right?" David asked.

"Yeah. They really haven't eaten much since you brought them dinner last night," Carter stated. My stomach began to turn as I thought of those animals being able to consume a human being. It really was an unsettling thought.

"Well, we'll just be a few minutes," David assured as it became clear that he wanted to end his conversation with his friend.

"Do you guys need help?" asked Carter, pointing back towards the car. I looked back at David with a slight look of concern.

"Nah, that's okay, that's why I brought him this time. Besides, I wouldn't want you to strain yourself, knowing how delicate you are," stated David with half a grin. Farmer Carter flipped his middle finger towards David, who laughed and gave him another hug.

"Alright. Logan, it was nice to meet you," he stated.

"And you as well," I responded as farmer Carter began to make his way towards his house.

"Thank God. I was afraid he'd be out here all night talking," muttered David as he went back towards his car and pulled out one of the bags in his trunk.

"Come on," he said as I walked over and began to pull a bag out of the trunk. We both dragged a bag over to a small pig pen. The pen was rather large, as I saw it contained dozens of pigs, several of which were asleep.

David then opened his bag to begin to feed the pigs, who quickly began to surround David and I. David began to feed them, but didn't look too thrilled with the situation that we were both in. He still had that same look of determination, like it was one of the more unpleasant parts of the job he knew he had to do.

As I opened my bag and saw the mess inside, it was only beginning to smell worse. My hands began to feel Clark's body. Which parts actually, I dared not to wonder.

"Okay, I don't think I can do this," I told David as he sat his bag and down sighed.

"Look, I understand that this really isn't the ideal way you were expecting the night to go, but it really isn't that bad," he stated as I began to stare at the pigs, who were eager to be fed parts of a human body. "Think of it this way, Clark was a bad guy, right? He hurt a lot of people, right? He can never hurt anyone, ever again. This is one of the few quicker ways to make sure that what we did tonight can never come back to haunt us, but we need to finish this."

I continued to stare at the pigs, who were continuing oinking, as I sighed and began to help David feed the pigs. The truth was that the experience was unpleasant, to say the least, and probably the worst part of our already horrifying day. Several of the sleeping pigs began to wake up to the sounds of their fellow omnivores, hoping to get a piece of the same action. After several trips back and forth between the truck and the pig pin, we finished giving the animals their late night snack. We put the empty garbage sacks in the back next to the one with Clark's clothes and the disc proving we were ever at the factory.

"What about this one?" I asked as David saw the remaining bag that we both knew contained Clarks' clothing and the security disc.

"Just keep it back there. I'll burn everything else along with the other bags later," he said. "Just put my cover over them to make sure no one starts snooping around back there."

I did as I was instructed as I made my way back towards the front of the car. David didn't stop to say goodbye to his friend, which I thought was kind of rude considering how great a service Farmer Carter allowed us to perform on his land with or without his knowledge, but I was in no real mood to share my opinions with David as we made our way back to Rockgate.

As we made our way back onto the interstate, we didn't say a word to each other. I looked over to David several times, who seemed to be solely focused on his driving. He wasn't saying anything, and the truth was that I really didn't want to know what was going through his mind. The fact that he was able to think of doing something so horrible this evening made me uncomfortable being in the same car as him.

After another few minutes of thinking about everything that the two of us had done the past two evenings, I found myself wondering more and more about David. Like why was he doing all of this? How could he? I mean, like how did he just so happen to think of getting rid of Clark in this most unsettling way I could personally imagine? Could he have been involved with something like this before, or had he continually thought about it?

When we arrived back at David's home, I sat frozen for a moment as he got out of the car. I didn't even realize the truck had stopped moving until David began to tap on the glass. I was still thinking about everything that we'd done, from the meat locker to disposing of Clark at the farm. I couldn't believe that I played the gruesome role I had in this evening's events.

I mean, considering the level of planning David put into this evening, it just left me with an amazing disbelief that he'd been able to plan all of this within the last twenty-four hours or so. Or had he already planned on going after Clark and I just so happened to serve as a sign that he was doing the right thing, or did my actions spark something dark inside of David, and if so, where would all of this end?

"So, what now?" I asked as I nearly followed him back into his house. He turned around and looked at me and smiled.

"Nothing. Have a good night," he told me.

"Wait. That's it?" I asked.

"Why? Did you want more?" he asked, raising an eyebrow.

"Well, no. I mean…" I stated, quite puzzled about the matter.

"Look, it's late. I mean, you do have school tomorrow, right?" he asked.

"Yeah."

"Well, go home. Try to get some rest. I'll talk to you in a few days."

"Okay," I said as I began to walk away.

"Wait," he said. I stopped as he made his way towards me. "I think it goes without saying that I would prefer that you keep the last couple of nights between us, especially around other people. It would be a real shame if something were to slip in front of Jess, because then I'd have to kill you."

I stood frozen, not really sure how to respond.

"Just kidding," he said. "Seriously though, if she asks…"

"We were hunting. I remember," I told him.

"Good. Because as her father, if you ever let that darkness come out and around her. I really wouldn't be kidding," he assured him as he began to stare sternly as he went back into his house. "Goodnight, Logan."

I stood there as I continued to wrap my head around everything. As I went back to my own car, I saw David begin to interact with his wife as they hugged. I just didn't understand how he could go in there and be a husband and father with all the darkness that I'd seen him unleash upon Jason Clark. It almost made me afraid for their safety. As odd as it may be, I was somewhat relieved to receive a threat from him in the event that I were to do anything to hurt his daughter, if for no other reason than to know that he knew where to draw a line.

As I made my way home, I began to think that what we'd done was murder. I mean, the actual premeditated act of taking another life. I'm supposed to be a criminal justice student, serving and protecting the law, not going out in the dead of night breaking who knows how many laws. Am I even still qualified to serve the law after participating in the acts that I have? Was David? Was he asking himself the questions or did he even care?

I mean, what would anyone say if they knew what we'd done? I'm sure that some would be able to appreciate what we were doing to a certain degree, but I think considering the amount of brutality and planning that went into these acts would snuff out a lot of our popularity. I know Jessica would never look at me the same if she knew what her father and I had done. What would my family say? What would my father say if he knew what I'd done since he's been gone? I can't imagine someone as religious as him being okay with the idea of his son doing such horrible things, no matter the reason.

Tired, and with enough uncertainty regarding who and what kind of situation I was really dealing with, I went home, figuring that it was an answer for another night. When I got home, I saw that my mother had fallen asleep on the couch, which I thought was for the best seeing as I really didn't want to speak with her on the chance that she could tell that I was agitated.

I took my shoes off the moment I saw her sleeping and crept slowly as quiet as possible, as I made my way into the kitchen. I snuck into my father's old stash of liquor in the hopes that the alcohol would ease my nerves and to help settle my overwhelmed brain. I took a strong swig from a bottle of whiskey. I knew I had no real business getting drunk when I had to go to school in the morning, but I decided to take another sip or two until I was calm.

After a moment, I felt the tension in my mind begin to ease itself and placed the bottle back where I found it. I then walked over to see a note that my mother had left for me.

"Dinner in the fridge. Love you," I read to myself as I looked in the fridge to see what she'd made or gotten. The truth was that I wasn't starving, but I knew that if my nerves continued to get in the way, I would likely develop digestive problems. As I opened the fridge, I saw the white Styrofoam box and pulled it out. I sat it down on the counter and opened it to see what looked like a pound of pulled pork. Pork? Of all the nights to decide to have pork for dinner. Even if it was dead, it brought me right back to Carter's pig farm, as I began to think of the irony that I'd just watched a pig eat a human and now this was left for me to consume.

Under the circumstances, and the fact that I wasn't a fan of this evening's slice of irony, I decided that I would skip dinner after all, my digestive track be damned. I placed the plate back in the fridge and decided to take one more swig from the bottle, before going to bed. The last little bit of liquor may have been just what the doctor had ordered, as I began to feel rather sleepy and tired all of a sudden.

I made my way to my bedroom and began to get undressed as I slipped under my sheets. I didn't look at my phone on the chance that Jessica had tried to get ahold of me to see how it went with David. This time, I wasn't going to let anything else matter. I just knew that I needed to rest and forget everything we'd done, and despite every act that David and I had committed together, I managed to get some rest. It was the first time in days I've been able to get any type of rest.

Chapter 9

Seeing things differently

As I managed to get sleep for the first time in what felt like forever, the one thing that I kept telling myself every time unpleasant memories decided to pop up in my peaceful dream-world was what David told me. Although, I wouldn't go as far as to say that what we had done was right, I knew that Jason Clark and Joe Walker would never be able to hurt anyone again; that much certainly couldn't be argued.

As bleak as that fact may have been, it was the only thing I could focus on to reassure myself. Just like when Arthur Phillips and the other Butchers were running loose in Rockgate. I put an end to their activities and because of it, people were safe.

The next morning, I woke with an odd feeling. It wasn't one of stress or fear over what I had done, and it wasn't sheer exhaustion from the fear of being caught. It was...normal. I really didn't feel any different from any other day, which considering everything that happened the night before was a little off-putting, I figured that shouldn't stop me from resuming my normal schedule, starting with getting ready for school.

It was kind of like when I...had taken care of Arthur Phillips and knew that his partner, Mason Thomas, was being charged for the crimes that I committed. Now, in my own defense, Thomas was a murderer, and many courts would agree that he deserved to spend the rest of his life in prison. All I did was ensure it, like any good Samaritan would, albeit with unorthodox methods. The point was that, for the first time in days, I felt like I was at peace.

Don't get me wrong, I won't deny that what David and I did was brutal and quite possibly evil, but I think I was beginning to understand that what we had done truly was a necessity. At this point, everything that David and I had done the night before just felt like a bad dream, something that was horrible to experience and yet something that has somehow passed from my conscious of guilt. Perhaps a better analogy would be a horror film, memorable and easily disturbing, but for some reason, it wasn't really phasing me like it probably should have.

As I got out of bed, I resumed my normal morning routine without a second thought. Although my diet had been more than a light the last couple of days, it remained the same as I really wasn't hungry. This morning, I was just completely normal. I took my shower. I brushed my teeth. I put on my clothes and gathered my belongings, before heading out the door without any sense of anxiety or any difference from the average school day.

As I made my way to school, I began to wonder why I didn't seem to be as bothered with killing Jason Clark as I felt like I should have been. I began to think about all the damnable acts that David and I had committed. As I look back on them, from the image of all of Clark's body to the sounds the pigs made as they disposed of the body, I still thought it was bad, but it was easier to live with than I felt like it should have been.

The truth was the only thing that truly disturbed me on the matter was how little I cared about what we had done. Normally, if I began to think of such horrors, I'd be terrified of the potential consequences. For the first time, I truly didn't even care. As bad as that may sound, it wasn't that I was taking what we'd done lightly. We took a human life.

I was still scared by the idea of losing everything in the event that we were caught or if someone we loved were to ever find out, even if they wouldn't tell a soul. It still scares me to think of a world where Jessica saw nothing but a murderer when she looked at me. It just didn't feel as wrong as I thought it probably should have.

Don't get me wrong, it's not like I would be eager to become involved in something so heinous, again. As dark as my type of thinking was beginning to become on the subject, I'm saying that if this steady feeling after taking my life was going to stay, I could easily live with what we did. I then began to ask myself a question that I was truly afraid to know the answer to, as I began to wonder…was this the way that other serial killers felt when they killed people?

I mean, after all the years of research and work I'd done on the subject, I always thought that many serial killers committed their acts out of some sick kick, whether they enjoyed the killing as a sense of pride in taking a life or if it was something else entirely. As horrible as it may have been, it just seemed like an easy thing to live with.

In truth, I really didn't feel anything. It was like my entire philosophy of what was right and wrong in the world was beginning to unravel itself. Was I starting to turn into a monster myself, or had I already crossed the line to where I was just as bad as the people I was wanting to dedicate my life to stopping. Surely, the fact that I was asking myself these types of questions meant that I was still a good person, didn't it?

As I continued my own personal thought process of my own sense of morality, I finally arrived at school. I arrived with only a few minutes before my first class and figured I'd swing by and see my friends who were no doubt hanging out where we normally would in the student center. I took a deep breath as I tried to prepare myself for any questions that Jessica may have had for me.

The official story that we both agreed on was an evening hunting trip, but what kind of animal? I don't think the two of us truly discussed the topic. I suppose I should begin by making sure that David already told her, by saying something along the lines of "Didn't he tell you?", if I wasn't sure on how to respond or take control of Jessica's potential nosiness by asking her what he father said and begin from there.

When I finally made it over to the student center, I noticed that none of them were sitting in their usual spots. I looked around the room and even made my way up the stairs to see if they were on the second floor, getting a bite to eat or something. I looked around to see many faces, but none were the ones I sought to find. I knew there was no way they were in class and decided that I'd try to get ahold of them, but then I realized that my phone wasn't even on and hadn't been on since last night.

There was no telling how many texts Jessica could've sent in the past few hours. I decided to bite the potential bullet by turning it on. As the lights began to flicker, it was only seconds before my phone began to buzz with various text messages from Jessica and one from Jacob. I then pulled it out and began to read from it, starting with Jessica's.

"Hey. How was tonight? Dad didn't say much," I read. The next one stated, "Hey, Jacob and Krista want us to go to breakfast together before our last day of classes, tomorrow, are you interested?"

In a much later text after midnight, she sent me another message. "Are you getting my messages?" Another one read, "Hello.". The fifth said, "Goodnight, Logan." The next one was a voicemail she left, basically the same theme of her trying to get ahold of yours truly. She also made a point of telling us that she'd gone with Jacob and Krista to breakfast down the street from the school.

The text from Jacob was likely sent by Jessica's request a few minutes ago while I was driving based on the time, as I read "Hey, man. Your girlfriend is worried to death about you. What up with you?"

I then texted Jessica back immediately, as I truly began to feel guilt again for having worried about me all night. "Sorry, babe. I turned my phone off last night and forgot to turn it back on. I'm fine. Sorry if I scared you."

I then began to sit at our normal hang-out area by myself for a moment. It was only a moment after I sent the text that Jessica decided to return the favor by sending me a picture via Snapchat. I clicked to see that she decided to punish me for my transgressions by sending a selfie of all three of them at the Eastcliff Waffle House to show off. Clearly, Jacob had the same idea, as he also decided to send me a picture. Unlike Jessica's, his picture included well-cooked bacon, hash browns, eggs, and a waffle, which I had little doubt Jacob would completely devour in a matter of minutes.

As I not only realized that I had missed a potentially great breakfast with my friends and made them all worry about me for no reason, I also began to realize that today was in fact the last day of regular classes. Ever. This is one of the last days I will ever roam the campus that I have had for the past four years of my life. I couldn't believe it. I mean, I knew that this day was coming upon us soon, but I hadn't even put any thought into it being this week.

It was hard to believe that this was going to be the last day of normal classes I would ever take. I mean, my education has been one of the biggest parts of my life since pre-k, but this was it. I mean…really it. It was an overwhelming feeling of both accomplishment and fear as I thought of everything that followed our upcoming graduation…the rest of my life.

I took a moment to enjoy my seat as I realized that it may very well be the last time I sat in it. But, it was kind of difficult to enjoy, knowing that I was sitting there all by myself. I then sighed for a brief moment as I decided to make my way towards my classroom. I sat around waiting for Jessica until it was time for class to start and figured, knowing her, that she would likely be late.

I then made my way to my Capstone class, where I sat with a familiar group of friends. I saw my friend Trevor Hatcher, a future homicide detective, or so he frequently told people. It would be unfortunate if he knew how defective his skills in deduction really were, not knowing that he was extremely close to an actual killer.

"What's up buddy?" he asked as I sat behind him.

"Not much, man," I told him. Next to him was another person I'd known for a long time…Jade Foster…a future public defender, who had enough connections, money, and good grades enough to begin her law school degree early.

"Are you excited about our last day?" Jade asked me with a grin.

"Honestly, I've been so busy. I didn't even realize it was the last day until a few minutes ago," I responded honestly as she scoffed.

"Have you at least begun studying for the final?" Hatcher asked as I once again began to feel the sensation of both fear and anxiety. The final. I mean, I had completely forgotten that I needed to study for our upcoming final exam, for both of my exams.

"No. I haven't studied for either of my finals, yet," I told him, scratching my head.

"Really? Aren't you the one who is usually on top of everything?" asked Jade, as I shrugged.

"He's probably got senioritis," said Payton Murphy, another friend of ours, as she sat her stuff next to mine. Our relationship has been sort of complex since high school, as she served as more of the sister I never asked for, and in many of my classes, a strange mixture of being a partner in crime or an intellectual rival.

"Well, I mean. I only have two more finals, this one and Advanced Criminological Theory, which sounds harder than it really is. The other classes are just research papers instead of actual finals for me, which I started the moment I heard about them," I told them.

"You lucky fuck, I've got like three more and have to drive all the way back over here, a different day for each one," stated Payton, looking less than thrilled.

"At least you get time to study for your finals," Trevor stated, sounding annoyed. "I work fifty-six hours a week on top of my classes."

"Sounds rough," she said as she cracked open an energy drink, which for her was like water to a fish, something neither creature could possibly live without.

"Well, my finals for my other classes at the other school aren't for another week or so. This is my last for Eastcliff State," she said.

"Same, closer to more papers than finals," said Trevor, fist-bumping to their mutual anguish.

"Where's Diaz?" asked Payton, looking around as the classroom began to fill itself without seeing our friend, Armando Diaz.

"Come on, now. Armando wouldn't miss the last day of regular classes," suggested Jade.

"Come on, we all know that Armando has never been on time for class a day in his life," pointed out Trevor with a grin. I began to question that statement, as I had known him to be here on time on occasion, but figured it'd be simpler to not add my opinions on the matter.

"Somebody say my name?" asked Armando as he made his way over towards us as he sat down next to me. "Sup, guys?"

"Hey, look who's here," stated Trevor.

"What's happening?" asked Armando, as if we hadn't heard him the first time.

"Well, it's the last day of classes before the final," stated Payton. Armando exhaled with a look of both shock and relief.

"I know. It's crazy. It'll only be a couple weeks before we never come back again," he stated.

"Here, here!" cheered Trevor, picking up his pencil as if it was worth toasting to, which I suppose it kind of was.

"You guys want to meet up tomorrow before class to study together?" asked Payton.

"I'm down," stated Armando as Jade and Trevor nodded. Payton then turned her on gaze me.

"What about it, Logan?" she responded.

"One last time," I responded, as I knew that after tomorrow, it was really going to be over. "Student center…an hour before class?"

"Sounds like a plan," responded Trevor. It was only moments later that our professor, Dr. Bonnie Nava, made her way into the classroom.

"Good morning, students," she stated as she made her way over to her desk. "I know that you all are eager about it being the last day of classes. So, let's get through this last lecture, and then you can all get out of here."

"Here, here!" repeated Trevor.

"Quiet, you," stated Nava to Trevor. Dr. Nava had a thing where she enjoyed roasting the students she liked, which was normally any of the students that were regular participants in class.

The only downside was that she was a retired police lieutenant who normally spent her lectures telling stories of her days in law enforcement. Sometimes the lectures were entertaining, and sometimes...not in the slightest.

Today was a little different than normal as she decided to spend our last day reviewing the key notes in this semester's material, which being a senior level class, was a little bit of everything we've learned in our entire college career. We discussed serial crime, collective violence, various different criminological theories, juvenile crimes, and etc.

After discussing the upcoming final exam expectations, my final college lecture ended. As much as I wish I could say I would miss college lectures, I couldn't bring myself to speak such lies and falsehoods. I knew that it wouldn't be long before my friends were out of class. I knew that Jacob and I were done for the day after this period, but I also knew I'd need to see Jessica before her next class.

I went back to our normal spot in the student center where my best friend, Jacob, was sitting there on his phone with his laptop sitting in front of him. I slowly approached him as he continued to text. I decided not to say a word to see how long it would take him to realize that I was sitting there. To my surprise, it didn't take long before he offered me a fist-bump as I sat down, without even looking over to see if it was me.

"Look, who decided to show up," he stated, as I gave him a confused look.

"What are you talking about?" I asked. "I was right here."

"Exactly! You should've been with us. Eating breakfast and being late to class," he stated as he put his bag down in front of us.

"Yeah? How did that go?" I asked as he put his phone down.

"It was freaking delicious, Logan!" he stated, staring directly at me. I chuckled as I heard his tone of both excitement and enthusiasm, even over something as simple as breakfast.

"Yeah? Did you bring me something back?" I asked, as the thought of eating was beginning to sound appealing, especially after skipping dinner.

"Yeah, but you may have to wait a few hours," he said, as he began to rub his belly.

"Thanks, but I think I'm going to pass this time," I told him as he shrugged and went back to his phone.

"We did miss you this morning," he added.

"Yeah, sorry about that. Long night, and I forgot to look back on my phone," I explained.

"Well, Jessica was worried that something went wrong when you went with her dad hunting. How'd that go?" Jacob asked.

"She told you about that, did she?" I asked.

"She sure did, until you finally picked up the phone. Since when do you hunt?" he asked.

"Yeah, it went alright. I guess, since last night," I lied, deciding not to count the times I went after the Boulevard Butchers or Joe Walker the night before last.

"That's cool," he stated. "Something to do, I suppose."

"How'd your last class go?" I asked.

"It went alright. I'm just ready to get out of here, you know. How about yours?" he asked.

"Same. It was mainly going over the finals," I said.

"Sounds about right," he commented."

"Hey, man. It's the last time we'll be able to go to the game-room. What do you say? One final game of pool? One final battle for the ages?" I suggested. He sighed.

"Ah!" he continued as he began to look over to his laptop. "I want to…but I need to finish this essay. It's due tonight and I have to work until eleven."

"So? Come play one game," I told him with half a smile. He continued to look rather disappointed and eventually sighed.

"I can't, brother. I need every minute I can use," he claimed. I could tell that he truly seemed to be stressing over this final assignment and figured he probably was telling the truth, but saw no reason why I shouldn't try to mess with him.

"Whatever…" I said, acting disappointed. "If you're afraid to getting your butt whooped by me, again, all you have to do is say so."

"Yeah…" scoffed Jacob. "That's it."

"Is it at least an interesting topic you're working on?" I asked.

"Depends…do you find Assessment and Curriculum interesting?" he asked rhetorically.

"No. I can't say that it does," I told him.

"Well, I'm almost done. I only need another couple hundred words," he responded.

"Don't let him fool you. He's been working on that essay since February," stated a familiar female voice, walking over towards us. I turned to see both Krista and Jessica, walking towards us.

"…He's going to be fine," finished Krista as the two began to sit next to us.

"Nope. He'd doomed," I suggested as Jacob decided to reply by extending his middle finger towards my way.

"Such vulgar expressions in the presence of such fair maidens," I responded after a fairly dramatic gasp. "Have you no shame, sir?"

Jacob decided to ignore my sense of humor as his only response was a scoff as he continued to type on his laptop.

"You are not right in the head, Logan," stated Krista, also having trouble not laughing.

"I try to defend your innocence and you repay me with an insult? You shock me madam!" I stated.

"Her innocence went out the door the day she met me," added Jacob, to all of our surprise. I must admit, I was usually the one with a dirty mind within our group, but when Jacob decided to visit my more perverted side, I had to admit that he really went all out. All of our mouths began to hang open as he laughed.

"You ass!" she exclaimed as she smacked him in the arm.

"What did I do?" he asked. I then began to shake my head in a solid mixture of both disgust and pride in my friend, as I knew Krista was likely going to destroy him.

"Hey, you," I said as I looked over to Jessica.

"Hey," she said with half a grin, as began to lean her head on my shoulder.

"I heard you guys had an excellent breakfast," I told them.

"Yeah, it was," stated Krista.

"It would've been nicer if you were with us," added Jessica, sounding as disappointed as she looked. I always hated it when she looked disappointed, especially when I knew I was the cause.

"I'm sorry that I wasn't there. I had a late night, I turned off my phone and I forgot to turn it back on," I claimed in sincere honesty. I'm sorry if I worried you," I told her, as she looked kind of skeptical.

"I don't know if I would go as far as to say that I was worried about you," she claimed, as everyone around her began to give her a skeptical look.

"Oh, sure you weren't. That's why you spent half the morning talking about him," said Jacob, as I began to chuckle at her embarrassment.

"Shut up," Jessica sternly ordered, looking as though she wanted to smack him as well.

"Yeah, shut up," Krista said as she smacked his arm again. I couldn't tell if she hit him to stick up for her best friend or if she was just looking for another excuse to smack him after his previous comments. Either way, I found it rather entertaining, especially when I wasn't the one in trouble.

"Abusive. That's what you are," Jacob accused Krista. As entertaining as their conversation was, most of my attention was still fixated on Jessica.

"Aw," I said to Jessica as I began to wrap my arms around her. "Deny it all you want, you love me."

"Yeah, yeah," I heard her softly say.

"These two are so adorable," Jacob stated as he began to sniffle in an attempt to mock us. "It just gives me a warm, tingly feeling inside."

"Yeah, that's probably one of your STD's. You should probably get that looked at," accused Jessica as I began to laugh, while Jacob began to nod. I knew he thought it was funny too, because he let out a large grin, trying to hold back his own laughter.

"Damn," I stated as the two began to stare at each other, ready to engage in their own battle.

"Alright, Kennedy. It's going to be like that?" he said with a grin as he began to put his stuff away. "Okay."

"You going to class?" I asked as Krista began to get up as well.

"Yeah, I'm going to walk her to her final class and then go to the library," stated Jacob. "You want to come with?"

"Nah, you go ahead and focus on your essay and your STD's," I suggested as Jessica began to giggle as Jacob put his backpack on his back. I myself began to stand up as Jacob walked in front of me.

"You too, Logan? You guys are assholes," he told me as he hugged me.

"Love you too, buddy. Good luck on your stuff," I told him as Jacob and Krista made their way out of the student center. I then looked down at Jessica, who was still sitting, and sat down next to her.

"You okay?" I asked.

"Yeah, I'm just tired. I didn't sleep well last night with all the work, and after Daddy got home last night, he got into it with Nicky," she said.

"Yeah, they were arguing a little when I got there last night. I didn't really overhear what it was about," I answered.

"Well…I probably shouldn't say anything," Jessica began to say, looking rather troubled. I could tell that whatever was the matter, it was serious; I could also tell that she wanted to tell someone.

"Hey, it's okay. You can talk to me," I told her.

"Dad found drugs on her," she told me. Out of all the likely scenarios I could've imagined, that really wasn't one I was expecting.

"What?" I asked in genuine disbelief, rather shocked by that concept.

"I mean, she had it on her. She wasn't acting any differently by the time I got off work. She stated that she was keeping it for a friend, but…" Jessica began to say, as her voice cracked. It was clearly something she was having trouble talking about, as would be the case for most families in this kind of situation.

"That still doesn't make it right. Yeah, I get it," I finished as I began to scratch the back of my head to try to think of a way to assure Jessica that everything would be alright.

"Exactly," she stated, looking as though she wanted to cry.

"Well, I'm sure it'll be okay," I claimed as I tried to comfort her during this somewhat stressful time. "But what do you think?"

"It doesn't matter what I think," she responded. "I just pray that is where her involvement with drugs ends."

"What type was it?" I asked. "If you don't mind my asking."

"Ozone," she answered. It suddenly began to make sense. David had been working on the Ozone investigation for so long and now his youngest daughter was bringing the same substance into his own home. Just another example of life's cruel sense of irony. "I mean, she knows what just happened to Jarrett. I can't believe she would do something like that."

"Well, Nicky isn't Jarrett. Hopefully, she will be able to understand the potential consequences when playing with this type of fire," I stated.

"If she doesn't, I'm sure Daddy will make a point of telling her," Jessica stated. I scoffed.

"I'm telling you, all the Ozone stuff will blow over soon," I told her. If it wasn't the police or the DEA, then something told me that it may be David who stopped Ozone, even if it took one drug dealer at a time. Now, what role I'd play in David's plans, if any, was still to be determined.

"I hope you're right," she said as she began to hold my hand. "So, how did your hunting trip go?"

"It went okay," I lied as I began to specifically choose every word that came out of my mouth so she wouldn't begin to suspect anything. "Why?"

"Why? Well, I'd like two of the most important guys in my life to get along, for starters," she stated firmly. "Second, I've never really known you to be much of a hunter."

"Well, I mean, it wasn't really much of a big deal," I lied again.

"What did you guys talk about?" she asked.

"Well, when you're out there in the wilderness, you're not really supposed to make a lot of noise, let alone converse with each other," I told her, which even I knew was Hunting 101.

"I know that you two didn't go the entire night without saying a word to each other. Spill it," she ordered.

"Look, aside from teaching me a few basic techniques for hunting, he asked me some questions about my future in the criminal justice system for the most part," I claimed.

"He didn't threaten you, did he?" she asked.

"Not really," I said, realizing that I should try to squeeze in a little honesty so she didn't continue to hammer me with questions. "I can say that I saw a little of his dark side."

"I knew it. He always does this. Whenever I've brought home a guy I like, he always tries to intimidate them," she said, beginning to sound aggravated.

"You've brought home other guys?" I asked. She gazed upon me with aggravation. "Okay, seriously. Look, last night wasn't bad. Honestly, we didn't really speak that much about you. I promise, everything is fine with us. It was mainly just us trying to get to know each other, like you wanted, right?" I asked as she shrugged.

"Yeah, I do want you guys to get along," she stated.

"Okay. Well, I just want you to be happy. That's the only reason I went," I lied as she smiled at me. I hated to lie to Jessica, but I knew that a lie was much better than her learning the truth about what her father and her boyfriend had done last night. "...and if he does decide to be a little overprotective, he's just going to have to get in line when it comes to you."

"Does that mean you've thought about...what we've been talking about?" she asked. I stared at her for a brief moment until I remembered that she was wanting me to move in with her. I admit, with everything I've been forced to juggle in the past few days, I still hadn't given much thought to the notion of moving in together like she's been wanting us to do.

I froze as I tried to think of an answer that wouldn't end with the two of us in an argument. I mean, to say that this was a life-changing decision was an understatement. There were still so many things to consider, from finances to actually moving. The concept of trying to find the best possible place had plenty of variables to consider alone, such as living within a reasonable distance to both of our future possible jobs and our families.

"Just forget it," she said as she tried to walk away from me. In an ultimate act of instinct, I grabbed her as I realized my answer. Despite all the recent complexities in my life and all the further complications that could result from this risky decision, I knew the one thing that was stone-solid was the fact that I loved her.

"Wait," I said, as I released her arm. "Listen to me, the truth is that it's a complex decision-making. However, when it is all said and done. I really don't care where we live. If you wanted to live in a bus station bathroom stall, I would move in there with you because you are so very important to me. Don't ever think that you're not just because I have a lot on my plate at the moment.

At the end of the day, I will always come home to you. If it would make you feel better for that to be literal, then fine. If moving in with each other really means that much to you... then make the appointment with that Adams guys and I will start getting stuff together," I assured her. She smiled as she grabbed my face and began to kiss it. She then began to lean her head back on my shoulder until it was time for her to go to her class.

As much as I wanted Jessica to be happy with me, it was becoming more and more difficult to juggle all of these problems. From needing to study for my final, to preparing to graduate, to preparing for the police academy, not to mention dealing with the death of one of my oldest friends, to dealing with my own personal darkness, and now David's involvement, seemingly wanting it to be more than a one-time ordeal, and Jessica wanting to move-in. I was beginning to get dizzy just thinking about all of the stuff on my plate.

Chapter 10

I'm moving out

After another few minutes of relaxing in the student center, possibly for the last time, I decided to walk Jessica to her final class one last time. Although I'd just agreed to move in with her, I was just having a hard time believing that this decision was going to be finalized like this. Not that I minded, it just seemed so sudden.

"So, you've been thinking about moving in together and have a place in mind, but have you thought about what you're going to tell your family?" I asked as she shrugged.

"Well, when Dalton moved in with Andrea, he stood his ground and told them that he knew it was time for the baby bird to leave the nest. I'll just tell them the same load of crap," she said with half a smile. I gave a soft chuckle. "What about you?"

I really didn't know what to tell her. I knew that it would not be an easy conversation to have with my mother, especially since it was only six months since my father's death. I truly hated the thought of her having to live by herself, even if it was bound to happen sooner or later, as with all parents.

"I don't know," I told her. "I mean, it won't be easy, especially since dad died."

"If you want, we can tell our families together," she suggested as we made it to her classroom.

I sighed as I kissed her forehead. "No. I'll take care of it."

"Okay, I'll see you later," she said as she walked into her class. With nothing left to do, I decided to go home and sort out everything that I had to deal with. After driving home from school, I knew that I had a lot of serious thinking to do. However, as I heard my stomach call out in its own special grumble, I decided that there should be no reason to think on an empty stomach and decided to pick-up lunch while I was in the area, Nothing could help me think better than a jalapeño bacon cheeseburger with a large side of fries.

After getting home and devouring the succulent meal, I decided to start looking at my notes. I admit, where Jessica's situation was involved, I was sort of hoping she would be willing to slow down on the whole moving concept, once she'd finally pressured me into agreeing, but I honestly didn't know if that really was the entire truth or not, because a small part of me was intimidated by the concept of being forced to make my own way in the world without training wheels anymore. Maybe this was the universe's way of telling me that it was time.

What was I going to say to my mother? I mean, she's always been a little protective and yes, as the years have passed, there have been days where I haven't even seen her, but that was different. I mean, possibly moving to another city miles away from the home where I grew up, it was truly overwhelming, to say the least.

If I didn't care about Jessica as much as I did, I don't think I would even be considering her request, at least not right now like I was. My life was already complex enough without having more things to worry about. My situation with her seemed to be one of the more complicated of my issues. I was excited, but with this sudden decision, I couldn't help but question the entire idea.

The more I began to think about Jessica and her desire to have us move in together, the more I began to think about her father; what about David? Why did he want the two of us to kill the way we did together? Was he trying to show me in his own way that what we were doing was the right thing to do, or was he wanting to see my reaction to see if I had my own darkness inside myself?

I knew that I had to think of the facts. Although I woke up this morning with a better understanding and acceptance of what he and I had done together, I can honestly say that I didn't enjoy it. Not one single bit. It was dark and quite fair to say…its own act of evil. I can't…I can't do it again. The act alone was almost more than my stomach could handle. As I think of the number of times that I've allowed myself to become involved with such heinous acts, it continues to make me sick.

I mean…I've deliberately murdered three people, and with the self-defense killing of Ryan Bailey…that's four. I was a serial killer, even if every single person I've harmed had their own victims. No, this wasn't the life that I was meant to live. The fact that I'm not in a jail cell right now proves that, right? It's all been just a horrible series of decisions that I've let go too far as it was.

Now, I've allowed David to become involved with my darkness, or allowed him to believe that it was okay to let it out. That's not right. I've done him an injustice. So, if David decided to ask me to help him "take out the trash" again, it would be nothing short of a hard pass. He just wanted me to hear him out, right? Hopefully, David will be able to handle my rejection as well as he could handle a dead body.

I was hopeful everything was settled where David was concerned, but I needed to focus on my upcoming final exams tomorrow. I'm not proud to admit that I haven't actually paid that much attention to the testing material as the previous tests were online and crammed for each exam as it came along, but this was an entire semester's exam, which was in-truth the Capstone where a little bit of everything since I began college was going to examined. As for my early exam, I was hardly worried about my theory test. I had a little doubt that I would ace it.

Over the course of the next couple of hours of trying to put everything behind me other than my school material, I studied until I knew my mom was coming home. I read the textbook's chapters and online notes, from the basics of the criminal justice system, such as the concept of deterrence to lessons on collective violence and the differences between each type of offense.

I then continued by reviewing a small amount of material on the juvenile justice system and the differences it has compared to the system of adult. Most differences were in areas such as terminology and court proceedings for minors who are arrested for more serious charges. I also gazed upon the laws enacted involving childhood cases that impacted the juvenile system, such as Graham v. Florida and Miller v. Alabama.

There was also a small chapter on criminological theory. The basic ideas of why people become involved in criminal activity. Was it based on their choices? Was it based on their own environment? I really didn't have the answers to my own actions, but based on my own criminal activity, the truth was that it's been nothing short of a large mess.

I decided to get back on topic and focus as I finished by going over the final pages of the notes discussing the judicial process, mainly court proceedings. From the day that someone is accused of a crime and arrested, to the various hearings and motions, to plea offerings, to potential trials, I figured that it would be best that I understand the process in the event that I found myself either working within it or I ended up in the clutches of it, defending my own life one day. Hopefully, it'll never have to come to that once I decide to put that darkness aside and move on to create a better and happier life for both Jessica and myself.

There were a few extra things here, but the problem was that there were several years of knowledge to go back over and memorize and understand while there were only a few dozen questions to test on the exam itself. Based on previous tests, I knew the likelihood that the majority would be multiple choice material, but quite possibly a few essay questions I'd have to worry about. Based on my college career, the one thing I could truly say that I've learned from all my classes is the concept of being prepared for anything. A lesson that I have been forced to learn the hard way several times over.

Eventually, I decided to indulge myself with a break. I knew that there was still a lot of material to go over, but after all of that studying and other stress, I had to worry about. I thought that I was entitled to a small nap. A small time where I can just close my eyes and drown out all of life's little problems.

I sat my notes to the side and decided to grab a blanket and just lay down on the couch, just hoping that a small amount of sleep would be enough to restart my brain and give me the energy boost to be able to obtain clarity on everything I had to worry about. I rested my head on a pillow and slowly closed my eyes as I decided to enjoy myself with the rest I would soon be able to enjoy.

Despite my goal of obtaining at least a few minutes of rest, it wasn't even a minute before I began to hear the front door open. In an act of pure instinct, I groaned and covered my head with the blanket as I realized that I was being cheated out of a perfectly well-deserved amount of sleep as my mother began to make her way through the door.

"Hi, honey," I heard her say as I uncovered myself, seeing her smile. I knew that the likely conversation the two of us would be having soon would be about me, I also knew that I'd promised Jessica that I would have it with her, but I knew I wouldn't enjoy it. I decided to respond to her with a fake smile.

"Hey," I responded to her as I reluctantly threw the blanket to the side.

"How was your day?" she asked as she down her purse and placed her hand on my cheek. It was warm and loving, as I suppose a mother's hand should be. I figured that I shouldn't tell her the complexities of my situation to start and figured I should just work my way up to the one involving my living situation.

"It was fine," I claimed.

"Are you hungry?" she asked me.

"I'm starting to be," I answered. Although it was only a few hours ago that I enjoyed one of life's pleasures in my burger, it was beginning to pass as I began to regain my appetite that I had been abusing the last few days.

"What are you in the mood for?" she asked. I figured that she would want us to simply dine on leftovers and still had little interest in eating pork after my actions the previous evening.

"Uh…how about Taco's," I suggested as she went into the kitchen and began to get out the seasonings and shells. I knew that the conversation I was going to have with her was going to be far from a fun or pleasant one and figured that I should at least be a good enough son to cook dinner. I decided to follow her into the kitchen and tell her, "Tell you what, why don't you go relax? I'll cook dinner."

"Do you even know how to make tacos?" she asked, as she gave me a look of skepticism. Although, I would normally be insulted by the skepticism I was receiving, I figured it was a fair question considering I had never actually cooked tacos by myself before. However, I have witnessed her make the meal several times over the years and figured that I knew what I was doing for the most part, as I responded with a simple smile and nod.

After several minutes of unthawing and preparing the meat, I began to get the refried beans and taco shells out of their small yellow box, only to find one already damaged. Needless to say, the odds of some of this food going to waste were unfortunately high, as only two of us were eating. As I smelled and heard the meat begin to sizzle on the pan, I tried to think of how I was going to tell my mother that I was going to be leaving home soon.

I knew the conversation wasn't likely going to end well and wanted to break the news to her as gently as possible. I then thought about what Jessica had told me about what Dalton had told their parents, something along the lines of the baby birds that eventually had to leave the nest. I figured that it was a bit of a cliché example, but it was the best idea that I could think of.

Although a solid answer was refusing to come to me, I decided to focus on the food, hoping its mystical powers of deep thought would be enough to help me think of something. As it became closer and closer to its completion, I prepared by getting the essential ingredients such as lettuce, tomatoes, cheese, and jalapeños, even if I was the only one of us that appreciated a little spice mixed in with our meal.

By the time the dinner had been completed, I managed to stop everything before anything decided to go against my wishes and allow itself to burn. As I removed the shells from the oven and the meat from the skillet, they both looked delicious enough to eat. I thought that it wasn't a bad presentation for a first-time attempt on my own, such as this meal.

"Dinner!" I yelled to my mother as I prepared my own dish. I made myself several tacos, which would normally be considered taco supremes by the time I was through with two jalapeño slices on each, one for each side, with refried beans on the side. I grabbed a drink from the fridge and sat at the table. It wasn't long before my mother joined me. Her plate looked similar to my own, other than the jalapeños.

"Well..." I started in the hopes that she would notice my achievement of not setting fire to the kitchen and making a seemingly appealing meal for the both of us. She decided to closely examine her plate. It was hard to tell what her thoughts were on the food, as her expressions implied that she was questioning, with a slight hint of pride.

"It looks good," she responded as she picked up one of her tacos and began to sniff it, clearly as a means to get a rise out of me.

"Don't be afraid. It won't hurt you, much," I assured her.

"I'm not afraid of a taco," she said.

"I was talking to the taco," I stated as she began to look aggravated as I smiled as we began to feast.

I must admit, the food did taste as good as it looked, better even. It seemed like the perfect mixture of both the tortilla shell and the meat. The cheese and lettuce gave it the extra flavor that cooled the steaming meat, while the peppers gave the dish the heat that tied it all together. As I dined on my first taco, I began to consider the idea that if I didn't like working in the field of law enforcement, I should contemplate the idea of becoming a professional chef. I then realized that probably wouldn't be a good idea on the off chance that I'd only had beginner's luck.

"Mm," I heard her say as she began to enjoy the first bite of my excellent cooking skills. "This is good."

"Thank you," I told her.

"So, how was your day?" she asked again.

"I told you. It was okay," I responded.

"It's nice that we're actually sitting together at the table for once," she stated. It was true that the stereotypical family meal at the table were a rare concept at our house, even before my father passed.

Assuming that one of us or both of us was home to enjoy a home-cooked meal, while it was hot and ready to be served, we would normally eat in front of our television. "What's the occasion?"

I froze for a moment as I had realized that I figured it would be an appropriate time to have our potentially life-altering conversation. I looked at her for a moment and figured that I should break the news to her slowly.

"Well, for starters...my last college finals before graduation are tomorrow," I told her. She nodded as she developed a large smile on her face.

"I know. I'm so excited for you," she stated as I tried to fake my own smile, knowing how fast that smile was about to fade away.

"Yeah. It's a big step where many things in my life are about to change," I informed her.

"I know. Have you heard back from the police academy, yet?" she asked.

"Not yet," I told her, as I took another bite of the food.

"Well, don't worry. I'm sure they'll call soon," she responded.

"Well, it takes time to do background checks and interviews. I should be expecting it within a week or two," I told her. She nodded as she went back to her food. "You know, with all the changes, Jessica was even thinking about moving out of her parents' house to get an apartment."

"Well, good for her," my mother said, paying little attention to me.

"I...uh...was also thinking about...the possibility of moving in with her," I said. My mother froze as she heard my news and sat her taco back on the plate. She then gave me a look that indicated that I not only had her full attention, but that I had completely ruined her appetite.

"How much thinking have you put into this possibility?" she asked sternly, but calmly. I sighed as I decided to push my way through this difficult conversation.

"It is in the talks, but we are looking for a place. She told me that she wants us to go look at a place near Birminghill," I told her as her expression didn't improve, at least not in a way that seemed favorable.

"Really?" she asked. I nodded. "Why are you telling me this?"

"It's kind of a big deal. I mean, I figured you should hear your opinion on the matter," I told her in a sort of obvious manner.

"You already know what my feedback is going to be," she said. "No. I do not approve of the idea of my twenty-one-year-old son moving in with his girlfriend. You don't even have a full-time job, yet. How are you going to pay for an apartment?"

"Well, for starters, I get paid for going into the police academy," I pointed out.

"You also have to pay them, don't you?" she asked. I could see a certain level of determination in her eyes that made me question whether or not she was trying to get me to back-down from the decision, but I didn't care.

"Well, Jessica's father works for the department; he may be able to help out." I thought of last minute. The truth of the matter was that it may have been a complicated request, given everything that David and I have been through together over the last couple of days. It hadn't even occurred to me how my relationship with him would only get more complicated if I were to move in with his oldest daughter.

"I'm sure he's going to be eager to do that when you're moving in with his kid," claimed my mother, sarcastically.

"Look, Jessica is a pharmacist and is making a decent salary without her degree, and I have saved a lot of money over the years working at the store," I assured her.

"Well, that's just rent. What about groceries and bills?" she asked.

"We haven't gotten that far," I responded.

"Okay. Well, you need to have a specific plan before you start going out, looking for houses with Jessica. Some places in this area aren't as safe as they used to be. There is gang violence around Eastcliff and Birminghill," she told me.

"Yeah, I know. The entire world is dangerous, mom. I'm not blind to that," I said. In the back of my mind, a tiny part of me wanted to tell her some of my deepest darkest secrets so she would know that anyone who was stupid enough to try to bring harm to me, or more specifically, someone that I cared about, would be in for a rude awakening. It wasn't long before I realized that type of comment wouldn't make her feel any better and decided to move on from the thought.

"I promise that this is not just an out of the bloom idea," I told her, even though that's kind of the way that's exactly what it was or the way that it seemed based on the way that Jessica pitched it to me. "We haven't made any definite decisions. We haven't even settled on a place."

"Well, good," she responded. "I don't think you're ready."

"Why not?" I asked. She looked at me as she decided to bring back her previous expression of sternness.

"You're too young, for starters," she claimed as she took another bite of her food.

"What are you talking about? You were twenty-two when you married dad and moved in with him," I told her.

"I'm done discussing this," she said as she attempted to go back to her food.

"Okay. I just figured you should know that the conversation has started, rather than just surprising you when the day comes and telling you," I told her.

"What happens if you buy a lease and decide that you don't like the place, or if something happened between you and Jessica?" asked my mother, beginning to sound rather concerned.

"I need you to understand this. I have always been smart. I wouldn't even be considering doing something like this if I wasn't serious about her, mom. I love her, okay. I want to build a life with her and I really want you to be okay with that because I want you to be a part of that life," I told her.

"So, you're saying that I have to just be okay with it if I want to be a part of that life?" she asked, beginning to look insulted and hurt.

"That is not what I said at all," I told her, feeling aggravated. "Do not put words into my mouth."

"You know what, I'm sorry. I really am. I knew that this wasn't going to be an easy thing to talk about because I knew you wouldn't like it, especially after what just happened to dad," I told her.

"Don't," she stated. "Don't bring him into this."

"Look, I miss him too, but we have to be able to move on after what happened. I'm not saying it'll be easy. I'm not saying we should forget about him, but it is time that we move forward. I have to move forward," I told her. "And like it or not, this is how, mom. It won't be today. It won't be tomorrow, but it will have to happen one day, and you're going to have to accept the fact that I'm moving out," I told her. She sighed as she stared off into the distance.

"You know what, okay. Fine," she stated as she picked up her plate and got up from the table. "You can do whatever you want."

"Where are you going?" I asked, beginning to feel slightly guilty.

"I'm going to my room for the night," she said as she threw away the food on her plate. The only solace was that she'd eaten the majority of the food on her plate, so the only thing wasted was roughly half a taco and what we hadn't put on our plates.

"It's barely seven," I pointed out to her, as she continued to walk away.

"Goodnight," she said, before I could even get another word in.

After she left, I sat at the dinner table for another moment as I looked at what was left on my plate, including an entire taco and some beans that looked like paste at this point. Although I really hate to waste perfectly edible food, I think we both knew that neither of us were in the mood to finish eating dinner after our little spat.

Despite the anger and concern my mother had expressed, I'm sad to admit that this conversation still went better than I expected it to. The only thing I could do was hope that I was doing the right thing and hoped that she would accept the decision that I'd made. I then went back upstairs to continue studying for the upcoming test, but had too much on my mind to even pay attention to the material.

I hated the idea of upsetting my mother, just as much as I hate to disappoint Jessica. It just seemed like whatever choice I made will end up hurting someone I cared about. I sat back and held my head as I began to wonder just how I managed to get myself into these kinds of messes. As many good points as my mother had made regarding this decision, she just didn't understand that I wasn't just trying to get away from home; I just knew that I wanted to start a new chapter of my life with Jessica.

After a moment or two of laying down and contemplating all of life's little problems, I heard my phone begin to buzz. At first, I thought it was Jessica, making sure that I had spoken to my mother as I had promised her I would. I was filled with a mixture of both shock and disturbance as I saw that it was actually David calling me.

Chapter 11

We can't

I must admit, I wasn't delighted to see David's name appear as an incoming call on my phone. I had enough on my plate to deal with without toying with the idea of becoming a serial killer during my free time. I don't know what David had in mind after what we did with Jason Clark and Joe Walker, but I knew that I'd need to make sure that I didn't allow myself to become involved with something like that, ever again.

At first, I decided to simply ignore David's call, and soon, my phone stopped ringing. I sat my phone aside as I decided to return to my studies. I knew that I didn't like the way that my last conversation with my mother ended and thought I should try to do something about it. I got up and walked over to her bedroom and knocked on the door.

"Mom?" I asked.

"What?" she asked. She sounded aggravated.

"Can we talk?" I asked.

"We don't have anything more to talk about," she stated.

"Will you just let me in?" I asked. For a moment, I heard absolutely no noise coming from her bedroom. I stood there for a few minutes, hoping that she was going to open the door at any moment in the hope that she would settle down long enough to discuss this important part of my life.

"Mom?" I announced once again.

"We'll talk in the morning. Goodnight, Logan," she stated. It was at that point I began to wonder at what point the child became more mature than the parent. I guess, I was being forced to learn the hard way as I decided to return to my notes and deal with that situation later.

When I returned to my room, I made my way over to my desk and returned my focus to my lecture notes. I then heard the phone begin to ring again. I looked to see that David was calling again. I sighed as I reluctantly decided to answer the phone.

"Hello," I answered.

"Logan, it's me," I heard David say sternly. "Listen, I think we need to meet up, tonight."

"I...I don't think that is a good idea," I told him. For a moment, I didn't hear anything except David's breathing on the other side of the line.

"It won't take long, but it is important," David insisted. "Listen, I'll be at my garage outside the house. Meet me here as soon as you can."

"Fine," I told him as I heard the phone disconnect. It didn't really take a genius to figure out what he was wanting to talk about. I knew that both Walker and Clark were bad guys, but I couldn't allow the same type of work continue any further than it already has. It wasn't that I was feeling guilty over what we did. In fact, it was just the opposite.

The truth was that I still remained sort of numb at the thought of what we had done to Clark, which debatably was much worse. The feelings of guilt and fear I had when I killed Ryan Bailey, even in self-defense, compared to the feelings of nothingness I felt over brutally disposing of Clark and Walker, frankly, scared the hell out of me.

Besides, I've already killed more people in this lifetime than I wanted, even if I have gotten away with it every time. It's best to not push my luck any further than I already have. The real question was how I was going to explain this to David. With any luck, he'll agree that what the two of us had done was a mistake, and he was just calling me to tell me that, and maybe that we never needed to do or think about it again.

But what if that wasn't why he was calling? What if he was wanting to meet up to inform me that we had a problem? What if we'd made a mistake at some point, or someone caught us, or someone was beginning to ask questions about Clark or Walker's whereabouts? That would certainly be unsettling indeed, especially if it's a problem that he was hoping that we'd be able to solve together.

These questions continued to rattle around in my head as I grabbed my essentials like my keys, my phone, and my jacket to go out to meet David. As I walked back upstairs, I approached my mother's door to inform her that I was going back out. I resisted the urge to knock, as I knew that she probably wasn't in the mood to deal with me at the moment.

Assuming that she really did go to her room to retire for the evening, I figured that it would be best not to disturb her. I then went back downstairs and decided to leave a note for her on the door in the event that she came out of her room, wondering where her son had gone in the middle of the night, again.

I went to my car and backed out of the driveway to make my way over to the Kennedy residence once more. While driving, I just kept praying and hoping that everything that was going on would soon be over. I knew that when it came to the unthinkable and possibly unforgivable acts, I had already crossed the line. I also knew that if there was any hope for redemption as far as I was concerned, I would have to tell David this, tonight. I still remained optimistic that the one-time experience was enough to settle his darkness once and for all. In the event that it wasn't going to go the way I hoped, I wanted to make sure he could except an answer that he may not like.

As I pulled onto their street, after a roughly ten-mile drive from my house, I saw a large cloud of smoke on the street. I pulled closer to see that the smoke was coming from a barrel in front of David's garage. There was also a man sitting beside the barrel. Through my own deductive skills, I deduced that the culprit behind the fire was coming from none other than David himself.

As I pulled closer, he began to signal to pull in right in front of the fire. I did as he requested, even at the risk of my car being covered in ash. I got out as I saw David continuing to put in a small item that I couldn't see. I walked closer to see that it was the disc from the meat-packing plant, as we watched it melt in the fire.

"Thank you for coming," he stated as I walked up to him.

"Where is everyone?" I asked.

"Well, Dalton doesn't live here, anymore. Jessica is at work, and Nicky…hell, I don't even know with her anymore," David said with a disappointing tone. "Wife is probably in the bed with a book or something. So, I'm out here."

"Having a bonfire…in the beginning of May?" I asked as I looked at the barrel.

"If anyone else asks, then yes. Look a little closer," he suggested. I looked inside the barrel. Although it was somewhat difficult to see the bottom over the bright yellow and orange flames, I managed to see parts of a shirt among the ashes.

"Clothes?" I asked as he looked back at me, nodding. I looked back and realized he was getting rid of further evidence. "Clark's clothes."

"Well, what did you think I was going to do with them? Donate them?" he asked as he scoffed as he continued to throw the entire bag into the fire. "I already burned Walkers. This is the last of it. Back up."

I took a step back as the bag began to melt on the fire, emitting an odor that made it difficult to breathe. I started coughing uncontrollably for a moment as David patted my back. I heard him cough only once or twice as I began to catch my breath again.

"You know you're not supposed to burn trash bags, right?" I asked.

"Well, the bag had all the other bags that had Clarks and Walkers' blood in them. Don't worry, that's the last of it. I'll put out the fire in a few minutes," he assured me as I stared at the fire for a moment.

"Was there something you wanted to talk about?" I asked.

"I just wanted you to be here with me. Just so you know the last of the evidence has been destroyed," he claimed. For some reason, I wasn't buying what he was selling as I stared at him for a moment. I then remembered that he may also have wanted to talk about Jessica, assuming she had already spoken to her family about moving out of the house to get our own little place.

"You said it was important," I reminded him.

"Well, I also wanted to ask you if you had spoken to Jessica today," he told me. I nodded.

"Yeah, earlier," I answered.

"I know she asked about what we did last night," he stated.

"She did," I added. It began to make me feel better that this was where the conversation was leading. I think it was safe to say that my relationship with David was complicated enough as apparent killing buddies without involving my relationship with his daughter into the mix of things.

"What did you tell her?" he asked.

"You already know what I told her," I told him. "Remember? We settled on the story. We went hunting."

"So, she didn't ask you about details or anything?" he asked for clarification.

"No. Why? Did she say something to you to make you think I said something I shouldn't have?" I asked.

"Not really. She kind of made it seem like I intimidated you though," he said as I shrugged, not really sure what to say.

"Well, considering that we're burning evidence of a murder. I can't imagine where she would get that impression," I said softly. David gave me a look of unease as he nearly jumped. "Don't worry. I didn't give her any reason to be suspicious. In the worst-case scenario, you threatened me to make sure I wouldn't do anything to hurt her, like any father would do."

"Are you intimidated by me?" he asked. Once again, not really sure how to respond to his question, I merely shrugged.

"Do I have a reason to be?" I asked.

"Not as long as you keep my daughter happy and keep your mouth shut," he said. We continued to stare at the fire for a moment, before he put it out with a bucket of water. "Come on."

"Where are we going?" I asked as we began to walk into David's garage. It was very dark in there for a moment, but it was still bright enough outside to see what was inside the garage. It was pretty much like you would expect a garage to have including a car, tools, a work table, and a lawn mower with quite a bit of dust inside. It also had a certain smell that was a rough mixture of musty sweat and gasoline, which I suppose is normal for most garages.

David closed the garage door behind me as he turned on the light over his side counter. On top of the counter, there was a small manila folder laying down next to a small drill. He picked it up as he offered me a seat in his garage and sat it down next to the seat he pulled up for himself.

"I also wanted to ask you, how are you doing, or I guess I should ask, how are you handling everything…from last night?" he asked, seemingly curious.

"I…really don't know what to say," I told him honestly.

"Well, what are your honest opinions regarding…what happened?" he asked.

"Are you asking me if I enjoyed it?" I asked. He nodded as I looked down.

"No. I didn't," I responded as I leaned closer to David. "I mean, we did kill a man."

"I understand," he said, looking slightly disappointed.

"But…" I started, looking back up at David. "…he was also a bad guy."

David began to nod as his look of disappoint began to shift into something else. As if he was almost forming a smile or a smirk. "Yes, he was."

"He even admitted it," I added. The truth was that I didn't think I would be able to relax until I realized what type of person David really was when it was all said and done. "How did you feel?"

David then leaned back in his seat as he exhaled. "Honestly, even though I'm not proud to admit it, it felt good."

"Are you saying you enjoyed it?" I asked. David stared at me for a moment and proceeded to scratch his head.

"Not the killing part, but…" he started looking unsure of himself.

"But what?" I asked.

"I've been trying to put Jason Clark away since he got out. Since he got back on the street, he's been smarter about his crimes, one of those guys that you can never prove to be guilty due to a technicality or some other form of bullshit," he said. "I'm glad that, after all these years, he's finally been stopped."

"Even if it *that* was the way that he was stopped?" I asked. I knew that this conversation was going to be harder than I thought when I figured out David's angle in all of this was, even if I was still slightly scared to find out the answer.

"Yes," he said calmly and definitively.

"I don't get it. I mean, you're a cop. Aren't you supposed to be preserving the law. You know, working with in it to stop guys like that?" I asked.

"Well, you're trying to become a cop, right? Should you not be working hard to learn the law and not murder people?" he asked. I sat silent for another moment as he began to scratch the back of his head. I think we were both seeking a common ground when it came to our work.

Whatever David's motives behind this unusual side of his personality, the real question was where will it end with him. The fact that he chose to have us kill Jason Clark, someone who for the most part a total stranger to the both of us gave me the impression that this would not be a one-time occurrence. But it has to be, David was right. Neither one of us had any business being involved with the activities that we've been involving each other with over the past few evenings. As I looked back over to him, who was now standing up trying to think, there was still something about this whole mess that kept bothering me.

"How did you know?" I asked David, who looked over to me.

"Know what?" he asked.

"How did you know that Jason Clark was guilty?" I asked. "You said you've known him to be guilty. How do you know?"

"Well, I've had my own suspicions about Clark going on for a while now, all the way back when he was first arrested for running over Anderson, a few years back."

"Why? It was an accident while he was under the influence, wasn't it?" I asked.

"I've been doing this for a long time, Logan. I find it kind of suspicious to believe that killing his ex-girlfriend's new boyfriend could be an accident."

"I see," I responded. Although I must admit that David had a valid point, he hadn't succeeded in reassuring me.

"I never had any proof of his drug-related crimes, not until the other night. After I took Walker's cellphone, I looked at his contact information to see who might end up missing him. He really didn't call anyone hardly, but his text history was filled with instructions from Jason Clark, including messages suggesting that he should take care of certain people that could hurt their business."

"Still..." I said.

"Logan, we stopped a murderer. According to what you told me about the Boulevard Butchers, you've stopped killers before too. We have stopped killers who wouldn't hesitate to do it again in a way that the law never could. Can you honestly tell me that some part of you doesn't feel like what we did was the right thing to do?" he asked.

I stood up from my seat for a moment, and I took a step away from David to collect my thoughts. I must admit that David had me. Although I didn't feel right after taking Ryan Bailey's life, maybe it was because I was afraid of being caught. After stopping Phillips, Walker, and even Clark, I wasn't filled with much remorse over what I had done.

I spent the last several months thinking that it was because they had taken lives of people including someone I had cared about…dad…Jarrett, both taken from this world sooner than they should've been. But what if David was right? What if this was the reason I've been able to live with what I had done as well as I have. Was it because deep down, I believed it was right?

He was right that every single one of the people that I have stopped, with or without him was indeed guilty of taking the life of an innocent person one way or another.

It was also true that stopping those guys was something that the law, the same law that David had sworn to protect, and the law that I was about to serve myself, had failed to do time and time again. As much as I hated to admit it, David was making a solid case.

I looked back over to David who gave me a stern look. It was as if he knew, as hesitant as I was on the matter, there was a part of me that knew he was right. I decided to sit back down in the seat as I tried to find the strength to face him and tell him he was right.

"Am I right or wrong?" he asked sternly again.

"You're right," I told him as I continued to face the floor in shame of what I was telling him, agreeing that the philosophy of vigilante murder didn't seem as bad as it should. "They were bad guys. They did bad things."

"And now, they will never be able to hurt anyone else," he added. "Right?"

"Yes," I nodded.

"You know that there are more people out there just like them, don't you?" he asked. I nodded once again as I continued to lower my head in shame. "People who continue to get away with horrible acts because there isn't enough evidence to prove they did it beyond a reasonable doubt or because there are small technicalities that allow them to continue to do those bad things.

"Yes," I repeated.

"Isn't the badge supposed to mean anything? What's the point of having all these laws if they don't do a fucking thing?!" he asked beginning to sound angry. I looked back up at him to see that his face was beginning to turn red. Once again, I found myself unable to retort or argue against David, no matter how much I wanted to.

"I don't know," I told him.

"Maybe I was meant to let you go. Maybe this is what we are supposed to do. When the law fails to do its job and bad guys, killers are able to get away with this," he said as he opened up his file and showed me the picture of a dead woman in the street wearing a teal colored hoodie and black pants. Although it was hard to tell what happened to her from the photo, there was a pool of blood around the victim's head.

"Who is that?" I asked. David looked at the photo as he sat back down in his seat.

"Her name was Chloe Jackman. She was murdered a couple of years ago. We caught the killer. This is him," he said as he handed me another photo. This was of a man had dark hair, but short, like a stereotypical lesbian haircut. He had a couple of freckles and his cheeks similar to Jarrett's and some noticeable facial hair on his square-jawed chin with an expression filled with anger.

"Who is he?" I asked as I handed him back the photo. He looked at it again and scoffed. "His name is Harold Reeves. We found out he was in the area the night that Ms. Jackman and her boyfriend were murdered. She used to date Reeves, and we figured it was a simple case of jealousy. We found the weapon that tied the crime back to him. However, because the investigating detective didn't get a proper search warrant like he was supposed to; Reeves walked."

"That sucks," I stated.

"It was bludgeoning in case you couldn't tell, with her…with a lead pipe," he added as he pulled out another photo. This one was much more gruesome. It was another dead body. The head was so horribly mangled that if David hadn't already told me it was Jackman's boyfriend, I might not have even been able to tell if I was looking at the face of a man or woman. As many pictures of dead bodies as I've seen, this was one of the most unpleasant, almost too awful to look at.

"Reeves hit Jackman many times, based on the injuries. Apparently, the first blow was enough to kill her. With the boyfriend, that was an entirely different story. The medical examiner couldn't even determine how many times he was beaten, clearly…he took his time," added David.

"Where are you going with this?" I asked as David scooted his seat closer to mine.

"Reeves now lives in Birminghill, still living his life a free man and the police haven't been able to catch him doing like this again, but…" he said.

"You think he's going to do something like this, again?" I asked.

"Well, you saw the same photos I did. Based on the level of violence, I think that someone who can do that is bound to do something just as bad eventually, if he hasn't already. Don't you think?" he asked.

"Maybe, maybe not. Either way, what exactly did you have in mind for Harold Reeves?" I asked as David stood back up.

"Well, I was kind of hoping, with your help, that we'd be able to get justice for Ms. Jackman and her boyfriend," he suggested. "It's been years since the case was thrown out, and no one would ever have to…"

"Wait," I interrupted as my head began to shake. "No. We can't."

David looked back over to me as face that almost looked filled of excitement began to fade. I took a step back at he sat his file back on the counter.

"Okay. I get it. It's too soon," he stated. "I mean, it's not like I'm suggesting we go take him tonight. I want to get my hands on the guy that's responsible for the Ozone epidemic, first anyways. That's who really…"

"No," I interrupted again. "I mean, we can't. We can't do something like that again, ever."

David looked confused as he crossed his arms. "I see. You do not think that what we are going is morally right?"

"It's not just that," I told him. "Well, first of all, we have already killed the same number of people as Reeves. How does that make us any better than him?"

"Because what we've done together has saved lives. It keeps guys like them from being able to hurt innocent people like these two, like your friend Jarrett, even your father," he claimed. I knew what he was doing. He was trying to use my anger towards what happened to both Jarrett and my father to try to manipulate me. It was the kind of move I'd expect from someone like Jason Clark or Arthur Phillips, but not from David.

"Don't," I said. "Don't bring him into this."

"I'm just saying, if you hadn't discovered Phillips and dealt with him the way you did…" started David.

"Then my dad would still be alive!" I shouted. David frozen as I took a deep breath as I tried to calm myself down. "On the night that I caught Phillips and the others in the act of…ya know. I tried to stop them. They saw me. They chased me. Ryan Bailey caught up to me, that is why I killed him. It was self-defense. Then…I guess Phillips and the others found my father and…"

"I didn't know," David said. "I'm sorry. Hang on, you said "Phillips and the others." How many Boulevard Butchers were there?"

"There was Ryan Bailey and Phillips. Mason Thomas, who took the warp for all the killings and…"

"And?" he asked.

"There was another guy. He was supposedly a new recruit who hadn't crossed that line, yet. I confronted him when he was trying to leave with his family. He nearly wet himself when I did. It was pretty clear he wasn't like the others.

"What happened to him?" David claimed.

"Once I was certain he hadn't actually killed someone, I let him go, and told him that if he ever came back, I'd kill him…guilty or not," I told him.

"What's his name?" David asked.

"Brian Mitchell," I answered. "Look, it doesn't matter. My point is that this vigilante life has already cost me my father. I want to get out before I lose any more of my humanity in the process. I just want to do the right thing, for once. If you want my help taking down both Ozone and Reeves, I will be happy to help you, but it needs to be done the right way."

"Logan…" he started, beginning to look disappointed, which also made me a little concerned.

"David, I appreciate you not turning me into the police for what I did. You saved my life. I want to repay you by showing you that it's not too late for either of us to be redeemed for our sins. We can be better. We have to be," I stated.

"Okay," David said as he began to nod. "I understand, now. It was wrong of me to ask you to become involved in this. I promised I would accept your answer after Clark, and I am a man of my word. I won't bother you again with my ideas on the matter, again."

"David?" I asked as he walked beside me and put out his hand to shake it.

"Everything we have done the last several nights will stay between us, including everything you've told me about the Boulevard Butchers," he reassured me. I shook his hand as he opened the garage door back. "Have a safe drive home, Logan."

I stared at him for a moment as I stepped out of his garage. David followed as he locked the door behind us and made his way into the house. I watched as I began to wonder if I should try to talk to him. He did seem rather disappointed, but I really didn't know what I would say. I mean, what would you say to cheer someone up after talking them out of committing a murder? After all, I knew that I was doing the right thing.

Neither David nor I had any business taking down murderers that way. I know what we did was wrong, even if it did potentially save lives. In the long run, no, no one has the right to play God and take life. As for the extremely gray area that we had been traveling within, I knew that refusing his offer to become any further involved in murderous acts was the step in the right direction to any possible kind of redemption.

I felt the warm spring air blow across my face and watched as the moon began to rise into the dark, starless sky. It was as if there was a bright light being shined on me in that moment. Despite all the darkness that was inside me and around me, I was still worthy of the light and good in my life. If David could not see that, well, that was his problem. My only hope was that he would be able to see things my way.

After a brief moment of collecting my thoughts on the matter, I soon got back in my car and began to make my way home from David's house. I walked through the door to see that the note I had left for my mother was still stuck there. I took it off and threw it away and figured by this point, she was likely asleep and did everything I could to not make any type of noise as I made my way back to my room.

I sat back in my room and just began to process everything that I needed to get done at this point. I saw the notes that were lying on my bedspread and realized that after a long day and plenty of studying, I was honestly just tired of it all.

I figured that if I got up early the next morning, I could ace my first exam without a problem and then meet up with my study buddies as we had planned and could just worry about it all tomorrow. I grabbed all the pages of notes and the textbook and placed it on a giant pile on my desk and just climbed into my sheets to fall into a peaceful slumber at the notion that I had put my darkness and the complications that followed away in the back of my mind to where they couldn't bother me any more.

Chapter 12

Last Day of School

During the night, I tried to focus on all the positivity in my life and how lucky and blessed I was to have all the people in my life that cared about me. Of course, I thought of my loving girlfriend, Jessica, who was somehow able to see past my own personal flaws and had come to accept me as her loving boyfriend and had proven herself to be one of the main reasons that I only desired to better myself.

It wasn't long before I thought of our close friends Jacob Breland and Krista Sholl, who've always made a point of keeping things interesting in our friend clique, never allowing things to get dull or boring. I thought of my mother, who, despite feeling down at the thought of me growing up and moving out and on with my life, would soon accept the reality and remain the loving caregiver I have always loved and cared for. I then thought of my father and the fact that, whether or not he was here or not, I knew he would always be with me in every step I took in my life.

All my friends from college from Armando, easily one of the biggest sweethearts around to even Payton, who I admit has had moments of annoyance in my life has become like the annoying sister I never actually had, but deep-down can honestly say that I cared for. I then thought of Trevor and Jade and everyone else I've come to know and care for over the years. It was hard for me to accept that I was soon going to be forced to say goodbye to all of them and all the others who'd had such a huge impact on my life over the last several years.

I figured that I owed it to all the people in my life who helped shape me into the person I am today. A person, who has made some rather gory mistakes, but who truly wanted to make the world around him a better place, not just for himself, but for the people that he cared about. Imagine it, it won't be long before I start going after the bad guys within the confines of the legal system. No longer continuing my vigilante career and no longer being scared by the idea that my darkness would completely consume me, until nothing remained but an empty monster of my former self.

I knew that if I had agreed to David's proposition, that would be the path I'd likely head down, intentionally or not. I knew I'd be letting all of those people down. This decision was nothing short of a second chance at life, a rebirth even. I was finally free to pursue a great life, filled with hope and happiness. It all began as soon as I graduated from Eastcliff State.

A few hours later, I woke with ease as I realized that this was the last day I would be engaging in my college morning routine and figured that I should savor every moment of it. I looked over to my phone to see, aside from a message from Jessica. Today, her message was pretty much summed up by the fact that she was planning on meeting with her classmates in the hopes of studying before her final exam as well, and had planned for the two of us to rendezvous later.

As much as I wanted to spend time hanging out with her, I knew that it was the right thing to do. I messaged her, telling her that I didn't mind in the slightest, as well as wishing her luck on her exam. I also noticed that it was actually half an hour earlier than I would normally get up.

Despite my warm-silky sheets telling my mind to enjoy a few more minutes in my bed. Not even to fall asleep, but just to stay in, relax, and enjoy the comfort while I still could. As devilishly tempting as the idea was, I figured I should get up and study for my first upcoming exam in a few hours. As painful as it was to do, I summoned the will to remove my sheets and get up.

I decided to take a moment to stretch as I made my way over to the shower, like I normally did. The hot water from the shower was almost as tempting to stick around and enjoy as my bed sheets. Unfortunately, as soon as I was sure I was clean, plus a few extra minutes of self-indulgence, I knew it was time to get out. I dried out and proceeded to get dressed.

Based on the time of the morning, I knew that my mom had already left for work, so we really didn't have a chance to talk about last night's argument. I figured I'd just put it off until my tests and college career were all taken care of. I then grabbed my notes, and my other essential items and headed out the door, still a few minutes ahead of schedule.

I then made my way over to the school, the last time I knew that I would be doing so for my education. There was a part of me that was feeling eager and triumphant, with the feeling that I was only a single small obstacle away from graduating. It was very similar to the feeling that I had four years ago when I graduated from high school. It also seemed rather bittersweet that everything was going to change. My routine. My friends. Everything that I had been developing into.

As I made my way onto the interstate, I decided to mentally focus on the course material, figuring I could let my emotions run their own course when I was actually done. I thought of the notes and material I had learned over the years. From the intro to criminal justice to the basics of criminal law and procedure to criminological theory to the other classes, everything that has led me to these last exams. I realized that I was indeed nearing the finish line of my college career to the point where I could see it with all my friends and family cheering me on.

I tried to focus on the material of my exam, but began to have trouble with the answers to similar questions that I knew I would likely be on the exam to trick and confuse my cognitive process. Had I let myself overstress on simple questions meant to confuse me, or had everything else in my life distracted me from my finals?

I began to feel a slight flutter of anxiety, knowing how important these exams were. Could I, of all people, begin to suffer from last day of school jitters? Me? The same guy who single-handedly took on serial killers and drug dealers who actually find myself worrying about an exam? Inconceivable! I knew that I knew the material, but I suppose it's just what the test represented that gave me an uneasy feeling. Maybe my friends were feeling the same way, and that's why we had all agreed to meet when we did.

Despite it being early, parking at the school has always been ridiculously poor. I had been forced to walk roughly half a mile away from my classroom. It was a walk I had taken many times over the years, from the freezing cold to the blazing hot. Rain or shine. Normally, I wasn't a fan of such exercise, but decided that I should try to make the most of them one last time.

As I made my way from the graveled parking lot, I walked along the sidewalk, next to College Road. The only sounds that accompanied me as I walked along, from my own breath, were the sounds of moving cars and trucks speeding beside me. As overwhelming as the thought of leaving college was, that was one of the experiences I really didn't plan on reminiscing on my college experience and the future.

I then headed over to the upper-level of the student center where we all agreed we would meet. When I walked inside, I saw dozens of college students sitting there, many eating breakfast or talking with their friends. Not really much different than any other morning to be completely honest. I searched to see if any of the others had also woken up early and decided to meet up, but I saw no one.

I decided to grab a booth near the cafeteria close to the main entrance, figuring it was the most likely place I'd be seen. I knew that I was scheduled to meet the rest of my classmates for our online Advanced Criminological Theory exam. I brought the exam up on my laptop and took a deep breath as I realized it was time to click on the exam. However, after starting the exam, I received a very welcome surprise when the exam turned out to be only a single question, reading, 'It's been a long semester and you've all worked hard. Click-Yes and promise not to mention it to any other classmates to receive a 100. Have a nice summer!' I felt a grin pop on my face as I happily accepted her terms and accepted a perfect score on the easiest final exam in college history.

Although I hadn't worried myself about this particular exam, I must admit I didn't think it would be this easy, but thought it best not to question the good things in life. After the first exam, I began to sit my laptop on the side and sat my notes on the table as I began to focus and study for my other exam that I knew wouldn't be as easy as my first. Although, I only needed a passing grade on the test to make an A, I figured that since it was the last day, I should give my all on the final and do the best I could.

After almost half an hour of studying, I heard a familiar voice saying, "Boo.", not even in the sense of trying to startle me, but just to get my attention. I turned to see which of my study buddies was trying to catch my attention, only to see that it wasn't any of them. It was Brice Katona, another student graduating with us and a good friend of mine. He was a big-built homosexual with a small blonde afro, currently wearing a teal tank-top with shorts and sandals with a rainbow bandana.

Brice and I had met during our freshman year, and we have had the occasional class together since then. He lived on campus since he's from South Atlanta, but I normally found him working at the school library or working in the student government. As I was majoring in criminal justice, Brice was a psychology major. While I wanted to focus my career on the things that people do, he chose to spend his life trying to figure out why people do what we all do.

"What's up, buddy?" I asked with a smile.

"Greetings, Earthling. I come in peace," he stated as he sat down across from me. "How goes your finals?"

"Well, I only really have one left since I'm done with all my other classes. I'm supposed to meet some of my classmates here, but I decided to get a head start," I told him as his eyes slightly widened.

"Oh, wow. Then today is your last day then, huh?"

"Yep, looks that way," I told him with little expression as I really wasn't sure on how I felt on the matter yet.

"Well, in that case…" he started as he stood up. He started walking closer as I stood up too, and he landed a hug on me. "…I'm really going to miss you, buddy."

"Yeah, I can honestly say that I will miss you too," I told him. Although I may not have always been one of his closest friends, he has always been a good one. He was one of the familiar faces that I knew I would likely never see after graduation, which I knew was going to make things harder when the day finally came that we walked across the stage and never looked back.

As we broke up our hug, I looked over to see a familiar face walking over towards us with a plate of breakfast.

"Payton!" exclaimed Brice as he nearly pushed me back to my seat as he jumped to give her a hug.

"Hey!" she greeted, with far more excitement than I'd had.

She sat her plate down on the table in front of me before she hugged Brice back. "What's going on?"

"Logan is being mean to me," he accused as the two looked over to me. I sat there looking completely innocent, with my mouth slightly open from the accusation. For once, I was actually behaving myself.

"Oh, yeah?" she asked, looking at me with her standard glare of irritation.

"Can we annihilate him?" he asked playfully, with glee.

"We can't right now. I need to study with him for our test," she explained, sounding slightly disappointed. "Wait until our test is done and then have fun."

"Torture him by making him do the exam first, brilliant," he said as he let out a giggle. The truth was that I was quickly losing interest in their conversation as I saw what Payton had brought to eat. Her plate contained brown and still sizzling bacon and sausage, yellow scrambled eggs, and perfectly buttered toast. The only thing missing from the delectable dish was a nice side of hash-browns, but the plate looked full enough.

Next to her plate was one of her signature Monster drinks; today's can was purple. Although I wasn't really familiar with energy drinks, I'm pretty sure that the color purple meant that it was Ultraviolet flavored. Although I've never been one for eating breakfast, the smell was tempting enough for me to look over and stare at the food with the idea that I might actually indulge myself on our last day.

"You both know that you love me," I told the two of them. They both gave me a skeptical look. I figured that since it was the last day, I should try to have some fun with them, and by fun, I mean try to annoy the shit out of him. "See, she even brought me breakfast."

As I made my way for the plate, Payton jumped to block my hand with her arm, crushing it into the hard table.

"Back off! I need this!" she stated, as pulled my hand back to see the damage it had sustained during the early cuisine crusades. Although, it was only slightly throbbing after being slammed into the table, I figured the minor injury was merely a warning. "Why don't you get your own plate?"

"Nah, I'm not that hungry. Truth be told, I was only going for the bacon," I told her. She stopped and ripped a small chunk of bacon and threw it at me. Although, I was only kidding, I knew that it would be unwise to not take advantage of this rare peace offering between Payton and myself.

"Oh, thank you. I knew you loved me a little," I told her with a grin. She rolled her eyes as she began eating her breakfast.

"Ugh! All this touchy-feely stuff is making me sick. I'll see you guys later. Good luck on your exams," he stated as we both waved goodbye to him.

"You too. See you, buddy," I told him.

"Later!" announced Payton. I decided to wait until she was halfway through her meal before I mentioned that we probably had to return our focus to the final.

"Have you been studying?" I finally asked as she looked up at me with her fork in her mouth.

"Mm-hmm," she nodded. "I studied for like four hours last night. How about you?"

"I…uhh…did quite a bit yesterday afternoon. Maybe two or three hours, give or take. I didn't study last night much," I stated.

After another moment or so, Armando Diaz came walking by us, looking a bit like a lost puppy. I figured that he was looking for us, but it looked as though he had no idea what he was doing when he walked past the two of us.

"Armando!" I announced. He stopped and turned to see the two of us sitting across from each other in the booth.

"Oh!" he said as he smiled. He then took the seat, right next to mine and greeted the both of us with a fist-bump. "How's it going, guys?"

"Pretty good," I said. "You looked a little lost for a minute."

"Yeah," he responded, as he began to look around the area. "This is probably my first time over here to be completely honest with you."

I couldn't help but grin, as I knew that when Armando and I usually met up to study or hang out, it was never up here and had just never realized it until now, on our last day of school.

"Really? Why?" asked Payton, as she finished eating her breakfast.

"I don't know," he shrugged as he began to pull out his notes. "I guess I just never really had any interest in coming up here."

"Are you ready for the test?" I asked. He gave a bit of a skeptical look as he shrugged again.

"I guess. I mean, I didn't really study much last night. I know the material. I'm not really that worried about it. How about you guys?" he asked.

"Well, based on what she told me, we have both been studying quite a bit. I'm not really that scared of it. I know that she's been stressing over it," I claimed.

"Have not!" she argued in objection, much to my surprise.

"What the hell are you talking about, Payton?" I asked, shocked by her denial. "You worry about everything related to school."

"Well, that is true," she said, as she began to nod in agreement. "I guess I am nervous because I've pretty much hit 'fuck it' at this point. Nava's exams are never hard, and as long as I do decently. I should be okay."

"Payton. We've been making nearly the same grades on every assignment. We don't even really have to pass the final to pass the class," I stated.

"Yeah, but you know, I like to do well on my exams," she stated.

"Which is why we're here," I pointed out, showing her one of my lengthy pages of notes. "Want to get started?"

She nodded as she scooted her plate, primarily filled with crumbs at this point, to the side as she began to look at her notes. Armando decided that his look through his notes online as he pulled out his Apple laptop, where we kept our online Powerpoint presentations filled with the material. One of the more convenient teaching methods of the 21st century in my own humble opinion.

After several minutes of studying through the material, Payton decided to break the silence among the three of us by asking, "Do you guys want to quiz each other?"

"Yeah, sure," said Armando as he scooted his laptop in front of Payton's plate so he could properly face her. "Who wants to go first?"

"I will," volunteered Payton, before I could ever think about answering. She scrolled through her own personal notes until she came upon a question she thought would be challenging for the both of us. Of course, she would never admit that's what was taking her so long. I've known her long enough to know the types of games she enjoyed playing.

"Sometime today, if you would be so kind," I requested as she gave me a slight look of irritation as she looked back at the paper.

"Okay. I got one," she said with half a grin. "What is the difference between specific and general deterrence?"

I was kind of shocked that this was the question she decided to go with, but maybe there was a sentimental side to her after all that she had decided to express on our last day of classes together.

"Well, specific deterrence is when the courts focus on punishing a specific culprit to show him that crime doesn't pay..." I started.

"...while general deterrence focuses on the rest of the population to show everyone else that crime doesn't pay by making an example out of the defendant," added another female voice, walking over to the table. We all turned to see both Jade and Trevor making their way over to join our group.

"That's right. Well done, Jade," she responded. Here I felt like chopped liver as she completely ignored the fact that I had answered the first part of the question. She then sat her page back down and saw me looking at her. "Yeah, you too, Logan."

Better late than never, I suppose. Jade sat her purse next to Payton. Armando, the sweetheart of the group, decided to be nice and took Payton's plate over to the dish washer's window.

"Thanks," she said as he came back to his seat. Jade took off her jacket, andunlike Trevor, who almost always wore the same red hoodie, pulled a seat up at the end of the table between Armando and Jade.

"Where are your notes?" I asked as he gave me a skeptical expression followed by a smirk.

"I don't need them. I got this. Go ahead, ask me a question," Trevor insisted. I must admit that his optimism and arrogance were truly remarkable, especially considering that he had the lowest grades of our entire clique, or at least suspected as much.

"Alright," said Armando. "What are the four main types of collective violence?"

Trevor stared frozen for a minute, trying to remember the answer. He squinted one of his eyes as he scratched the back of his head.

"I know that one of them is terrorism," he stated, sounding unsure. The majority of the group continued to gaze in amusement as we waited to see if he would ever finish his answer.

"Good…go on," I insisted. He then looked over and tried to sneak a peek at Payton's paper sitting on the table next to him. Payton then smiled as she snatched her notes from where he wouldn't be able to see them.

"Uh-uh," she said. "You said you've got this."

Trevor squinted his eyes at her as another minute passed, waiting for Trevor's response. By the time Jade finished pulling out her notes on her own laptop, she had apparently grown tired of waiting to see if Trevor could actually finish the answer. She then tapped his shoulder as he raised his index finger to the rest of us. He then looked at her laptop and returned his attention to her with a large grin on his face.

"Terrorism, rioting, vigilantism, and lynching," he answered, before quickly turning his attention back to Jade's computer. I must admit, I began to worry about Trevor, not for not knowing the answer, but for taking so long to answer it. The exam was only seventy-five minutes long. At his current pace, he'll never finish on time.

"Correct. Thank you, Jade," responded Payton, as Trevor looked insulted as Jade merely smiled and winked at him. "Okay, which form of collective violence is considered to have high levels of organization and individual liability?"

"Vigilantism," I responded. I figured, given my recent activities with David, I would be in trouble if I didn't understand the textbook concept of vigilantism. Still, it seemed a little ironic that I should be the one to know the answer at the top of my head.

"That's right, Logan. Thank you for actually answering quickly," responded Payton.

"Okay, my turn," stated Armando, who stared at his laptop for a moment, before he grinned and nodded. "Okay, what is considered to be the most common type of criminal offense in this country, today? Is it A…petty theft, B…vandalism, C…prostitution, or D…drug crimes?"

"Drug crimes," responded Trevor, surprisingly quickly compared to his last attempt to answer a question. Perhaps my concerns weren't as necessary as I had previously thought. It was true that drug crimes were the most common type of criminal act in the country.

It was also true that the Ozone Mist operation that David wanted my help with wasn't making things any better. Apparently, the D.A.R.E. operation didn't have a large impact on kids once they grew up. We lived in a much different day and age from when we were little to adults, I doubt that even McGruff the crime dog could even have any impact.

"Figures, that's the one you would understand the most about," muttered Jade. He looked over at her, giving her a scoff.

"See, that's how you do it, Payton. He actually gave us options. Thank you," responded Trevor.

"Shut up," she replied. "Go to the next question."

"What criminological theory suggests that crime is a result of a lack of integration with social groups? Hint: It can also be classified by the neighborhood crime rates and ecological characteristics?" asked Armando, completely reading from his computer screen.

"Social disorganization theory," answered Jade, in a matter of seconds.

"Right," he said as he sat his paper down.

"I got one," stated Trevor. "What is the difference between a misdemeanor and a felony?"

"You really think that the easy one will be on the final?" asked Jade with an expression filled with skepticism.

"Maybe," he stated as he shrugged. "You never know."

"Well, a felony can be punishable by up to one year, whether it's probation or prison time. While a misdemeanor is a lesser offense, it would more likely result in only jail time or punishment of less than twelve months," responded Armando. I looked around and noticed that I wasn't responding to the answers. I knew the answers, but they were all answered before I could get the chance to speak, I almost began to feel left out, or worse, like a referee.

"Okay, my turn. Name the court case that stated that criminal defendants have the legal right to an attorney if they can't afford one?" I asked.

"Go ahead, Foster. You're the law school student," responded Trevor.

"Gideon v. Wainwright," she responded, looking smug.

"What year was it?" I added.

"1963," she added.

"Is she right?" asked Trevor.

"Yep," I responded feeling slightly disappointed as Jade who proceeded to gloat with a dab, the first time in years I've actually seen someone perform such as move, but I suppose it was reassuring to know that some things would never die.

"Okay. Let me do a couple before we head to class," requested Jade, looking more serious as she picked up her notes.

"Alright. Bring it on," stated Trevor with a smug grin.

"What are the four types of serial killers?" she asked. I figured that I was the only one of us who actually *was* a serial killer, more or less, I figured it should only be fair that I answer.

"Uh…hedonistic, visionary, power and control-based, and…uh…" I started as I tried to remember the last part when it hit me all of a sudden. "…mission-oriented."

"Very good. Now, based on our notes, what are the seven types of hedonistic killings?" she asked. Trevor began to look shocked.

"Dang, you want us to list all of them?" asked Payton, sounding shocked by the question as well.

"Well, we're in a senior level class. She'll probably ask us that and have us describe them as well, right?" asked Jade. It was true that the exam would more than likely have a lengthy answer such as this on it. I could appreciate why Jade figured it would be a good question to review.

"Do you want us to describe them as well if we answer?" I asked.

"No. I think if you just know what the seven types are, we should be alright," she responded.

"Well, there is the black widows, contract killers, revenge killers…" started Armando, beginning to count off the different types of murderers with his fingers as if he was counting to ten back in elementary school.

"…there are also Angels of death and lust killers," added Payton, who began to look confused herself.

"That's five. Two more," responded Jade.

"Hang on," I stated really quick as I went down the list in my head until I went through the process of elimination. As everyone started going through their notes, the answer hit me. "Cost cutters and lethal caretakers."

"That's right," she said, as Payton smacked herself in the forehead for not remembering the answer. "We got about ten minutes. Do you guys want to head over?"

"Hang on. I got one more question to ask," I suggested. Trevor and Jade looked at me as Payton and Armando began to put their stuff back up before class, "What sounds good for lunch?"

Trevor scoffed as Jade proceeded to put her own notes back in her bag.

"Uh…tacos," suggested Payton.

"Tempting, but I just did that for dinner last night," I informed her.

"Get a burger," suggested Trevor. "I think that's what I'm going to do after the exam."

"Maybe," I thought out loud as we all finished putting our belongings away as we all made our way to our classroom, one last time. We all went over to the liberal arts building and made our way into our classroom, located on the second floor of the building, where several other students were already sitting there studying their own notes for the coming exam.

Chapter 13

What am I doing?

Today, I sat in between Payton and Jade. Jade decided to spend her last few minutes before the exam, posting a selfie of herself on Snapchat. I later saw on her story that she was talking about the fact that it was her last day of Eastcliff State and how emotional the whole experience was for her. Personally, I was skeptical about how emotional Jade really was because she was, in a fact, a future after all, not to mention the fact that she wasn't really a big fan of school. Although I suppose it's fair to assume the last day of school hits everyone differently.

Payton decided to spend her free time pulling her notes out one last time. She also decided to guzzle down the last of her energy drink in the hopes that the concoction of ingredients would not only give her the energy she needed but help her focus as she studied as much of the material as she could before the test.

I looked up in front of us to see that Armando and Trevor were both on their phones. Although it was hard to tell exactly what they were doing, I figured that it was safe to say that at least one of them was playing a game from the sounds that started to come from one of their phones. If that is what they wanted to spend their free time doing, it made no difference to me.

I then decided to pull up the online notes on my own phone. After I did, I saw all the different chapters and categories I needed to focus on and internally felt like I was being stretched in several different directions. I began to really feel my heart race as I began to feel the pressure as I realized that this test was the last part of my entire college career. I just couldn't believe that everything came down to this. I knew that I wanted to do well, and I knew the material for the most of part, but there was still so much to cover in so little time. I didn't even know where to begin.

Although the class had an easy professor for me to not usually have to worry about the exams, the material still gave me an unsettled feeling. I then decided to take a deep breath to analyze my current situation. I thought about all the material that I already knew, and I decided that it would be best to quickly go through the material that I wasn't as familiar with. Then it hit me, criminology, the subject that focuses on all the different theories on why criminals commit the acts they do. Surely, if I were a professional on this type of material, I would understand how I ended up in the situation that I had with David.

Wait! Now, take it easy, ol' boy. Come on, Logan. You need to focus on one thing at a time, starting with your final college exam. You can worry about David and all your other problems later. You owe it to yourself and to everyone else to do your best work. Just one more time. That's what I kept telling myself. I then took another deep breath as I began reading the material regarding criminological theory.

I began to read from word to word. Sentence to sentence. Slide to slide. The material started with social disorganization theory. I knew that material as I had written about it several years ago in my actual criminology course. It seemed easy enough to understand and then proceeded to Labeling theory.

It was a theory that also seemed relatively easy, even if I wasn't as familiar with the concept as much as some of the others. I began to quickly look through several other theories, such as Strain theory and the social bonding theory. I tried to read as much about it as I could as I tried to work through the selective differences in the material.

After several minutes of quiet studying and slight inward panicking, Dr. Nava made her way to the head of the classroom with a stack of papers in her hand as she stated, "Good morning, students."

The majority of the class, including myself, looked up as Nava sat down in her seat with a smile and a faint chuckle. "Well, this is it, isn't it? The end of the line for most of you."

This was the point when I realized that study time was officially over. Although I have had several distractions keeping me from spending more time focusing on my studying, I figured that after several years of hard work, I was finally ready to take this final test and move on with the rest of my life. I looked around to see several students who couldn't help but express their own excitement over graduating with a gigantic grin on their faces, including Trevor and Payton. Several students even began to nod as Nava began to laugh again.

"Okay. Well, I won't keep you guys any longer because I know that all of you are probably ready to get out of here. To those of you who are graduating, I would like a chance to wish you all luck as you go serve the community as officials in the criminal justice system, and I also want to tell you all that it has been a pleasure to teach you all. Well, most of you," she said as she looked at Trevor. Trevor looked around, beginning to look singled-out.

"Are you ready?" she asked.

"Me. Oh, yeah. Bring it on," he suggested.

"Why don't I do that? Now, I'm going to pass out your test. Put your name. Student ID number, and date. Fill in the blanks. When you're finished, bring the test to me and then you can leave."

As the answer keys were passed out, I felt my heart begin to pace faster as I began to fill out all the necessary information. I didn't really understand why I was nervous, but I figured that I should just try to remain calm. It wasn't but a moment later that Nava passed out the actual exams. Jade passed it down the line, and I moved the others past Payton.

The test felt thick, as if it was at least several pages long. I decided to look at the back of the exam to see how long it was, to see that there were approximately fifty questions, all multiple choice. The good news was that the last question seemed to be a free past as it read, "I'm tired. It's been a long semester, so just fill in A." It wasn't as satisfying as my morning exam, but I suppose one question was better than none.

As I began to feel the assurance that I knew I would at least get one question right on this exam, I turned it back to the front and got to work. My method when it came to these types of exams had been the same since I was in middle school. I would go through, carefully read the question. If I knew it at the top of my head, I would answer it immediately and move on.

If I wasn't entire sure, trying to determine between two possible answers due to my inability to remember which answer was which, I decided to go back to it later and put a small unnoticeable dot by what I think the answer could be. If I had no idea at all what the answer was, I would work to try to remember and leave it completely blank, and ultimately guess if it came down to it.

There was a large variety of material that we had been learning and that I knew to expect when taking my exam. Fortunately, for the most part, the test was material that I had gone over recently and knew. The majority of the exam involved the judicial system, which I seemed to understand more than any of the other chapters. Perhaps I should skip the law enforcement division and simply follow Jade to law school.

By the time that I had gone through the exam, I had answered the majority of them. There were roughly ten questions that I was skeptical about answering immediately and maybe three that I had absolutely no idea about. As I tapped my pencil against my face, I saw several students begin to get up from their seats, already done with the test, including Armando.

After he turned in his test, he went back to his seat to collect his bag as he offered both Payton and I a fist-bump as he softly whispered, "See you guys, later."

Jade was the next member of our little group to finish. She looked confident when she turned in her exam, or at least when she got up from her seat. As she began to leave, she chose not to say anything, but gave us a simple smile as she walked out of the classroom. After several more minutes, I knew that I wouldn't be able to get a completely certain answer on the questions.

I knew that I would have to base my answers on my instincts. One of the ones that I wasn't sure about one of the true or false questions, based on a possible technicality. Nava was known for being devious enough as she used specific wording in the possibility of tripping up one of her students. I've always hated these types of questions when it comes to true or false as the odds were completely equal. I'm just as likely to be right as I am to be wrong. I read the questions over and over in my head and simply decided to go with what I figured to be the best possible answer.

As I continued to try to remember what the remaining answers were, I noticed that Payton had completed her exam as she got up and grabbed her bag. Her expression suggested a small amount of concern as she went to turn in her exam. However, it seemed to change as she grinned when she walked by me to leave. I suppose she was glad to know that it was finally all over. By that point, I was only three questions away from completing my final college exam.

I looked around the room to see that almost everyone had already finished, as I noticed that there were only five people left in the room, including Trevor, Nava, and myself. Two students in the back also seemed to be having trouble. Although I wasn't entirely sure how long I had been sitting there, I knew that it had been somewhere around half an hour.

It was shocking that so many people had already completed the test. Maybe it was because everyone else didn't have so much on their plate to worry about, like moving out or being a serial murderer. It was also equally likely that everyone went through the test as fast as they could, just hoping to get college over with once and for all. I admit that since high school, I was frequently one of the last few to finish. It's not that I didn't know the material, but I liked to take my time when it came to these exams and usually tried to go back over them when I was done.

I then watched as the next person to get up from the exam was Trevor. He walked over to Nava and turned on his exam with the biggest grin I had ever seen on his face. He then walked past my desk as he left and patted me on the back. He then whispered something to me. I couldn't quite hear, but I'm almost positive he said, "Good luck, buddy."

I offered him a fake smile as I had trouble completing the final question. It was based on material that we hadn't gone over in the last several months, and I didn't get a chance to look at it before the test this week. I decided to go back and closely look at all the other questions and answers I had already submitted to make sure I was content with what I was turning in. By the time it was over, I was faced with this one question that I'd narrowed the answer down to two possibilities.

Eventually, I had to come to the realization that, despite my best efforts, I had no idea what the answer was. I realize that it was a lot of thinking over a single question worth only two percent of the exam, but the way I figured it was still two points, which could be two points away from passing or succeeding with the degree I wanted.

I eventually decided that I had plenty of other things to worry about instead of this single question. I simply decided to bubble in the first possibility and stood up to turn in the exam. I cherished every step I took over to the professor as I realized it was the final exam I would be turning in at Eastcliff State College.

"Have a nice day," I told her as I handed her the exam.

"Yeah, you have a nice life. I expect great things from you, Mills," she stated as I began to walk away from her. I grabbed my folder of notes and threw them away as I made my way out the door.

And that was that. I was officially done with college. I walked out the front door to see the halls were completely empty. I then walked out the front door of the building with the overwhelming sensation of both relief and anxiety in the knowing that I was final finished. On this beautiful sunny day of May, I was officially done with college forever. I took a deep breath as I turned around at the liberal arts building, where I had taken so many of my classes over the years.

As I realized that my college life was coming to an end, it made me feel a little sad as well. I realized that I wasn't really as ready as I thought I would be and certainly not as ready as many others. I figured that after all this time, I owed it to myself to at least have one finally stroll around memory lane, or at least one final walk across the campus.

I decided that I should begin my tour by walking back inside the liberal arts building. Although I had spent perhaps even half of my college classes in this building, there was only one that held true significance for me. I walked over to the classroom right across from Nava's final exam room. Room 102.

I looked in there to see that nobody was inside. I walked in to see an empty classroom. Although it may seem strange to most to find me here, this room had significance to me. In my freshman year, it was where I had taken my speech class. Although, it wasn't really the best class I had ever taken, it held a lot of memories. It was the place where Jacob and I had taken our first college class together. It was also where I met Jessica. It was crazy to think how far we had all come over the last several years.

I decided to sit in my old seat. In the first row, the second closest to the right. Sitting in between Jessica and Jacob. Next to us was also where I met another good friend of ours, Andrew Wallace. Andy had graduated last year, one year earlier than the rest of us, but the time we all had together. I can truly say it was one of the biggest highlights in my college experience.

After a moment of sitting and thinking back to all the fun times I had in this room, I knew that it was time to leave it behind. I walked out of the room and walked over to the main lobby of the building. There was a small room where many students were sitting in between multiple vending machines containing a variety of treats. Although it was rare that I would partake in the school machines, I decided to indulge myself on the last day and bought myself a cool, refreshing bottle of Dr. Pepper.

I then made my way out of the liberal building for the very last time and made my way over to the student center. I walked through the side door of the first floor to see all the seats that were provided for the students socializing, studying, or whatever they frequently chose to do with their spare time. I made my way over to the table that my social group normally used, which was currently empty, as were many seats currently. This came as little surprise during finals week. Instead of sitting in the chair that I had sat in so many times before, I merely felt the top part of the back of the chair and proceeded on my last look around the college.

The next part of my goodbye route was going to be one of the most difficult as it was one of my favorite places on campus, the campus game room. Although I wasn't technically supposed to go in, as the front door was locked and a sign on the door said it was closed for finals, I decided to go in through the side door under the side door stairs that the administrators never think to lock-up. I figured they wouldn't mind since I wasn't planning to do anything really wrong other than briefly saying goodbye.

As I looked around to make sure no one was paying any attention to little old me, I opened the side door and made my way inside. It was dark when I first went in. It took a moment, but eventually I found the light switch. The first thing I saw was multiple televisions and seats where many students have spent the last several months trying to alleviate their problems and stress through video games. I've never really been one for playing with game consoles and quickly made my way over to the air hockey table in the very back corner of the room where I had played many games with friends.

I then made my way over to the other side of the game room, where the campus held three pool tables, neighbored by a room with two ping-pong tables. I'll admit that I had never mastered the game of ping-pong, but I figured that I should still enjoy myself, even if I wasn't exactly good at the game. After a brief passing glance, I stood frozen in the pool room.

This was the room I spent the majority of my time in when it came to the room, even when I didn't have someone to play with. Even on the first day of college, when I really didn't know anybody and had far less experience with the game, the upper-classmen welcomed me with open arms, or more specifically, a pool cue.

Since then, I've played many-a-game in this room. Although I have played against many worthy opponents, such as my girlfriend Jessica, and my friends Andrew Wallace and Nathaniel Figgures. My most common rival was Jacob Breland. Ever since our freshman year, even when his older brother Jack attended Eastcliff State, we had been each other's perfect rivals as our skill levels matched the others. For some reason or another, I could never get any of my criminal justice pals over to play pool against me, except maybe Jarrett.

Come to think of it, it was also the last place I had seen Jarrett Weldon alive, before his untimely death. I couldn't help but feel like I'd failed him by refusing to continue working with David, but I knew that there was a right way and a wrong way to do things. If I was ever going to get a chance to do Jarrett justice, it needed to be done the right way.

As I realized that maybe I wasn't okay with the way I had handled the David dilemma, I scratched my head as I left the game room for the very last time. I turned off the lights and shut the door behind me as I made my way upstairs. The only thing the upstairs of the student center was used for was the cafeteria. Despite the overpriced, mostly mediocre food, I had little doubt that I was going to miss the jalapeño bacon cheeseburgers. Beginning to remember that I hadn't eaten yet, I decided to get one last burger to enjoy. I always loved the spice mixed in with the sizzling crispy bacon that really made the burger as decadent as I felt it should be.

After the meal and a brief moment of relaxing, I made my way past the campus bookstore and left the student center behind as well. I then found my way out into the campus courtyard, which was considered to be the very center of the campus. Many activities and events have been held in this area, including the occasional movie night when they would put a large screen and offer tickets to see a film, which is what Jessica and I did for our first double date with Jacob and Krista. It was also where the campus would hold job fairs, which promoted many companies to come by and try to basically recruit students.

Roughly half of the booths had little to offer, while some

frequently gave away free stuff, which is what most students looked around for. Whether it was small amounts of candy or a free bottle of water. The best booth had to have been when Outback Steakhouse even came by and gave away small pieces of sirloin steak. The yard held so many fun memories, but alas, it was time to move on, both literally and figuratively.

The more places I began to say goodbye to, the harder I knew this whole thing was going to be for me. Although I would never admit it to anyone, I was a bit of a sentimentalist. I had already made my way through the majority of the campus, and every location continued to fill me with so many memories that I knew that I'd never be able to have again. It just seemed crazy. Despite all the headaches and stress that practically made me homicidal, which given the last few days may be a poor choice of words, I began to realize that there were a lot of things about this place I was surprisingly going to miss.

I then made my way past the campus library. Although I did have a few nice memories in that building, I decided to skip it. I sat outside for a moment to simply stare at the large tree that was right next to the building. After a few minutes of thinking back to all the time I had spent working and hanging out with friends, I knew I had to make my way past the building and begin to make my way back to my car.

The only locations left on campus at this point that meant anything to me were the science building and the gym. I had never really been a fan of science, even back in grade school. Instead of going in one last time like the library, I decided to simply look at the building and pass it. Although I was tempted to go in and see if Jessica was inside and done with her classes, I figured that I should keep my word to ensure that she isn't distracted in the event that I was wrong.

After passing the building, I came to the last building on campus, the gymnasium. Another place that our friends would go occasionally to stay in shape and get exercise. Technically between Jacob, Krista, Jess, and I, I am what some people would call lazy in succumbing more to sitting around and relaxing more than the others. I will say that I still had some fun times despite my preferred laziness. I made my way past the gym a couple hundred yards to the next parking lot where I had parked earlier.

As I unlocked my car, I took a single moment to reflect that as I drove away from the college, I was literally and figuratively driving towards the future. As excited as I was about completing this step, I knew that it was time to get to the other problems surrounding my life. I knew that at some point this afternoon, I was going to have to speak with my mother and try to make her understand why I needed to take this next step in life by moving out, even if she doesn't like it.

Then there was David. Even if I knew I wasn't going to continue to work with David in the vigilante methods of justice, I knew that I would also need to make things right with him so he would come to understand that what the two of us did with Clark wasn't the only way to ensure that justice was served.

After getting off the interstate on my way home, I passed the cemetery road where they buried my father after he died. I'm not entirely sure why, but I felt like I needed to go by and see him. Talking with him always made me feel better growing up, maybe paying him a visit may have helped me focus on what needed to be done from this point off.

I got off the main road and turned onto Cemetery Road, where I drove for several minutes until I began to see a large field filled with hundreds of headstones. The cemetery was beautiful today, very green, fitting for a beautiful day in the middle of spring. I parked my car next to an older gray Volkswagen.

I got out of the car to see the only person at the cemetery was an older woman wearing a blue dress, lying on the grass in front of one of the headstones that I would assume belonged to her husband.

I paid little mind to the old lady as I made my way towards the edge of the cemetery where I knew my father was buried. I knew exactly which one belonged to him considering how often I had come to visit, even if I hadn't really made the trip in the last week or two with all of life's little problems beginning to pile up on me.

I finally stopped as I came upon the headstone that read Paul Benjamin Mills. I stood frozen as I stared at the hard headstone, not really sure what to say or really where to begin. I scratched my head and then decided to lean down to properly look at him.

"Hi, dad," I uttered to the tombstone, hoping that wherever he was, he could somehow hear me trying to speak with him. "I'm sorry that I haven't managed to come by recently. You know how busy I get with everything going on."

I heard no response as I finished my statement. The only noise that I could even hear was the wind whistling, as I felt it barely go past my face.

"I…I wanted to tell you that I finished up college today," I said, as I gave a brief chuckle as I imagined how he would've responded. "Yeah, it is cool. It's taken a lot of work, but hopefully it all ends up paying off in the end. I…uh…I really wish that you were going to be there to see me graduate. I know that you would've wanted to, if you could've." I sighed again. I began to lick my lips as I thought back to the real reason that he wouldn't be able to. The reason that he'll never get the chance to see his grandchildren or ever get the chance to take another breath in life…because of me.

"I also wanted to…" I started as I began to feel my heart begin to feel heavier and took a deep breath in the hopes that it would make things easier. "I just wanted to tell you that I'm sorry. I'm sorry for everything. For what happened to you and what happened afterwards. The way that I…"

I felt a tear begin to slide down my cheek as I tried to get a hold of myself, but the more I thought about it, the more I was forced to accept that I was responsible for what happened to him. It didn't matter how many tears I would or wouldn't shed or how many times I tried to apologize to him, I knew that nothing would change that fact.

I didn't know if, wherever he was, he knew about everything that I did afterwards with The Butchers and with David more recently. I knew that if he did know, then he would be ashamed of me, which I knew would only make things worse. It took a moment longer than it probably should have, but I wiped my face and stood back on my feet. "I just really wish you were still here with me."

"He is," I heard a voice coming home from behind me. I turned to see my mom, still in her work clothes, walking over to me.

"Hey," I said as she approached me and gave me a hug.

"Hi," she responded with a smile as we both turned back towards the headstone. "I didn't know you would be out here."

"It felt like the place to be," I responded. "…if that makes any sense."

"Yeah. I understand completely," she stated. "I came out here for the same reason. And as much as I don't like it, that place for you isn't just with me," I turned my head in confusion as she gave me a smile. "It's with Jessica."

I completely turned my body as I wanted to make sure I understood what she was stating. "Are you sure?"

"No, but I know what your father would say," she said as she looked back over to his headstone.

"Let me guess, something along the lines of letting me follow my own path and make my own mistakes."

"Actually, I was thinking more along the lines of him stating how we would always turn your room into a home gym when you moved out," she said. I let out a chuckle as we hugged each other, knowing there was no possible way that statement was true.

"Well, I'm not leaving just yet. Jessica and I still have to look for a place that we both like," I stated.

"Okay," she said as she began to rub my chest. "How'd your test go?"

"I'm not really worried about it," I told her.

"I know. You never really are. You work hard and I am so proud of you, and I know that your father is too," she said. I looked back at her as I kissed her on the forehead. As we continued to stare at the headstone, I felt another small gust of wind pass through me, as I began to believe that he was not only really there, he knew everything that I had been dealing with, but that there was a part of him that understood. The truth was that I couldn't ask for much more than that.

"You see, I told you. He's still here," she said. I looked up at the tree a few feet away as we saw a few of its branches that began to blow around the both of us.

"It's time for me to get back to work," she said.

"Okay. It's about time I get going too," I stated as we both went back to our vehicles.

I hugged her before getting into mine. She waved at me as she pulled off and made her way back towards her work. I sat there for a brief moment as I began to feel glad that I had come by to visit my father. It gave a sense of peace that everything really worked out for the best and maybe there was still a part of me that was still worthy of leading an honest life, filled with love and hope.

As I started my car to head back to my house, I heard my phone begin to ring. I looked at it to see that the caller was Jessica. No doubt calling to see how my test went, along with telling me how worried she was about her exam until she saw that she'd made an A, just like on every other test. I picked up the phone and then answered, "Hey, how'd your final college test go?"

"Logan..." I heard her say. It was kind of difficult to hear her speak as it sounded like the phone was moving.

"Jessica? I'm having trouble hearing you," I asked.

"Logan!" she repeated. This time I began to hear her much clearer. I also heard that she said my name. She sounded out of breath and in more of a panic.

"Hey, Jess. Can you hear me? What's going on?" I asked.

"It's...it's Nicky," she stated.

Chapter 14

I'm going to finish this

After several minutes of trying to calm Jessica down, I came to understand what had happened. Apparently, after she came home from school, she saw that her sister Nicky was lying on the floor, seemingly unresponsive. She panicked and immediately called nine-one-one and they were in the process of taking Nicky to the hospital as Jessica called me. Given the fact that Jessica had told me her sister had been in possession of Ozone recently, it didn't take a detective to put two and two together, but I continued to pray that I wasn't going to have to attend another funeral for someone else I cared for.

I immediately rushed over from the cemetery to the county hospital, which was in the middle of Birminghill, roughly fifteen minutes away from their house and an additional ten minutes away from the cemetery. I figured they had taken her to the emergency room side which is where I looked for parking for an additional five minutes. Why in the world the hospital would be so packed in the middle of a weekday was beyond me. After finding a parking spot, I rushed inside, looking for Jessica.

I looked in the waiting room to see several people sitting around waiting to be helped. After another several minutes of searching, I finally found Jessica in another waiting area down the hall, scouring and pacing with a frightened look. I could tell that she had been crying, but I was still hoping that she would have some news.

"Hey," I announced, to let her know that I was here to comfort her. She nearly jumped the moment she heard my voice. She then ran into my arms as she began to silently cry. All I wanted was to hold her and tell her that everything was going to be alright, even if neither of us knew exactly what was going to happen.

"Thank you for being here." she said softly. As I felt her shaking, I began to hold her tighter in the hopes that my arms would magically help calm her and make everything alright. Unfortunately, my arms didn't function that way, no matter how badly I wanted them to.

"Of course, I'm here," I told her as I looked at her and let her go. "Come on, sit down. Tell me what happened."

I held her hand as the two of us went back into the closest waiting room and sat as close to the hall as we could in the hopes that we might somehow get news faster by being as close as we could. As Jessica sat down, she couldn't even bring herself to look at anyone, not even me. I could also see that she had clutched her hands together. I think she was just trying to calm herself down to speak after the shock. I could see that she was still shaking, and I put my hand over her clutched hands.

"It's okay. Take your time," I assured her. Eventually, she nodded and took a deep breath as she began to talk to me.

"Well, I came home after school. I opened the door and saw her lying at the foot of the couch. She was just lying there," Jessica stated, sounding disturbed.

"I don't understand. She should've been in school, right?" I asked as Jessica began to nod.

"I don't know. She must've played hooky or something. I then called 911 and then I called you because…" she said as she began to rub her head, as she let out a small chuckle with a small emotional crack in the back of her voice. "I don't even know why I called you, before my own parents."

"Maybe you just needed someone here for you," I stated. She looked over to me with a smile that was clearly filled with emotional turmoil.

"We then got here and they took her back into surgery. Shit. I haven't even told my parents, yet. I have to call them," she said as she jumped up from the seat. I grabbed her hand.

"Hey, you go ahead and take a minute. You can be here if there is anything. I'll call," I assured her as I got back on my own feet. She nodded as I walked away from her.

I decided to walk outside to make sure I had good reception and proceeded to call her family, starting with her mother. To make things a lot easier, I told her what had happened and that I was calling while Jessica waited in the hopes that she'd be able to hear something from the doctor. Of course, her reaction went about as well as expected, with nothing short of extreme panic. I told her where we were and she assured me that she was on her way.

I then proceeded to call their brother, Dalton. I was quickly able to get a hold of him since he was on his lunch break. I told him everything that I had just told his mother, and he reassured me that he would be there as soon as he could.

I then called David last. I sighed, I knowing that as if our last conversation was already complicated enough, now we had this to worry about. Despite everything that David and I were going through together, I felt obligated to inform him of what was going on and proceeded to call him.

"Hello," he said, not sounding too thrilled.

"David. It's Logan," I told him.

"Logan, I'm pretty busy here, right now. If you're calling right now to talk about…" he started. Obviously, given the urgency, I decided to stop him before he could finish.

"David, listen! Nicky is in the hospital," I told him. For a moment, there was nothing but silence at the other end of the phone. I couldn't even hear him breathing and looked to see if the two of us were still connected. "David? Did you hear me?"

"What do you mean, Nicky is in the hospital?" he asked, sounding extremely skeptical of what he was being told.

"I mean, Jessica came home and she found Nicky on the floor, unresponsive. I'm at the hospital with her. You need to get down here," I stated.

"I'll be there as soon as I can," he stated. He was surprisingly calm as he hung up the phone. I must admit that it was somewhat unsettling to hear him like this. I couldn't tell at this point if he seemed calm because he was angry with me or because he had already been exposed too much to the darkness and it was starting to affect his judgement where his family was concerned, but I figured that his reasons really didn't matter at the moment.

I then walked back into the waiting room, where I saw Jessica sitting there. She didn't look at me as I sat back down, but I think that she could tell I was still there. She just continued to stare off into space with an expression filled with both worry and shock, and I really couldn't blame her. The truth was that I couldn't even imagine what she had gone through, seeing her sister completely unresponsive and on the floor like that. For all she knew, her sister could be dying. With nothing left to do, I gently pulled her head to lean on my shoulder as I put my hand on her kneecap as we continued to wait.

After roughly another twenty minutes of waiting for some sort of news or diagnosis or anything to change, we heard footsteps coming down the hall. Although, Jessica wasn't really paying attention, I looked and saw Dalton in the doorway. I gently tapped Jessica's side as she nearly jumped, looking around to see her brother. She quickly got up from her seat as she gave her brother a similar hug to that which I had received when I had arrived. She wasn't sniveling as much this time, and I'd like to think I had helped her calm down, even if she was still tense.

"Hey," he said, and began to squeeze her. I could tell that he was still in his work uniform and kind of dirty as he rushed over. "I got here as fast as I could. What happened?"

Jessica began to explain to him everything that had been going on. By the time we were both finished, both of their parents ran through the door. Mrs. Kennedy looked more startled, as if it was life or death that she hugged both of her kids as quickly as she could. Her expression was roughly similar to Jessica's when I'd arrived.

David, on the other hand, didn't look as concerned. He was still in his work clothes too, and I noticed that he looked rather angry. I couldn't tell if it was because he was sore because of what we discussed the night before or because of this whole new mess, but I knew that either way, he was not in a good mood. Dalton volunteered to tell their parents what Jessica had already explained. I think he just didn't want her to have to keep reliving the ordeal.

After a couple of minutes of explanations, we heard footsteps making their way down the hall that I had found Jessica startled in. We then saw a man in light blue scrubs coming down the hall as he began to look around for everyone in the waiting room and called, "Nicky Kennedy?"

Jessica and her parents immediately rushed to the doctor as Dalton stood up as well. I decided to continue to sit there and listen in on the official prognosis; hoping for the best.

"How is she?" asked Mrs. Kennedy.

"It was touch and go for a moment or two, but we were able to stabilize her. She is going to be okay. It's a good thing we found her when you did, otherwise I don't know if I would be able to say the same," he said, with a sympathetic look on his face.

"What happened?" asked Jessica.

"Well, we're still running a few tests to be certain, but we think that she overdosed on Ozone," stated the doctor. I then sat up in my chair to make sure that I was hearing him right. Ozone? How was that even possible?

"Are...are you sure?" asked Mrs. Kennedy, who quickly glanced over to David, whose stern look began to turn into more concern.

"Well, we've had a lot of people in the area dealing with Ozone overdoses. This is the fourth case today," he said.

"Jeez," said Jessica, who began to hold her head as they all looked at her.

"Can we see her?" asked David.

"Well, she's not awake, yet. But we're taking her to a room as we speak," he repeated as he signaled us to follow him. We made our way down the hall to an elevator. We then went to the third floor, where we made our way down another hallway and turned to see an open door as we stopped.

Mrs. Kennedy and Jessica were the first to slowly make their way into the room. Dalton then walked in slowly behind them. Then David. I walked in last to see Nicky lying in a bed in the middle of the far wall as a nurse was making sure she was still set-up properly. The nurse didn't say a word, but walked past me as we were all left to watch Nicky while she lay there with an IV in her hand. I wish I could say that she was looking peaceful, but in reality, she looked really pale, as if she was at death's door.

In her defense, that may have just been the lighting because that's the way that I knew a lot of patients in the hospital looked. It was rather disturbing to see her so lifeless. It was similar to the lifelessness that I noticed when I last saw Jarrett. I began to wonder how much more it would've taken for Nicky to end up just like him, but thought it wouldn't be appropriate to wonder such things when it was a miracle that she was still here.

Mrs. Kennedy sat down in the small cushioned chair, looking like she was going to break down in tears at the sight of her youngest child in this situation. She then looked down and clapped her hands together as she began to pray for her daughter's well-being. Dalton and Jessica were right next to her mother, both just hoping for the best for Nicky.

David then glanced over to me. It didn't take a genius to know what he was thinking. He was angry. He was thinking about what he had just said about the Ozone continuing to spread, and he wanted me to know that, probably in the hopes that I would change my mind about helping him take down Ozone permanently. I must admit that the idea became more tempting the longer that I looked and saw Nicky suffering in that small bed.

I then thought of what the doctor has said, Nicky had been the fourth person today in the exact same shape. So many people continuing to suffer as the pieces of shit who created this garbage were probably enjoying themselves at the moment.

It was a thought that filled me with a very strong sense of fury. The type of fury that made me desperately want to jump in the car with David and go find the shit-bags who created this narcotic and wipe them off the face of the Earth. For Nicky. For Jarrett and everyone else that has been hurt by Ozone Mist.

Unfortunately, as angry and filled with temptation to once again take the law into my hands, I knew that I couldn't. The fact that I had done it so many times already and hadn't already received life without the possibility of parole, or worse, was nothing short of luck and good fortune. I began to take a deep breath as I began to remember what I had to do.

I was still only a number of days away from graduating from Eastcliff State with all of my friends and Jessica. Hopefully, Nicky would be able to be released soon enough to see us walk across that stage. As much as I cared about them both, I knew that I still had to do right by myself. I had to move in with Jessica. I had to go to the police academy and then eventually make my way into a forensics program and make an honest career that could provided for a family one day, one that I hope that both Nicky and David would both be a part of.

As much as I hated to see Nicky like this, now, I knew that it was only a matter of time before the ozone dealers that did this would face justice, hopefully the right way. The last thing I wanted was for David to be caught doing something so heinous that it would not only ruin his life, but the lives of his family. They were all good people who shouldn't have had to pay for their darkness, or mine.

I then looked back to see David continuing to look at me, as if he was waiting for my answer, hoping these circumstances would change my mind on the matter. I gave him a sincere look in return and shook my head. Telling him one final time that I couldn't sink any deeper into my own darkness. He lowered his head in what I would assume was disappointment. He then walked past me and made his way back over to his wife, who didn't take her eyes off of Nicky.

"I'm got to go back to work. I'm going to find the bastards that did this," he stated as he put his hand on his wife's shoulder. She didn't say a word. She just put her hand on his and nodded, knowing that he would keep his word. "Keep me posted on her condition and call me if anything happens."

"Okay," she said softly. The both of them stared at their daughter.

He then made his way over to see his daughter, giving the most sincere look of overwhelming love for his daughter that I'd seen on him in several days. Although no one else would've seen it, I could see the anger behind his worried eyes and the deep desire to kill the people responsible for Nicky's current condition.

He touched the top of her head and brushed her hair before kissing her forehead. He then made his way out of the hospital room. Wanting to make sure that David wasn't actually leaving to do something reckless, stupid, and/or dangerous, I signaled to Jessica that I would be right back as I followed David out of the room. He had almost made it to the emergency room exit by the time I managed to catch up to him.

"David?" I asked. He stopped for only a brief moment and continued to walk away from me. He didn't even turn around to face me.

"I'm busy, Logan," he finally stated as he continued on his merry way out of the hospital entrance towards his car.

"Hey," I told him as I tried to stop him by jumping in front of him before he could get into his car. "Where are you going?"

"I'm going to work to stop these assholes. Not that stopping them seems to matter to you," he accused me, as he got past me and jumped in his car.

"Come on, you know that's not true," I said as he began to start his vehicle, ignoring me. I then began to tap on the glass to make sure he was really hearing me. He then looked down, as he rolled down his window, realizing that he was at least going to hear me out. "Look, they killed a friend of mine. Nicky is in the hospital right now because of the same people…"

"You think I don't know that?!" he shouted at me as he finally looked up at me. His face was cherry red. I couldn't tell if he was about to cry or was just really angry. From the way that he was looking at me, I think it may have been both. "That's my little girl in there!"

"I want them off the street just as badly as you do," I told him. He scoffed as he put on his sunglasses.

"That, right?" he asked as I heard him unlock his car. "If you really want them gone as much as I do, then get in the car and help me stop these fuckers once and for all."

"How?" I asked.

"I'll find somebody that knows something. Jason Clark wasn't the only lead I had on Mister Mist," he stated. "Are you getting in or not?"

"I'm not going to help you, unless it ends with the bad guys in cuffs," I told him. He locked his door and began to nod.

"Then we have nothing further to discuss. You may want to take a step back," he said as he began to pull out of his parking spot. I ran back up to his side of the car, before he could hit the gas.

"Do you really think that Nicky would want you to do?" I asked.

"Well, I don't know and since she's not really in a position where I can ask her…" he started as he hit the gas and sped out of the parking lot, leaving me staring at David, driving away, knowing he was going somewhere that I was unable to follow.

As ashamed as I was to admit it, a small part of me was still hoping that David would be able to find the creators of this garbage that would choose to make money over choosing the well-being of others and wipe these scumbags off the face of the Earth. It really didn't help that David was literally tempting me to join him in his vigilante crusade.

But I knew that the more I continued down the dark path, the more likely that the darkness would consume my soul until nothing but a monster remained. As I began to hope that it wasn't too late for David, I made my way back into the hospital to console Jessica during this desperate hour of need.

Over the course of the next several hours, we all just stood pacing around the small hospital room, hoping for any kind of development with her. More specifically, we were just wanting her to regain consciousness. Mrs. Kennedy spent a lot of time praying for her daughter's well-being. Jessica, Dalton, and I soon joined her, hoping that if God was really out there; watching over any of us, he'd know that Nicky was meant to recover from this whole ordeal and had a long life ahead of her.

A few minutes after I came back into the room, Dalton stepped out to take a call from his boss to explain why he had just run out. I'm sure that, given the circumstances, his boss would understand, but Dalton didn't seem too concerned about whether or not he had his boss' approval or not. He soon began to text his girlfriend, Andrea, who would arrive later than the rest of us before he told her what had happened.

Based on the amount of time he was texting while in the room with us and the fact that it took a few hours for her to arrive, I'm pretty sure he'd given her some of the details already, if not the full story, and told her to stay at work, since there was nothing more any of us could really do except try to console each other. That's all I was really doing there, just trying to be there for support for people that I cared very deeply about, and hoping and praying that everything was going to work out.

Although it may not have been allowed, I snuck over to one of the nearby empty rooms and grabbed a few extra chairs for the rest of us to sit in. As we continued to sit around the hospital room, I then decided to call my mother to let her know what had happened. She also showed deep concern for Nicky and stated that she would come after she got off work.

I told her that there was no point in arriving until Nicky was actually awake and really in a position to see anyone, which really wouldn't happen until she was actually conscious. I told her that I would be home soon, but I figured that I should be there as long as Jessica was. That's the kind of support that we are supposed to show our loved ones, isn't it?

As more time passed, Krista started texting Jessica. And of course, Jessica told her best friend everything that was happening. Although it technically wasn't any of my business, I peeked over to see what exactly Jessica was telling her. Krista also offered to come over for Nicky, stating that she was like the little sister she never had. Jessica told her that she should just wait until Nicky was actually awake. Krista stated that she would do what Jess thought was best and said that she would come as soon as Nicky woke up. Krista continued to send a few messages afterwards, but I eventually stopped reading as it was more along the lines of their normal gossip chats.

As more and more people, including some of Nicky's friends and friends of the family, learned about what happened, it kind of became a sort of rinse and repeat ritual. Everyone started with shock after learning the news, followed by curiosity as everyone asked what happened and how she was doing at the moment. The final step is their condolences or asking either "if you guys need anything, let me know," mixed in with the frequent request of "Keep me posted."

It got to the point where the entire situation seemed almost like a cliché. The more I thought of it, it was actually a normal human reaction to such news. That's usually the way that this sort of thing goes, isn't it? Maybe because when it's all said and done, nobody really knows what to say in that type of horrible ordeal. They all meant well and hoped for the best, but there's not much anybody can really do at this point.

After several hours of sitting around, the room was just completely dead silent. No sound coming from Nicky. No sound coming from anyone typing or texting. The only sounds we could hear were our own heartbeats and breath. Mrs. Kennedy soon fell asleep in the seat next to her daughter. Dalton continued to scroll around on his phone. He wasn't making any noise while he did it, though.

Eventually, Jessica, who was lying with her head against my arm, began to nod off as well. I figured that the stress of everything that she had been experiencing all day, after probably spending the majority of the night studying for her final exam, was eventually enough to make her pass out. As glad as I was to know that she was finally getting some rest, it was kind of a complication, to have her lying on me as I was unable to move without waking her.

Without any shred of interest at the idea in sleep, eating, or even grabbing a drink of water, I simply stared at Nicky in her hospital bed. I thought about how lifeless she looked in the bed and how close she was to dying. How close she was to being in the exact situation that so many people, including one of my oldest friends, Jarrett, had found himself in…in a coffin.

The more I thought about all the people that continued to be hurt by the drug that continued to plague the area, the more I hoped for the worst for the people that did this. As bad as it may be to think, it got to the point where I honestly hoped that the people who caused all of this met a horrible demise. If it was anyone else other than David that I knew was going to do it, I'd be extremely delighted to hear that those bastards were dead.

It was around five-thirty in the afternoon when I began to hear footsteps coming down the hall, loud footsteps that seemed like heels. I turned to see footsteps at the door as I began to hear knocking. Jessica began to wake up as Dalton and I saw Andrea walking through the door. Dalton immediately jumped up to greet her, waking his mother in the process.

As much as I enjoyed having Jessica resting on my arm, I was happy that I would finally be able to get up and go to the bathroom without disturbing her. As everyone got up to catch Andrea on everything that was happening with Nicky, I quickly decided to relieve myself. After I finished my business, I walked back into the room to see she was talking with everyone while sitting in my seat. Figuring that I needed to stand up anyway, I just decided to go with it.

As Andrea began speaking and getting comfortable, a nurse knocked on the door soon after Andrea to check and see how Nicky was doing. She didn't look too excited about the fact that so many people were in the room, crowding the room with more chairs than there were supposed to be, but she clearly didn't care enough to say anything about it. After fiddling with the machinery to make sure that everything was still working properly, she decided to leave us.

After the nurse left, Mrs. Kennedy decided to go down to the dining hall to get something to eat. Andrea and Dalton went with her to get supper, leaving Jessica and I alone with Nicky. By this point, we weren't sitting next to each other. There wasn't any real discussion for a few minutes after they left the room. She simply stared at her sister, holding her head. I decided to walk closer to her and continued to rub her sister's arm.

"Hey," she said, looking slightly startled as if she hadn't even realized that I was still here. She then rubbed my side. "Are you sure that you don't want to go downstairs with my mom and them?"

"I ate before you called earlier. I'm more worried about you," I told her. "You've been pretty quiet."

"I just can't help but wonder, what would've happened if I hadn't come home when I did…" she started as she sounded like she was going to begin crying again.

"You can't think like that. She's alive and she will wake up before you know it," I assured her. She nodded, rather hoping I was right, whether or not she truly believed me was an entirely different matter. "When was the last time you ate?"

"I don't know," she scoffed, followed by a soft chuckle. "I had a coffee early this morning at school and a granola bar."

"Do you want to go downstairs and join your family?" I asked.

"No," she said as she shook her head. "I just don't want to leave her alone."

"If you want to go get something to eat, I'll watch her," I told her. She looked up at me and smiled.

"Thank you," she said with a smile as she patted my arm. "I think I will get something from the vending machine down the hall."

"I won't leave her side," I promised her. Jessica took a deep breath. I could tell that she felt bad for leaving her little sister during this difficult time. She watched the both of us as she left the room, leaving me alone in there with Nicky.

At this point, the sun was beginning to get lower and twilight was upon us. I knew we had maybe another half-hour before the sun would begin to set. I looked back at Nicky and after being angry at the people who had created the drug, I felt another emotion as I was beginning to feel bad for Nicky. I mean, for someone who has so many people that love her, she ended up on drugs. Why? Peer pressure? Stress reliever, if so, for what?

I've known Nicky Kennedy for months and never would've expected this type of behavior from her. On the other hand, I suppose she never would've expected her sister's boyfriend to be a killer either. It just goes to show you that you never really know what's going on in people's heads.

I then looked back and saw Jessica coming back into the room with a bottle of Sprite and a small bag of sour cream and onion chips in her hand. She then sat back down in the seat next to her sister, but the curious thing was what happened next. The exact moment that she opened her bag of chips, I saw Nicky's eye flutter. Jessica didn't notice.

"Hey," I said, as I tapped Jessica. She looked up at me as I pointed to Nicky, whose eyes began to flutter again. She immediately dropped her bag, jumped back up, from her seat and began to hover over her sister, with a large hopeful grin on her face.

"Nicky?" she asked softly. After another brief moment of her eyes trying to open and a head shake, Nicky was finally awake. She had a bit of a confused expression as she began to see that she was in a hospital room with just the two of us.

"Jessica? Where are we?" she asked, trying to make sense of what was happening.

"You're in the hospital," she responded. She looked around again and briefly stared at me for a second as she looked back at her sister.

"Why?" she asked, still looking confused. "What happened?"

"Nicky," I said as I began to stand next to Jessica over Nicky. She began to look confused by the entire ordeal. Instead of interrogating her immediately about the drugs, which I'm sure she would receive later, I decided to avoid those questions.

"What is the last thing you remember?" I asked her. She closed her eyes and put her hand on her head, looking like she was having trouble remembering.

"I...I decided to play hooky and I..." she said as I think it began to come back to her on what had exactly happened, "Oh, God."

"Yeah, it's a good thing *He* was looking out for you," I responded, pointing upwards. Jessica glanced at me with a skeptical look, before quickly turning back to her sister, who began to realize why she was in her current situation.

"Nicky? Did you take any drugs?" asked Jessica. Nicky's expression changed from a look of confusion to one of shame as tears began to run down her face. She covered her eyes as she couldn't bear to face either of us. She then nodded, confirming what we already knew to be true.

"Nicky," said Jessica as she began to hold her sister's arms. "Look at me."

Jessica then slowly pulled Nicky's arm away from her face so she could properly face her sister, whose face was beginning to turn red, filled with tears and shame in her eyes over what she had done. Jessica then hugged her sister and began to hold her as she softly began to whisper, "It's okay."

"I'm sorry," Nicky started saying over and over again in front of her sister. "I'm so sorry."

"I know. It's okay," repeated Jessica, who continued to hug her sister. "We're going to get you help, okay."

It was really one of those touchy-feely moments you would've expected at the end of an episode from a nineties sitcom, that warmed people's hearts. It was that kind of love and hope that I knew Jessica provided to her sister and everyone she came into contact with that made me want to be a better person. It was also why I could never allow her to see my dark side and why I owed it to her to try to be a better person. After a moment of the two sisters hugging each other, I walked over to the both of them.

"I'll go let everyone know that she's awake," I told Jessica, who looked back at me with a smile and a nod as I left the room. As I made my way out of the room to the elevator, I saw Mrs. Kennedy, Dalton, and Andrea getting off the elevator, who all paused the moment they saw me.

"She's awake," I told them. They all hurried back to her room as I followed behind. Mrs. Kennedy quickly dashed into the room, followed by Dalton, and then Andrea. As I glanced back into the room, I saw Mrs. Kennedy holding all of her kids as Andrea watched the same way that I was watching from the hall. It was the kind of moment you couldn't really help but be happy for.

Knowing that their family was back together, but still incomplete, I figured that after all David and I had recently been through together, I at least owed it to him to fulfill his request to let him know when Nicky was awake. I once again stepped out and began to dial him. The phone rang for a minute.

"Hello," I heard David whisper.

"David. It's Logan," I told him, wondering why exactly he was whispering.

"What is it?" he asked.

"I just wanted to let you know that Nicky was awake," I told him.

"That's great," he said, still whispering. "Tell her, I'll be there as soon as I can."

"Hang on. Why are you whispering? Where are you?" I asked.

"I just got a lead on a big Ozone deal tonight," he said softly.

"How big?" I asked him.

"Well, let me put it to you this way. I heard it's going to be one of the biggest drug deals in state history. The big guy himself is coming out tonight for this one," he stated, beginning to sound more confident.

"That's great," I told him. "Get backup and storm the place."

"I can't. I didn't exactly get the information legally," he said.

"David, what did you do?" I asked, feeling slightly disturbed as I now knew what David was capable of.

"It doesn't matter. It's already done, now. Now look, I'm about to put an end to Ozone Mist, once and for all. I know you said you didn't like my methods, but I'm sure that there are going to be a lot of guys here soon and I would appreciate the help," he said.

"David..." I started to tell him, not really sure what to say.

"I'll send you the address in case you change your mind," he said.

"David," I uttered again, but before I could get another word out, he hung up the phone.

Chapter 15

A War on Drugs

As I realized that David was off on his own personal vendetta to take down an entire drug cartel single-handedly, I stood frozen with my phone in my hand, not really sure what to do next. I figured that the most obvious choice was to try to call David back and try to reason with him and tell him why going after the head of the Ozone organization like this was a bad idea. I tried to call him back, more than once, but every time his phone only went to his voicemail, until I realized that he wasn't going to pick up.

By the time that my second call went through, my phone buzzed. I saw a text from David with the address and read, "578 Higgins Street. Eastcliff, Ga."

I thought about calling the police, but I knew that even if they found out about the drug operation, there was a chance that David could get caught up in the middle of all of that in a less than desirable way. If David were to get caught because of me, what would stop him from trying to bring me down with him? Even if he decided not to bring me down, he still had a family that needed him, now more than ever before.

I knew that I couldn't just leave David by himself to take on the entire drug operation, he would likely be killed in a matter of minutes. Even if I did decide to go with him to take down Ozone, there was no telling how many people that would involve stopping. There could be dozens of armed assailants making sure that nothing went wrong. Even if I was stealthy enough to get in there without being detected to get David, stop Ozone, and get out without dying in the process, which would certainly be my preference, it would mean that I would likely have to dive back into the darkness that I've been so eager to leave behind lately. I didn't want to be the kind of guy that had to do bad things, even if I knew it was for good causes.

I knew that if Jessica knew I let something bad happen to her father, she would never forgive me. None of them would. Plus, I still kind of felt like I owed David for saving my life. As much as I hated the idea, I knew what I had to do, even if it meant that I might end up getting killed in the process.

I went back to Nicky's hospital room. When I walked into the room, I saw that Nicky was actually sitting up and talking with her family. It was reassuring to see her recover so quickly. As I slowly made my way back into the room, Jessica glanced over and smiled. I couldn't offer the same sentiment with her father's situation on my mind, and I merely stood in the doorway, wondering what I was going to say to her.

Before I could think of something to tell her, she made her way over to the doorway and pulled me out into the hallway.

"Did you get ahold of my father?" she asked.

"Yeah," I nodded. "He said that he was going to try to be back here as soon as he could, but..."

"But he's working," she said, with a slight look of disappointment, something that seemed to be a feeling that she was used to where her father was concerned.

"He said that he may have a lead on the head of the Ozone organization," I informed her. I'm not entirely sure why I told her so much about what David was up to, but I figured if I kept most of the details under wraps, it shouldn't come back to haunt me.

"Let me ask you something," she said, beginning to look rather troubled. "I know that you are going into the same line of work, but do you believe that you will ever put your work before your family?" I couldn't say that I was surprised by such a question given everything that she'd been through. I also couldn't give her an answer easily. I certainly never wanted to lie to Jessica, but I knew how complicated the truth of the matter really was.

"I can't answer that one, Jessica. I promise you that you are a priority in my life and sometimes there may possibly be pressing matters, but I promise you that everything I do and have ever done, I do it for the people that I care about," I told her. She gave me a low-key smile and kissed me on the cheek. "Look, I'm glad that she's up, but it's getting late and my mom wants me home. If you want me to stay a little longer, I can, but…" I told her. Before I could finish speaking, she nearly jumped.

"Oh, of course," she said as she nodded. "You've been here all day with me. Yes, absolutely."

"I'll talk to you later, honey," I told her as I kissed her on the cheek. "…to make sure that she's doing alright."

"Okay," she said as I made my way down the hall to the elevator. I knew that I should get to the address David had sent me as soon as humanly possible, preferably before David ended up getting in over his head. I figured that it may look questionable if I was seen running out of the hospital, so I quickly paced myself towards the exit and passed the nurse's station nearby. I saw that there were several people waiting to be checked in, but I saw there was a woman at the desk, who I assumed worked there, as I made my way to the door.

"Have a good night," the nurse said to me. I smiled and waved as I continued to make my way to the door. I then continued to quickly pace my way back to my car. Despite the fact that it was beginning to get dark, there were many cars still in the parking lot by the time that I was leaving. I had to press my key button to remember where I had parked. I heard a small honk a few feet away and unlocked my car and started it as fast as I could.

I then pulled out of the parking lot carefully and made my way towards Higgins Street. It was in Eastcliff, which meant that I was going to be getting on the interstate for a few miles. I wasn't entirely sure where in Eastcliff the address was located and typed it into Google Maps, where my phone told me that it was going to be nearly a twenty-five-minute drive.

I made my way onto the interstate ramp and drove maybe twenty miles over the speed limit, which at the moment was about an average speed of ninety miles-per-hour, hoping that I wasn't going to be pulled over as I watched closely for nearby patrol cars as if I were still driving with a dead body in my car.

After several minutes of driving, I made my way past Eastcliff State College. I figured that was the exit I was supposed to take, but my phone told me to take the next exit to get there faster. I zoomed past the college and hoped that my phone knew what it was talking about. After another few miles, I heard the phone state, "take the next right off I-75 and onto Eastcliff main street."

I did as I was told and the phone guided me through another street that I was unfamiliar with until I had finally made it to Higgins Street. I must admit that the city of Eastcliff was smaller than I thought it was. Since I lived in Rockgate and was closer to Birminghill, I didn't spend much time in Eastcliff and never really took the time to look around the city. As interested as I was in seeing what Eastcliff had to offer, I knew that now wasn't the time. I was in a hurry to help David.

As I made my way down the road, the buildings got smaller, to the point where I saw a large factory in the middle of it. I looked around and saw that the gate was closed, but there were over a dozen vehicles, including several vans, behind it. I then looked at my phone and glanced at the screen reading, "You have arrived at your destination." Score one for Google Maps.

I knew that I was here and David was too. I then decided to turn off the lights on my car and try to find somewhere nearby I could park in case I had to get out of here in a hurry, which I had a feeling was going to be very likely. I saw a parallel parking spot a few-feet away from the factory gate and took it.

As I got out of the car and began to make my way around the factory, I saw a familiar light brown Dodge Chrysler, that I knew belonged to David. He was already here and inside. I knew that if I could find out how he got in, I could do the same. I then saw that his car was parked over by a tree that was leaning over the top of the gate and found my entrance.

The tree had many branches and edges, so it was very easy to climb, but I was forced to jump on top of David's to reach the first thick branch I could grab. It wasn't so different from the trees that I would climb with my friends before we realized the joys of technology in our teen years. It took me a minute to climb, as I almost slipped, but after maintaining my balance and getting a better grip on the largest branch that I could hold onto without breaking.

I then pulled myself up and climbed another and then another until I was high enough that I could see over the factory gate. This factory was gray on the outside, with light poles that surrounded the building. It was much nicer than any of the factories that resided in Rockgate, probably because this one was still in operation.

As I looked around, I began to wonder if the factory was still open or if David had given me the wrong address. However, as I looked a little closer, specifically at the ground, I looked closer towards the vans, one of which was black and two were white, nearby. Outside the factory, I saw several men holding weapons, big ones, but I was too far away to tell what kind of weapons they were holding and I was too preoccupied to care. The important part was what seemed irrefutable at this point, I was at the right place.

I began to crawl to the edge of the tree branch and slowly made my way over the gate. By the time I was over into the branch territory. I noticed that I was roughly nine or ten feet off the ground and maiming myself. I then noticed that I was standing near the factory's dumpster.

I began to lower myself and tried to swing myself over to the dumpster. It was maybe only a foot away, but I figured that landing onto it may be a lot smoother than landing on the ground, which I was still pretty high from hitting with ease. I soon began to move my legs and swing myself. Unfortunately, mother nature decided to pull the rug out from under me, as it were, in this case, letting the branch snap from above me.

As I heard the tree snap and found myself still trying to make it over to the dumpster, I ended up flying onto the top of the dumpster, right on my back. It wasn't a very pleasant experience, to say the least. As if it wasn't bad enough that my back was beginning to ache from my shoulders to my spine, it made a louder noise than I was expecting it to.

I slowly climbed off of the dumpster and hid myself in case one of the thugs in the yard decided to investigate the potential sound of my back breaking. However, I was hopeful as it was a large area to work with. I slowly peeked my head from behind the dumpster to see that one of the men holding guns had in fact heard the sound. I saw him begin to make his way over to the dumpster.

I took a deep breath and figured that my best bet was to ambush him, which I knew could end up getting me killed, but knowing that a bullet would more likely have the same effect. I then glanced again to see that he was coming over towards my right. I wasn't entirely sure if he was going to check behind the dumpster, but I began to prepare myself for the possibility.

I felt my heart begin to race as he made his way closer and closer. I then heard something coming over a small radio, but couldn't quite make out what was being said. I peeked my head out again, only to the point where I could only see the man, who had finally stopped in front of the dumpster. He wasn't even looking at it. He was trying to hear his orders coming in through his walkie-talkie.

"Yeah," I heard him say from behind the dumpster. "Okay. I got it. Yeah, I'll be right over."

I continued to see that he was beginning to turn back around towards the factory. As he began to turn around and go back to his bosses, I slid my belt off my pants as quickly and quietly as I could and figured that taking him out through a surprise would be my best bet. I then made my way from behind the dumpster and began to strangle the man with my belt.

He began to fight against me, but I heaved as hard as I could to ensure that he wouldn't be able to get away. After a brief moment, he stopped struggling all together and dragged him back around the dumpster. I checked his pulse to see if he was still alive. His pulse was slow, but it was still going. Although, I really had no idea who I'd just attacked, I was glad that I didn't really have to bring myself to the killing line again if I didn't have to.

It then occurred to me that I almost did end up crossing that line. I wasn't entirely sure why I attacked him. He was walking back towards his factory, just doing his job. I then remembered the type of work this guy was involved with. Even if he was just a goon, he was still working for some seriously bad people, according to David's information.

I then peeked my head out one more time to make sure that no one heard the two of us struggling. Fortunately, all of the other thugs were making their way into the factory, just as my unconscious friend was no doubt about to do, but why? Why were they were suddenly going in? I knew that there was only one way to find out.

I looked down at the thug lying at my feet and realized that he wasn't much larger than myself. It also occurred to me that if I was about to break into a factory involving who knows what, I had better not be wearing a button-down short-sleeve shirt and a pair of denim jeans. I then decided to change and take the thugs' clothing in the hopes of blending in.

Since his pants were close enough to mine, I decided to leave him with his dignity and took only his shirt, gloves, and weapon. I looked to see how much ammunition I had to work with, only to discover nothing more than a single bullet inside his pistol. Now, honestly, what kind of goon carries around a gun with only a single bullet inside? I had half a mind to march in there and complain to whatever crime boss had orchestrated this meeting, but I knew I'd likely need more than one bullet to face them. When I was sure that no one else was watching, I decided to open the dumpster to take out the trash. Afterwards, I made my way into the factory. I knew that I still didn't want to be seen and made my way around to find an entrance, other than the one the other thugs had been using.

On the side of the factory, I saw a stairway that led to a door on the second floor. I climbed up the stairs and made my way up to the door, pleasantly finding that it was unlocked. I slowly turned the handle to see that I was in an office. I figured that it was the factory manager's officer as it was filled with several filing cabinets and a large window that showed the entire factory floor from this one room.

I could also see the entire railing on the second floor, which also to my surprise, was completely empty. I then made my way out of the office to see that all of the thugs and dealers were on the ground floor facing each other. It was kind of difficult to see them, but I could tell that most of them were wearing the stereotypical gangbanger clothing, including bandanas, gold chains, and hats that weren't in their intended position. I could also tell many of them had weapons with their fingers on their triggers.

I continued to make my way across the second-floor railing to try to get a better angle of what was happening down there. I saw that in the middle of the division, there was one guy who was wearing a long brown coat, unlike the men behind him. It was difficult to see his actual face because the lights in the factory weren't on, but I could also tell he had dark skin.

A moment later, I was startled as I saw the garage begin to open and four more vans pull inside, along with an SUV. Several more men who looked like they were thugs quickly jumped out of the vans, before the backdoor of the SUV opened and a man wearing a fancy suit walked out, who I could have easily assumed was the one who orchestrated the whole Ozone Mist operation and the one Clark referred to as Mister Mist.

The lights of the SUV were bright enough that I could actually see the man in the suit, and I realized that he looked familiar to me. It took me a moment to process that the man in the suit was none other than Jordan Adams, the real-estate salesman that Jessica had been wanting us to meet with. I couldn't believe it.

All this time, Adams' so-called real estate dealings were all a front for his drug operation. I tried to stay as quiet as I could to try to overhear the conversation that was beginning to happen as Adams walked over to the man in the large coat.

"So, you're Mister Mist?" asked the man, who sounded as surprised as I was to learn that Adams was Mister Mist.

"That's the name that's been going around. I'll be honest, it's growing on me," Adams replied, as he smiled and shook the man's hand. "I take it that means you're the head of the Black Skull gang?"

"My friend's call me Reaper. If you have what you say you have, you better get used to calling me that," he said while smiling.

"I have your supply as long as you have the money," responded Adams. Reaper snapped his fingers as one of the thugs behind him brought over a large suitcase. Adams then opened it and smiled. I couldn't exactly tell what was inside, but I figured it was money. Adams pulled out a large bundle of bills.

"So, where's the stuff?" asked Reaper. Adams sat the money back in the briefcase and closed it before snapping his fingers. Seconds later, one of his cronies soon came over with a similar suitcase and sat it down next to the case of money.

Reaper opened it up and pulled out a small baggie. It didn't take a genius to know that the bag contained Ozone. The two men both stared at the baggie and began to laugh as they closed their brief cases and shook hands.

"Pleasure doing business with you, Misty," said Reaper with a large grin.

"If you like that, maybe you'll be interested in my new little product," added Adams.

"Whatcha got?" asked Reaper. Adams then turned and signaled another one of his goons, who came over with a small square patch.

"I call it Double O-zone. A lot of the crew like to call it Ozone Extra, though," responded Adams. "It's a little something that my guys have been working on for a few weeks. It comes in the form of a patch, making it easier to handle and work twice as well as the original batch."

"Is it good?" asked Reaper.

"Well, we have yet to test it on a human, but the animals seemed to enjoy it," Adams stated, with a grin.

"Well, as it happens, I have you your first test subject," said Reaper, who then signaled his thugs again. This time, two of Reaper's goons made their way towards the drug leaders, dragging a man, who had clearly been beaten. After they threw away the back of the beaten man's head, I realized that he also looked familiar. It was David.

As I was afraid of, David had found himself captured by drug-dealers after deciding to go straight into the lion's den when they were hungry. Adams and Reaper looked down at David, who looked up at the two of them. I could see he'd been beaten by the black eye and what looked like a small amount of blood.

"Who is this?" asked Adams.

"Somebody that my boys caught poking around before you even got here. At first, I thought he was one of yours, but now, I see you wouldn't be this sloppy," Reaper stated.

"No, this man is not in my employ," Adams stated to Reaper, before turning to David. "Who are you?"

David spoke not a word. One of Reaper's goons then pulled the back of David's hair, forcing him to look up at the two drug lords.

"Are you a cop? DEA?" asked Adams. David stared at him for a minute, before spitting on him. Reaper laughed as Adams pulled out a handkerchief and wiped the saliva from his face, before smacking David.

"Doubtful. There's no one else here. If he was law enforcement, they'd be storming the place by now," pointed out Reaper.

"Well, whoever you are, you're about to be the first in human trials for my latest creation," said Adams, who walked over and pulled over to grab the Double O-zone and began to walk back over to

David, who was beginning to put up a struggle against his captors. Reaper then signaled for his goons to shoot David.

"Wait," interrupted Adams, as Reaper looked disappointed. "I want him alive."

I knew that I had to think of something fast, before David ended up becoming the next victim of Ozone. It quickly occurred to me that I was technically not prepared for this, as I only had one bullet with a single bullet against what seemed to be two gangs of goons. I also knew I would have to get their attention, but how? I looked around to see an office and made my way back there. As I looked in the office and looked at the desk, there was nothing. I began to look through the drawers when I saw a letter opener, hoping it would come in handy.

I figured that my best bet would be the element of surprise, even if I had to surprise every thug one at a time. I then made my way down from the office as quickly as possible and began to make my way down the stairs. There was one goon standing far enough behind from the rest that I dropped a small dirty penny I saw lying on the rail and dropped it on his head.

I backed away from the rail to make sure no one could see me. I then noticed that he was beginning to make his way upstairs. I then went back to the office and hid, leaving the door partially open, hoping he would follow me inside. I heard every step he took on the railing, before he made his way into the office.

I immediately pounced behind him and began to subdue him as I put the thug in a chokehold. He put up a bit of a struggle. I then began to wonder, if this would be the appropriate time to use the letter opener I'd found in the office. I knew that I really didn't want to have to use it as I was trying to leave my own personal darkness out of this. However, the thug quickly gained the upper hand as he budded my face with the back of his head.

He succeeded in getting me off his back as he went for his gun.

Before he got the chance to fire it at me, I pulled out the letter opener and stabbed him in the back, placing my hand over his mouth before he could let out a scream. I then stabbed him again to make sure he understood I meant business. After the second time, he quickly began to seize with his struggling. I then dropped his body as I saw blood begin to ooze from him. I wasn't entirely sure if I had killed him, but I knew that he would've killed me if I hadn't.

I then took his weapon. Luckily, this time I was able to find a more competent gunman who knew to keep his weapon loaded. I then made my way back out onto the railing. I saw that they had several guys working to hold David down as they began to slap their new drug patches on him. I looked up at the lights and had a new idea as I began to shoot them, hoping it would be enough to startle Adams before he could completely poison David, while keeping him from seeing me for a moment.

I was able to shoot out the first few lights. The problem was, the farther ones were harder to shoot at and despite how many westerns I'd seen, I wasn't exactly a professional marksman. Almost everyone on the ground began to jump after hearing the first shot fired, but the dealers saw me and began shooting in my general direction from both Adams men and the Reapers gang. By that point, I was forced to duck for cover, with only one or two lights still shining above the factory floor, as the rest of the floor was far dimmer and harder to see.

Although it was hard to tell what exactly was happening, I noticed the gunfire had begun to seize. I began to wonder if they were planning on returning fire. I then began to hear tires moving out. I peeked my head out to see if they were retreating. I glanced and saw as Adams rushed for the briefcase of money. Knowing I didn't want him to get his hands on that money, I began to fire towards the suitcase; inches away from Adams. It took the rest of my ammunition, but I was able to scare Adams away from the money as he came to the obvious conclusion that the money was useless to him if he was dead.

I managed to run to the factory floor during the confusion and saw that the only person that was still there was David, lying on the floor. I kept the gun on me until I was sure that all of the goons were really gone, as I tended to David. David was lying on his stomach. I turned him over to see that he seemed to be really out of it.

I then saw that there were several small patches placed on his arm and face, lying underneath him. As I realized that David had already been drugged with the Double O-zone drug, I began to panic. I checked his pulse to feel that it was not only still there, but it was going disturbingly fast. Part of me wanted to go after Adams and Reaper, but I knew that if David didn't receive medical attention immediately, he was surely going to die.

I knew that standing in this factory with this much damage would probably be a bad place for the two of us to be found, especially for a police officer that didn't work in this particular area. I then pulled David from the floor. He was heavier than he looked. He then began to struggle. I figured he was trying to pull himself together. Although he didn't actually say anything, he did point back at the table, where the suitcases had been sitting. The one with the drugs was already gone, but the one with the cash was not. I could tell that he wanted me to grab it, so I did.

I then remembered that if I should try to check to see if there was security footage that could compromise both David and myself. Surely, if Adams showed his face, he was going to make sure that it was in a place where he could've done it without being caught. Hoping he took care of that for both of us, I returned my focus to my girlfriend's dying father.

After a quick struggle holding both David and the suitcase, we made our way back towards my car as the large gate was now open. Before I could get David in my car, he began to pass out again. I knew I had no choice and called him an ambulance. I dialed the phone as fast as I could before I heard a female operator say on the line, "nine-one-one, what is your emergency?"

"I'm outside the Twilight-water factory where a drug deal just took place. I'm with Detective David Kennedy, and he's down. Officer down, hurry," I stated.

"Okay, an ambulance is on its way," the lady said. I quickly hung up the phone, before she could ask me anything else while trying to keep my attention on David alive and awake. He kept slipping in and out of consciousness, but he began to slip again as the lights began to flash as I heard the ambulance sirens. Two paramedics jumped out of the ambulance, one holding a bag. They flashed a light into David's eyes as they began to quickly get him on the gurney.

They asked me several questions about David. I knew only some of his personal information, but there was only so much I could answer about him. It took us several minutes to get to the hospital, but he was rushed back into the emergency room. I stood there for several minutes. I realized that I was right back at the same hospital where I was earlier.

I knew that whether or not David was going to make it, I needed to think of a reason why I was the closest person to respond to his current predicament. Maybe something along the lines of him going off the rails where his daughter was concerned, but wanted to think of something that wouldn't end up getting him fired or me arrested. The more I thought about it though, the more I realized that his job wasn't what was important at the moment.

I scratched my head as I texted Jessica, "Hey, I'm back at the hospital, in the emergency waiting room. Do me a favor and come down here."

I began pacing as I tried to think of a way to break it to her that now her sister and her father were both being admitted to the same hospital. I then felt my phone buzz as I read her message "Why are you down there? Are you alright?"

"I'll explain when you get down here. It's important," I responded, as I sat down in the same seats that we had sat in earlier. It took her almost half an hour before she made it back to the hospital. Given the short notice and the long day we'd both had that I knew was going to get better for her, I suppose the timing was understandable, Jessica made her way back into the room as I stood up.

"Hey, what's going on?" she asked. I took a deep breath as I tried to think of a way to break the news to her. It was hard to do when I knew she'd already suffered more than her fair share of panic for the day.

"Um, tonight, before I left, I called your dad. He told me that he had found a lead on the Ozone dealers. He sounded pretty out of it, so I followed him," I told her as I licked my lips.

"What do you mean, you followed him? I don't understand," she said. "What are we doing back here, Logan?"

"I tracked his phone," I lied, as I took another deep breath. "And I found your father on the street, partially beaten, and drugged with Ozone."

"Oh...oh, my g..." started Jessica, who looked as if she was about to become sick and began to shake again.

"He's in there," I added as I pointed towards the emergency room doors.

"Is he...?" she tried to ask as she began to breath erratically. I shook my head.

"No, they don't know anything, yet," I added, as I held her hands to try to calm her once again. "The ambulance got there pretty quickly, but he's still hanging on."

"I need to go tell my family," she said as she jumped back up from the seat. This time, I didn't stop her. I knew they would hear about it eventually, but I knew that I would still likely need time to think about what our story should entail when David woke up, assuming he ever did. After Jessica left me in the waiting room for almost twenty minutes, a woman wearing scrubs and holding a clipboard came into the room.

"David Kennedy?" asked a different physician from earlier this afternoon. This one was a woman with dark skin, wearing only scrubs. I stood up this time as I walked over to her.

"Yes, how is he?" I asked.

"Well, the compound he was injected with was a little different than the normal cases of Ozone we've been dealing with lately," she said. I crossed my arms to prepare myself for any kind of upsetting news she was prepared to tell me.

"So, what does that mean?" I asked. "Is he still…?"

"Well, this is actually going to sound odd, but he's actually recovering faster than expected. When he was brought in, his heart completely flat-lined, but we were able to revive him, and now, his vitals are completely normal," she said with a comforting smile.

"So, he's okay?" I asked, a bit confused. "Just like that? How is that even possible?"

"Well, I don't get to say this often enough, but I would call it nothing short of a miracle," she said. "Are you related?"

"Uh, no. I'm a friend of the family and the one who found him," I told her, licking my lips again. I heard several footsteps approaching us. We both turned to see Jessica, Dalton, and Doris Kennedy walking over to us as fast as they could.

"How is he?" asked Mrs. Kennedy, who sounded completely out of breath.

"As I was just telling this young man, it was touch and go for a moment or two because he was injected with a drug that shared many of the characteristics of Ozone, but we were able to stabilize him."

"Thank the lord," uttered Dalton, as they all began to look relieved.

"He's not out of the woods completely. He hasn't woken up, yet, and it's still early," she said. "I won't lie and tell you that something can't change, but I will try to remain optimistic. If he wakes up soon, you may even be able to take him home within the next few days."

"Can we see him?" asked Jessica.

"We are about to put him in a room. However, if you want to go home and get some rest, I'll be happy to call you the minute he wakes up," suggested the nurse.

"No, my daughter was admitted a few hours ago," Mrs. Kennedy stated, holding her head in clear distress. "I'd like to go check on my husband, though."

"Very well," said the nurse. "I'll inform you when we get your husband in a room."

"You guys go on home. Please, just try to get some rest," suggested Mrs. Kennedy.

"You can't really expect us to go home?" asked Dalton.

"Yes, please," pleaded Mrs. Kennedy, who began to look quite startled. It was understandable given everything the poor woman had been forced to endure in the last few hours. Jessica and Dalton both hugged their mother as I watched.

The four of us went back to Nicky's room, where Jessica and I tried to explain what had happened to David. Needless to say, the family continued to ask me several questions as to why I was even there. Although I wasn't really comfortable with giving the specific details, I continued with what I told Jessica, that David had sounded a little erratic on the phone when I told him that Nicky was awake. I managed to get one of my buddies from school, who was pretty much a hacker, to track his phone for me. When I got there, I found David at the factory, partially beaten and unconscious.

This was a convenient story since Jessica knew Brice, and knew that he did in fact indulge in certain hacking programs. It was also easy to believe that as David was indeed acting a little odd when I called him earlier, I had deleted the messages he'd sent with the address while in the ambulance. Eventually, the family stopped questioning my side of the story and just appreciated the fact that I was there in time to save David.

After my interrogation was over and the case was pretty much closed, we went back to the Kennedy house. Although Dalton had already moved out, he wanted to make sure that Jessica wasn't home alone tonight, and neither did I. He called Andrea, as I called my mother and told her that I was going to be spending the night at Jessica's after explaining that her father was now in the hospital after a crazy night at work. I really didn't feel like telling the story all over again and pretty much gave her the suggestion of not talking about what had happened to Jessica or her family.

Although Dalton and I were spending the night over at Jessica's, Jessica was pretty much wired. I think that after everything that I knew was going through her mind at the moment, she just couldn't find it in herself to relax. At around one in the morning, Dalton decided to sleep in his old room as Jessica and I shared hers.

As much as I would have liked the idea of spending the night in my beautiful girlfriend's bedroom, the thought of any hanky-panky didn't cross either of our minds. We didn't even take off our clothes, other than our shoes. We spent a few minutes talking as I held her and tried to convince her to try to get some rest. Although it wasn't an easy task by any means, she eventually managed to relax enough to the point where she was sleeping in my arms. Personally, I found myself in a similar situation of not being able to rest.

I couldn't help but think about what the nurse said to me. A miracle? She called David's vitals a miracle. Was it really? I mean, both David and Nicky had both had a near death experience and somehow miraculously, both seemed to recover from a drug that had left dozens of people dead in its wake. I just didn't know how it was possible. Maybe someone or something really was looking out for David tonight, because as crazy as it may sound, it's the only conclusion I could think of. The nurse was right. It was indeed a miracle.

Chapter 16

House Hunting

At some point during the night, I actually fell asleep in Jess' bed. I only knew this because, by the time morning arrived, I found myself waking up next to her, which was something I could definitely get used to. She looked too peaceful for me to intentionally wake up. I then decided to just lie in bed for a few minutes as a way of relaxing. It wasn't long before I realized that I didn't have that much to relax about.

Jordan Adams was still on the loose, making more Ozone Mist and even his new concoction of Double O-zone that he was looking to sell more of, not to mention the fact that there was little that David or I could do to stop him.

Nicky was still in the hospital with her unconscious father. I knew the moment Jessica woke up, the sooner she'd have to face that terrifying reality, all the more reason to let her sleep in a little longer. As pure as my intentions were of wanting her to stay in bed a little longer, my hopes were cut short by the sounds of her phone beginning to ring.

I looked to see that it was indeed beginning to wake her as she began to turn and groan as the phone rang. She then tried to block out the noise with her pillow. I then got out of bed to look and see who had the audacity to call this early. It was Jessica's mother. I figured it may not be the best idea to answer her phone and figured it should just go to voicemail. If Jess wanted to answer, she could when she wanted to get up.

"Who is it?" she mumbled from under her pillow.

"It's your mom," I told her as she removed the pillow from her face. She then pulled herself out from under the covers. Although I must admit that her hair had seen better days, she still looked cute as you could see her still half asleep.

"I'll take it," she said as I gave her the phone, which had stopped ringing. I figured it really was about time to get up as I looked outside her window to see that the sun was out. Given all the bad and complex situations of late, it was truly a beautiful morning.

As Jessica began to speak with her mother, I tottered over to the bathroom next to Jessica's room to relieve myself. As I finished, I glanced at myself in the mirror for a brief moment, realizing that my hair looked surprisingly well for someone who just woke up after a hell of a long night and without even a shower. I didn't understand it, but decided to not question the good things in life.

After a moment of hearing Jessica mumbling through her bedroom while speaking to her mother, she made her way back through the door, looking more awake than she had a moment ago.

"What is it?" I asked.

"Dad's awake. We need to get over there. I mean, I do," she said as she started putting on her jeans.

"Hey," I told her, as I tried to calm her down. "It's okay. I'm coming too. Go ahead and get ready. He'll still be there waiting for us."

She nodded with half a grin as she went into the bathroom to get ready. Once again, as true as my intentions were to be there for Jessica during this stressful turn of events, I knew that it was also important to get there soon to make sure that David didn't accidentally say something that would complicate either of our stories. I got my shoes back on as fast as I could as I waited for Jessica.

Fortunately, I knew she was in a hurry too, so it didn't take her long. I walked over to where Dalton was sleeping, only to see that he wasn't there. I walked outside to see that his car was no longer in the driveway. He had probably already went back to the hospital to check on his family or went back home to Andrea. Either way, it was one less thing to worry about.

It only took Jessica a few minutes to get ready. She then put on a cap so she wouldn't have to worry about her hair. She grabbed her belongings and followed me out the door. We hopped in my car and made our way back to the hospital. As we drove back to the hospital, I noticed that it was almost ten o'clock. I admit that I hadn't intended to sleep that late, but I must admit that it was nice.

When we finally got parked, we rushed through the doors. The truth was that I really had no idea where I was going and was forced to follow her, which was becoming complicated considering I wanted to be the first person that David spoke to when he woke up to make sure that our stories lined up.

Eventually, we made our way down the same hall that Nicky was being held in and went down the hall a few more rooms to see her father in the bed, sitting up. In the room with David was his wife, Dalton, and Andrea, and Nicky, who was still hooked up to her own IV.

His partner, Detective Michael Russo, was also in the room with their boss, Lieutenant Wade Pierce, a few feet away from the family. I must admit, it was unsettling to see how many people had already spoken to him, before I could.

"Hey, there they are," announced Dalton. Jessica quickly rushed over to her father's side, filled with a look of worry as they gave each other a huge hug.

"I'm so glad you're okay," I heard her tell her father.

"Yeah, I'm okay, sweetheart. Thanks to Logan," stated David as he, along with everyone in the room, began to stare at me. I managed to fake a smile as I was still unsure of what was going to happen next.

"Hey, I'm just glad you're alright," I told David as he smiled, looking around at his family.

"So, you were the one who found him?" asked Pierce. I didn't say a word and simply nodded.

"That's right. He saved my ass," clarified David.

"So, how did you know he was in trouble?" asked Detective Russo, looking skeptical.

"Well, the truth is that…" I started to say as I was going to continue with the same story I told his family the night before.

"Hey, take it easy, alright," interrupted David, before I could say another word. "He saved my life. The interrogation can wait until later, don't you think?"

Russo looked over to Pierce, who merely shrugged as he closed his small notepad, "Alright, fine."

"Thanks," David said.

"We'll come check up on you later, partner," said Russo he patted the end of David's bed as the two made their way out of the room. Russo then walked past me, giving me a skeptical look. Pierce looked over at me with a smile as the room got less tense.

"So, how do you feel?" asked Jessica, to her father.

He began to shake his head. "It's all still a little fuzzy to me."

"So, do you remember what happened last night?" I asked him as I took a step closer to him. His family turned to him, who began to hold his head.

"Bits and pieces," he stated. "It was like I just told everyone before you guys walked in. I remember following an Ozone lead after leaving the hospital yesterday. I remember Logan calling me later to tell me that Nicky was awake. I went to speak with one of my informants, who gave me information on a deal going down and…nothing."

"Well, we're just glad you're alright, daddy," said Nicky, who slowly made her way over to her father's side.

"I'm just glad that you're alright," he said as he looked up at Nicky, before looking around the room. "All of you."

"We love you," Doris Kennedy said as she leaned over to kiss her husband on the forehead.

"I love all of you," he said, with a smile. "Do you mind if I talk to Logan about something really quick?"

"Of course," Mrs. Kennedy stated as she approached me. She then gave me a hug as well. "Thank you for saving my husband's life."

"Of course," I told her, with a far less fake smile.

Dalton and Andrea then made their way out of the room, as he patted me on the back. Jessica helped Nicky back to her room. They shut the door behind them, leaving David and I alone.

"So, how are you really feeling?" I asked him. He exhaled before giving me a brief chuckle.

"I feel like shit, but I know I'd be a lot worse if you hadn't been there," he stated.

"Well, I knew you wouldn't be alive, right now, if I hadn't. We were lucky, you know," I told him. He nodded.

"I'm sorry," he stated.

"No, you're not," I responded. I couldn't help but grin a little bit. David let out a soft chuckle. "I'm curious though, what exactly was you're plan, if I hadn't shown up."

"I don't know," he stated.

"Your family needs you, David. You do get that, right? Now more than ever," I told him.

"Yeah," he responded, as he lowered his head in shame. "But those guys had to be stopped, don't you get that?"

"Yeah," I told him as he looked back at me. "The drug that Adams injected you with was a new concoction of his that he called Double O-zone. He said it was supposed to be like an advanced version of the drug that everyone else has been taking."

"That probably explains why my head is still spinning," interrupted David, beginning to hold his head again.

"There's no telling what will happen if Adams manages to get that shit on the streets," I stated as he nodded.

"I know," he stated.

"So, what now?" I asked.

"Nothing. It doesn't matter anymore," he stated as he shook his head. I looked back at him as he scoffed.

"What do you mean?" I asked.

"We saw what happened when I tried to take him down myself," he said. "...and we can't arrest him, now. Even if we were able to find him and make something stick, he saw my face. If he found out that I worked for the police, I'd be just as done as him."

"Maybe not," I told him. "Believe it or not, I actually have a plan to take down both Adams and Ozone."

"Tell me," he requested.

"Later, we'll talk more when you get out of here. From what I heard, that could even be tomorrow," I told him. He scoffed again. I patted him on the back.

"Do you want me to bring everyone back in here?" I asked as I started towards the doorway.

"Hang on," he said. "I heard a little rumor that my daughter wants to move in with you."

"Is that right?" I asked, shocked in the realization that Jessica had indeed mentioned it to her family already.

"You know that she can never know the truth, about either of us," he stated. I nodded, agreeing that was truly the last thing I wanted. "Do you really love my daughter?"

"Yes. More than anyone or anything in this world," I told him. He nodded as he smiled, whether it was sincere or not I couldn't quite tell.

"Okay, then you promise me that you will never stop working to make her happy," he requested. I nodded once again as I began to nod as well. "Alright, bring them all back in."

"Okay," I responded.

"Hey, Logan. Thanks for saving my life," he yelled back at me. I nodded as I walked out of the room. When I looked in the hall, I saw everyone was standing outside, waiting for the two of us to finish up.

"He's good," I told them.

Mrs. Kennedy helped Nicky back into David's room, as Dalton

and Andrea followed. Jessica, on the other hand, stood outside for another moment with me as I began to lean against the wall. She then began to stand next to me.

"Hey," she said as she nudged my arm.

"Hey," I responded.

"The doctor says that Nicky is going to be alright. They're going to let us take her home tomorrow," she said.

"That's good," I responded, as I looked over to her to see her smiling. I looked back over at her as she began to softly chuckle.

"What?" I asked as her laugh made me smile.

"I really don't know what I should be thanking you for first. For staying with me and comforting me last night, or for saving my father's life," she said.

"Well, you can start with one and then later thank me for the other," I told her with a grin as she started smiling.

"Okay," she said as she began to press her lips against mine. "Thank you."

"You're welcome," I told her.

"So, what did he want to talk to you about?" she asked next.

"Uh, he wanted to say thank you, and he basically gave me his blessing on the idea of the two of us moving in together," I told her. She lost her smile and began to fiddle with her hair for a minute. "That is what you still want, isn't it?"

"I don't know," she said. I stopped leaning on the wall as I began to pay her my full attention.

"Talk to me," I requested. She began to look disappointed.

"I want us to move in together, but after all of this. It's just that…my family clearly needs me. I just don't know if I can handle being away from them, right now with all of this," she said. "I also know that I've been the one pressuring you about moving in together. I just got caught up in the idea so badly and…I'm sorry."

"No, hey…" I told her as I began to hold her in my arms. "You don't ever have to apologize to me. It's okay. We'll get there one day. If you still feel this way later, when Nicky and your dad are taken care of, we'll find our place together."

"Thank you. It's just that I already set up an appointment with Jordan Adams, too," she said as she began to hold her head.

"Don't worry. Just tell me the address and I'll be sure to take care of it," I told her.

"Here," she said as she handed me a home magazine with Adams' face on the cover, with one place circled in the apartment's section. "The appointment was supposed to be this afternoon at four. Call that number and tell them we're cancelling our appointment."

"Not a problem. You go be with your family. I'll handle Adams," I said as I smiled and winked at her. She kissed my cheek as she walked back into the hospital room.

I watched for another brief moment as she began to surround herself with her family. As content as I was to know that Jessica and her family were still alive and well, it infuriated me to think that Adams was still on the street, selling his drugs. Fortunately, as I told David, I did have a plan to deal with that pesky little problem, and, lucky for me, Jessica just gave me the ticket to make sure everything went accordingly.

As I made my way back to my car, I saw that it was almost noon at this point and knew that a few extra hours would be more than enough time to make sure everything would be in order. Even though Jessica expressed no intention of attending the meeting with Jordan Adams this afternoon, I had every intention of going there. I knew it would be the one place that Adams could let his guard down after last night's fiasco and would be the perfect place for me to stop him once and for all.

I knew that I had been telling myself that I wasn't going to allow myself to become further involved in any vigilante acts, but with so many people I cared about continuing to suffer because of Adams and his damn narcotics and his latest creation, Double O-zone, about to hit the streets, I needed to ensure that didn't happen again. If I could take down Adams and get him to lead me to his supply, I could end them both once and for all.

I decided to take advantage of the extra time to get a bite to eat while I was out. Nothing special, just something to settle my stomach to where it wasn't growling any longer. After picking up a fast food chicken sandwich, I decided to go pick-up supplies from my house before changing into clothes that I thought would be more appropriate for my meeting that would be less likely to accidentally leave behind any potential evidence. I decided to grab gloves and a long-sleeved shirt, even if it was May and summer's heat was quickly on its way. I also grabbed some tape and a few other tools that could also come in handy in the event that things were to go off base and was forced me to improvise.

As I began to place these tools in my trunk, I remembered the suitcase that I'd taken during all the chaos of last night. I opened it to see that the case was filled with money. With no one nearby, I decided to count and learned that the case contained approximately three-hundred-thousand dollars inside. A serious amount of money to just have lying around in my trunk. I then took a moment to think of what all this money could do for me and my family. I mean, this was more than enough money to buy a house with, even if Jessica wasn't ready. It could easily pay for both Nicky and David's hospital expenses with some left over. The more I thought about it, the more I realized where that money came from. It was money that was made off of the suffering of others.

I had no right to take that money any more than Adams or Reaper did. I sighed as I placed it back in the trunk of my car to try to think of an alternative use for the case and decided to return my focus to where it truly belonged, stopping Jordan Adams once and for all. Before I knew it, it was three o' clock, and I decided to call Adams' office to make sure everything was still in order for our meeting, truly wanting to make sure he wasn't still startled or too paranoid to help a seemingly happy couple find their dream home. The phone began to ring, and then I began to hear the familiar deep voice of Adams himself as he answered, "Hello. Adams Apartments and Homes. How can I help you?" I knew it was Adams himself, as I recognized his voice from the night before.

"Hi. My girlfriend booked us an appointment this afternoon to look at an apartment in Birminghill. Name of Jessica Kennedy," I told him, feeling only slightly uncomfortable mentioning Jessica's name.

"Ah, yes. As a matter of fact, I was just about to head over to make sure everything was set-up for the two of you. At four o'clock, correct?" he asked, sounding rather upbeat; as a good salesman would be expected to.

"Absolutely. I did want to inform you that she will not be able to join us due to a family emergency, but I will still be there to look at the place."

"Well, that's fine, but I do hope everything is alright. We can reschedule if you need," he stated, sounding genuinely concerned, unaware that he was the cause of all of her current heartache.

"No. That's okay. However, we did begin talking about looking at an actual house instead of an apartment. The ad said that you were selling it too. The address is Eighteen Maple Street. It's a small brick, one level home with a garage," I began to suggest.

"Yes, of course. I know the one. It's a beautiful property for the price. I'll be happy to show you both if you want," he offered.

"Yeah, okay. I was hoping that I could possibly meet you there, first, instead of at the apartment. Is that okay?" I asked.

"That'll be fine. We are still meeting at four, correct?" he asked.

"Yes, sir," I responded.

"And what's your name?" he asked.

"Jarrett. Jarrett Weldon," I uttered, deciding that it would be more convenient to give him a false name rather than my real name in the event things became more complicated than I'd like.

"Alright, Mr. Weldon. That being the case, I'll see you shortly," he stated.

"You got it," I told him as I hung up the phone. With my trap in place, I knew that I needed to make it count. I figured that I should try to make it over there before he could to try to get a layout of the place to ensure that I maintained control of the situation. Before I drove to Birminghill to meet with Adams, I decided to stop in Eastcliff, specifically outside the Twilight-water factory where I knew David's car was still parked.

When I got there, I was lucky to find that it was still unlocked. I looked in his backseat to see that the rest of the drugs David and I picked up at the pharmacy were still hidden away in his truck. I grabbed it as I figured it would be a convenient tool to subdue Adams with, before manually locking up David's car before we could come pick it up. I figured it would be a shame if someone were to try to take something from the empty vehicle.

I then made my way over to the house to meet with Adams. It was indeed a small home, but it did look like a nice neighborhood. I pulled into the driveway to see that the home had a two-car garage, which I knew would also prove to be useful in my endeavors. I pulled in front of the right-side garage door as I saw Adams standing outside the home in a suit similar to the one I saw him in last night.

"Hi, you must be Jarrett," said Adams as he approached my car to shake my hand. I shook it off and managed to fake a friendly smile. I knew mine wasn't as convincing as his though.

"Yes, sir. It's very nice to meet you," I responded, as the two of us began to gaze upon the house, as I noticed the sun began to glare down on the two of us. "So, this is the place?"

"This is it," Adams responded. "Shall we go inside?"

"After you," I stated as we both walked through the front door. Despite it being a small home, it looked a lot bigger on the inside. We entered the large empty living room with fairly nice carpeted flooring.

Although I was here with the primary purpose of taking down Adams, there was a small part of me that couldn't help but try to picture Jessica and myself living here. I mean, it was a very nice home, but I knew that there was no possible way that we could afford a place this nice for at least another few years, even with my new suitcase filled with cash. I then tried to focus my mindset and remember why I was really here.

"So how long have you and Jessica been together?" Adams asked.

"Uh…little over a year, but we've been pretty close for nearly four," I claimed.

"Ah, that's nice," I heard him state. I glanced over to fake another smile for a minute. "I'm sorry to hear that she wasn't going to be able to join us. She sounded very nice over the phone."

"Yeah, she is. Actually, her sister is in the hospital," I told him.

"Oh, my. I do hope she'll be okay," Adams stated, sounding

sincere. I must admit that I almost felt a certain sense of admiration for Jordan Adams. Throughout our entire conversation, he seemed calm, cool, and collective when it came to his sales pitch. If I hadn't personally seen him in the middle of a drug deal with Mr. Reaper only hours earlier, I would've never suspected that Adams would be capable of being the creator of Ozone Mist. Then again, a psychopath like him probably found it easy to lie and fake and pretend, like he actually gave a shit about the people that he sold houses to, making him more dangerous than anyone I've ever come up against; truly a wolf in sheep's clothing.

"Yeah, she's a little shaken up," I stated as I looked over to see his true reaction. "We found out that she actually overdosed…on the drug Ozone."

"That's awful," he stated. I could tell that there was little to no remorse in his eyes as he looked at me, although he tried to fake it. "I'm sorry. This is none of my business. I should just focus on showing you the house."

"No, it's fine," I told him as I noticed him beginning to distance himself for the first time since I'd arrived. We both made our way into the kitchen. I could tell from all the cabinets and drawers that were built into the wall that they were made of very nicely crafted wood. I then let out a small chuckle as I realized I was once again getting sidetracked.

"Something funny?" he asked.

"Yeah, I just like it, that's all," I claimed as I began to scratch the back of my head. "Please, continue."

"Well, the house has plenty of space and a perfectly working stove oven," he said as he opened the door to the stove.

"It's very nice," I said, as I began to take more pictures in front of him to keep up appearances for the time being. "Do you care if we check out the garage next?"

"Ah, the most important place for a man is in his garage. I can appreciate that," he said, regaining his smile as we walked over towards a door in the kitchen that led into the garage. I began to take another couple of pictures with my phone as I continued to look around the place.

"Do you like it?" Adams asked me.

"Yeah, it looks great," I told him. "Hey, this may be an odd request, but do you care if I try out the garage door to park my car? I just figured that if we're thinking about it, I should get used to parking my car inside, you know."

"Well, it's a little unorthodox, but I see no harm," he said as I opened the garage door and pulled my car through the garage door. As I parked my car in the garage, I grabbed the needle from under my seat and hid it inside my sleeve before getting out.

"Well?" he asked, with a grin on his face. I began to nod, trying to show an impressed expression.

"It feels like home," I told him as I took a step back and began to close the garage door.

"Well, if you like the garage, I'm sure you'll love the bedrooms. They…" he started to say as he made his way from the garage. With his back turned, I slipped on my gloves and pulled the needle from my sleeve and injected him with only a small part of the dosage.

He let out a single loud groan, before he hit the floor. He began to breathe deeply as I turned him on his back. I watched as he continued to try to squirm for another moment, but soon the drugs began to run their course until he was completely immobilized' lying unconscious in front of me. I took a brief moment to revel in the fact that the man who'd been the cause of so many people's anguish, was lying at my feet and at my mercy.

"Well, I appreciate you showing me around the place," I told Adams' unconscious body. "But it really is outside my intended price range. I'm afraid we'll need time to think things over."

I then went back to my car and got the rest of my supplies. I wasn't sure how long the drug would keep Adams out, but knew that I really shouldn't waste any extra time. I tied his legs and his arms, and taped his mouth shut, and threw him in my trunk. I pulled my car out of the driveway and saw Adams' car still sitting there.

I then thought it would be best if no one else saw it just sitting outside until I could come back and deal with it. I then got out and grabbed Adams' car keys and his phone from him in the trunk and decided to back his truck into the garage where no one would expect it to be.

After covering my bases, I got back in my car and drove Adams to one of the few places on earth where I knew I could hide him away where no one would likely come looking for him, the same place that I dealt with former problems I've had in the past, like Arthur Phillips and Joe Walker.

Chapter 17

Mister Mist

The entire drive down to the Rockgate factory, I decided to crank my radio up in the unlikely, but still possible, event that Adams decided to wake up earlier than I planned. Although it was very loud in my car listening to Metallica, I drove with extreme caution to make sure that I didn't end up getting pulled over with Adams' unconscious body in the trunk. Although I've managed to get away with murder in the past, it would be far from ideal to end up slipping up and getting a kidnapping charge instead.

Fortunately, fate decided to work with me once again as I arrived at the old, worn down Green-Star factory in Rockgate. The only problems I faced now were the fact that I was going to have to move Adams in the middle of the afternoon and the less than likely possibility of someone deciding to stop by the factory and stumble upon Adams here before I could come back to handle the problem.

I backed my car as close to the entrance as I could without drawing any unwanted attention to myself and pulled Adams' unconscious body from the car. I then made my way back into the factory and ended up placing Adams on the same table that both Phillips and Walker had died on. Luckily for me, Adams was still completely out of it. I knew I wanted it to stay that way and went back to my car to get more rope and tape to ensure Adams couldn't go anywhere until I could return.

After several minutes of work, Jordan Adams was completely tied down to a table. I wanted to make sure it stayed that way in the event that fate wanted to test my luck and decided to put a giant tarp over Adams. There was a small part of me that wanted to simply get it over with here and now. He was unconscious and wouldn't be able to fight me.

It would also be considered a more humane way of taking care of him, like putting an animal to sleep. After everything Adams had done, did he really deserve to go out so easily? Was that even really my call to make? The sad thing was that I actually knew the answer to both and still found myself standing over Adams with what I admit was malicious intent and a serious temptation to finish him off that became more and more tempting to partake in.

The only reason I spared his life for the moment wasn't because I wanted him to suffer longer, but because I knew that it wasn't time for him to go, just yet. Two things were missing before we could take care of Adams: his drugs and David. David was the one who wanted to take care of Adams, all I was doing was making sure that Adams couldn't flee anywhere he couldn't be found. The only question I found myself asking was how I was going to get him to tell me where he kept his drug supply.

I then felt something begin to vibrate in my pocket. It was Adams' phone. I had realized that I'd left it active. I pulled it out with every intention of simply smashing it against the factory wall so no one would be able to track us. Then it occurred to me that maybe Adams had incidentally kept some kind of clue as to where he kept the majority of his drugs. I knew that because his operation was so small and growing, there wouldn't be many places to make it. I figured that it was all being kept in a single location, but where?

I began to look through Adams' phone to try to find a specific location. Surprisingly, for a man who runs a soon to-be multi-million-dollar drug operation and a somewhat bogus real estate venture, he had absolutely no security on his personal phone.

Although there was no kind of security, there was also little to find. I saw messages from associates of his and found out that his business was run through him. For example, if he had a shipment transfer, he would call his specific associates. There was a large group message among associates detailing directions to meet at what he referred to as 'the special place', likely because the shipment was so large for him. Unfortunately, it didn't include the whereabouts of his Ozone supply.

He did have a convenient app on his phone called the GPS Tracker, which included in its settings, previous destinations. I began to look at the address and began to compare it with his previous destinations. Several of which were of the homes that were in his real estate catalog, one of which was his personal home address, one of the Eastcliff factory from the previous night, but just before was another factory in Goldmarsh, Tennessee, which was maybe twenty miles outside of Rockgate. The address was listed several times in the GPS and I hoped that it was the place that I was looking for.

I covered the still unconscious Adams with the tarp before leaving and hoped that my luck wouldn't run out long enough for me to get what I needed. I wrote down the address and began to make my way over to Goldmarsh. It was a peaceful drive as I made my way into the city. While driving, I did notice that I had been getting text messages from Jessica and my mother. I decided to tell them both that I was busy with one of my other college friends but would be home to see them both soon.

As I got closer to the address, I noticed that it was in fact a shut-down pharmacy, on the edge of Goldmarsh. I noticed that there were no trucks or cars nearby and figured that there was no one home. However, I did find it interesting to find that the building was locked. Although I could understand why an abandoned building was locked, but the lock itself was clearly new; far too shiny for a run-down old factory building. Luckily, I knew how to pick a lock and opened it with ease, making my way inside. For a building that looked like it had been shut down for many years on the outside, it was quite clean inside.

It wasn't like any of the other rundown buildings in the area. There was no dust, no rats, not even a spider web. I made my way down a hallway into the back slowly and saw a small office. It had many chemicals inside and papers lying on a table. I glanced at them and realized that they included Adams' notes on his Ozone narcotic.

On top of the table was also a contact book and a list of clients that listed known drug dealers and associates, including Joe Walker, Jason Clark, Harold Reeves, and Grim Reaper. This was all enough evidence to lock up Adams for the rest of his life, if I could find a way to tie it to him. Unfortunately, the only proof that Adams was here was on his phone's GPS, which would never likely hold up in court, even if it were admissible.

I knew that all of this was for his formula, but I still wanted the supply. I then looked over towards an office and saw that the building had its own garage that included several vans. I decided to make my way down there and was surprised to find that the garage was also empty. I then went down the stairs to see that inside the vans was enough to take Ozone on a nationwide scale. However long it takes to make Ozone, it was clear that Adams had been working on all of this for years. This place was the entire Ozone operation, or at the very least, the head of the snake.

That's when I realized what I had to do and what I knew had to happen. I destroyed Adams' phone by running over it with my car a couple of times, before leaving and making my way home. I then received a message from Jessica, who told me that David and Nicky were expected to get out of the hospital in the morning. I thought that would be perfect and I had a special welcome home surprise for David when he got home.

I went back home and began to text David and told him that I wanted to meet up after he got out of the hospital. He knew that I had something in the works, but I'm curious to see his reaction when he sees how productive I've been this afternoon.

After spending the next day with my mom, my friends, and with Jessica's family, both David and Nicky were home from the hospital. Later the next evening after the rest of the family went to sleep, David managed to sneak out to meet up with me outside of the Green-star factory in Rockgate. Luckily, he knew what I had in mind as he dressed in a similar fashion to me.

"Okay, you said you had a plan to take down Adams? What is it?" he asked.

"Oh, not here. We're just here to pick up a package," I informed him, feeling a slight sense of irony considering it was only a few days earlier when David told me the same thing for the exact same kind of situation. I think he knew it too; he scoffed.

We went inside the factory, and he saw the tarp moving. The truth of the matter was that I was somewhat surprised to see Adams still struggling. I hadn't attended to him in over a day, and with no food or water, I honestly expected him to be rather weak. David looked at me with shock.

"Is that?" he asked. I nodded. David began to look eager, even grinning, as he knew he was about to get his revenge against Adams. There was a small part of me that wanted it to be over, but I figured with all the time and effort I'd already put into this, why should I spoil it now?

"No, not here. We're just moving him," I told him.

"Where?" he asked, sounding confused.

"You'll see," I told him, with half a grin on my face. Although he seemed rather reluctant, we left the tarp over Adams and took him over to his factory. Oh, of course, he tried to fight and struggle when we began to move him. He even let out a few muffled screams, but it made no difference to anyone. He was ours, and he was going to suffer for the pain he'd caused so many others. When we arrived at the factory in Goldmarsh, David and I moved Adams onto a table in the factory.

"What is this place?" he asked as he began to look around.

"This is Ozone Central," I told him. "Go ahead. Look in the van."

David opened the van to find it filled with Ozone. He looked back over at me with a large grin, knowing that we were about to put an end to it once and for all.

"You've been busy. I mean, how the hell did you find him? How did you find this?" he asked, beginning to look amazed.

"It's a long story. I'll be sure to tell you later. Right now, we have another matter to attend to," I claimed as we made our way over Jordan Adams. David removed the tarp to see Adams' terrified expression. He saw the two of us standing over him. His eyes began to flutter as they began to adjust from the black tarp, he'd been staring at for over a day. He was also breathing rather hard, probably because he'd spent so much time underneath the tarp and in a car trunk. As we both knew that this was the end of both Adams and his Ozone operation, I decided that he should at least be entitled to speak before he died. I removed that tape over his mouth.

"Ah! What is this?" asked Adams, sounding as if he was struggling to piece together what was happening.

"This is the end," answered David. As I watched him walk around the table to taunt Adams, the words he said reminded me of when I'd killed Arthur Phillips, not even a year ago. He said the exact same words in the exact same chilling tone. The tone of disgust with personal pain the back of his voice. A pain that could only truly be rectified in blood. It made me wonder if I'd had the same expression on my face when I taunted Phillips that David had on his face. "The end of your business. The end of your damn drug. The end of you."

"You?" asked Adams, squinting his eyes and recognizing David. "You should be dead. That dosage alone should've…"

"It didn't," interrupted David, leaning closer towards Adams as he glanced over to me with a smile. "Thanks to him."

Adams then looked over and saw me standing over him, right across from David. By this point, he knew he was doomed. I could see it in his eyes. I also noticed his sweat began to slide on the table. The only thing that bothered me was the slight amount of satisfaction I had in seeing that look of terror on his face.

"Look, I don't know who you guys are, but just listen. Look over there," he stated as he began to lean over towards his parked vans. "That supply over there is worth millions. Just take it."

"We don't want your drugs," I told him.

"Okay. Well, I have money, lots. Seriously, just let me go. How much? Give me a number," he continued to plead.

"Fifty-three," stated David with disgust still in his voice. It was clear that Adams didn't understand, as his face turned from terror to confusion. I then thought that if he was going to die, he should at least understand why.

"You look confused," I stated as he looked back over to me. I then looked over to David. "Doesn't he?"

"Yeah, he does," stated David.

"Well, let me explain it to you. You see, that's the number of confirmed deaths from your poison over the course of the last few months, and that's just based on the state's record," I said as David handed me some of the police files from work as I decided to list some off. "Robert Hamilton. Curt Anderson. He was a veteran who came home from war damaged and was hoping for a way to ease his painful memories, not completely end them. Brittany Hall, a mother of four."

"That's terrible, but it's not my fault," muttered out Adams, with no sympathy in his voice. I continued to flip a few of the files as I began to get angrier.

"What about Rebecca Kerns? She was a twenty-year-old college dropout, peer-pressured by a few of her friends to try something new. Jarrett Weldon, another college student, twenty-two-years-old, about a year away from graduating from Eastcliff State with a law degree. He wanted to protect people, but college tends to stress kids out; life stressed him out. Nicole Kennedy, a seventeen-year-old high school student dealing with the same kind of stress of growing up, and she was almost robbed of that chance when your drug caused her to overdose and put her in the hospital."

"You're wanting to kill me because a few stupid kids decided to do stupid things?" asked Adams.

"Oh, careful…" I started as David completely lost his patience and punched Adams in the face.

"Ow!" cried Adams.

"I tried to stop you. You see, that seventeen-year-old that I mentioned, that's his daughter," I said as I watched him turn back over to David, who was nearly red with fury.

"Look," started Adams, as he tried to spit away the blood from his running nose into his mouth. "I'm sorry about your daughter. I am, but I can't be held responsible for what someone else does, especially when I haven't even met them!"

"Even if you're responsible for creating the drug that's killed so many people?" David asked.

"So, what? If you take too much of anything, it'll kill you. Drugs, alcohol, even water. You know what they call that? Drowning! You don't call the water company if someone drowns, do you? Just like you can't blame a gun company if someone is shot and killed after it's purchased. I don't force anyone to do anything they don't already want to do. If you're looking for an enemy here, it's the human condition."

"Oh, for the love of…" started David, who walked away for a moment as both Adams and I watched.

"People are always going to choose to do drugs. Killing me won't change anything!" shouted Adams as David walked back to us with a needle completely filled with Ozone as he handed it to me, much to Adams dismay.

"Well, that's where you're wrong, because there will be one less drug on the streets," I told him as I injected him with his own brand of human healing. "I figure you should at least reap the fruits of your labor once before you die."

Adams sat on the table before he began to thrash in front of the both of us. I must admit, it was somewhat disturbing to actually see someone begin to overdose before my very eyes. I looked over to David, whose eyes didn't blink once as Adams continued to struggle and squirm. After a moment or so, Adams eventually stopped thrashing. I wasn't sure if he was dead or near death or even care enough to check because I knew either way, he was done.

"What next?" I asked David. David looked at me for a brief second and then looked past me and began to point at the vans filled with the drug behind me.

"We destroy it. All of it," he answered in a disturbingly calm tone.

"How?" I asked.

"Burn it," he suggested. "We need to burn it and make sure it all goes up in smoke."

"What about him?" I asked as we looked down upon Jordan Adams.

"Him too," he responded. We began to collect our files and then left Adams there for a moment to buy gas to burn Adams and his drugs. We decided to drive a few blocks so no one would ever be able to make the connection between us and the fire we were about to start.

It wasn't long before we returned to the factory. We began to pour gasoline all over the floor and inside and around the narcotic-filled vans. I stopped and watched as David began to pour the rest of the canister on Adams, before throwing it aside. We left the office intact in the hopes that the police would discover it and tie the Ozone back to Adams. David was the one who lit the fire as we quickly made haste on our exit.

By the time we made it out, the building was beginning to smoke. It took us a matter of seconds to leave, and we did not even look back on our work. We figured that once the fire was tied to a drug operation, the police would believe the fire was started by a rival gang in the area, someone who'd been pissed off by Adams, which really wasn't a stretch. We then made our way back to his house. I got out and decided to make my way home.

"So, what are you planning to do with the money you took from Adams?" David asked. It occurred to me that I still had put little thought into the money I had taken.

"I don't know. You were the one who told me to grab it," I told him. "I assumed you had a few ideas."

"I just figured that it would be such a waste," he stated.

"Actually, I do have an idea. You do still have the files for those who had overdosed by the Ozone, right?" I asked. David nodded.

"You want to give it back to the people he hurt?" he asked as I nodded. I then pulled it from my trunk and pulled out a few bills, before closing it and handing it to him.

"Some of it, yeah. It may be a little short of what they deserve, but I also figured it would be enough for Jessica and I to put down a deposit when we decide to look for a place together."

"You're a good man, Logan," he told me as he began to make his way to his own car to handle the money.

I couldn't help but think about what he said. Was I a good man? I mean, I'd still like to think so, but I did just help murder a man, and not for the first time. I knew that there was a line between good and evil. I'm just afraid that I've already crossed it. Was I still a good person for doing something bad to worse people, or was I truly just as bad as them? I figured that after everything we'd just been through, it was a question that was better suited for another day.

Chapter 18

New beginnings

Over the next several days, the news broadcast the fire in Eastcliff, primarily because of the drugs that were found in the area. Eventually, they were able to identify Jordan Adams as the deceased body through his dental records. They found some of the remaining records that proved that Adams' real estate business was a front for his drug operation. I must admit, I didn't keep tabs on the total amount of drugs that had survived the fire, if any.

Although the police were still investigating the fire, they thought, as we'd wanted, that it was a gang-related incident or that a pissed off member of Adams' staff killed him and burned the place to the ground. There was also speculation that something went wrong and Adams committed suicide by overdosing on the drugs, before setting the fire. No matter what theories surrounded the fire, none of it could be traced back to David or myself.

Now, both the Ozone epidemic and Adams were behind me. It was time to move on with the next chapter of my life, and it all began tonight. After several years of sleepless nights, ridiculously long essays, and enough stress for several lifetimes, I was finally graduating from Eastcliff State College with my bachelor's degree in criminal justice.

As I found my way standing around in the hallway in my own blue cap and gown, I saw easily a hundred more students and professors wearing the same as all of our friends and family sat in the auditorium waiting for us.

It was only slightly more overwhelming than when I graduated from high school, probably because I knew at that time that I was going to college, but this was it. Many of my fellow graduates were taking pictures with each other. Some of them were crying and hugging each other as they began to come to the realization that they would likely never see each other again. I slowly made my way around as I began to say goodbye to some of my oldest college friends. I walked over to see Jade and Trevor, who were taking pictures of each other, along with another classmate of ours, Chloe Cassidy.

"Hey, buddy," said Trevor, who surprisingly approached me with a hug. Jade and Chloe then proceeded to give me one as well.

"So, this is really it?" I asked as they all smiled with a hint of sadness.

"Yeah, I guess it is," stated Chloe.

"So, we all know that you're going to law school," I stated, looking over to Jade, before turning to the other two. "What about you guys?"

"Well, I'm thinking about going to work for victim advocates," stated Chloe.

"Well, I hope that goes well for you," stated Trevor, looking skeptical. "I hear that can be a tough job."

"Well, that's why somebody needs to do it," she stated, as he nodded. "What about you? Still thinking about becoming a homicide detective?"

"Well, to tell you the truth, I've actually been thinking about becoming a private investigator, and starting my own business," Trevor stated.

"Really?" I asked, actually surprised by that concept, as it seemed so different from everyone else's.

"You sound surprised," he stated. I shrugged.

"More because of the fact that you're graduating, not so much because you're starting your own business," I told him with half a grin.

"You're an asshole," he said as he hugged me again.

"You're a punk," I responded.

"All of the emotions are so real over here," stated Payton, as she began to walk over with Brice Katona and Armando Diaz. Everyone exchanged their new set of hugs and handshakes as we all began to come to the realization that we had all made it. We all began to take our fair share of pictures with each other.

"So, what are you guys up to?" asked Brice.

"We were talking about what we're going to do from this point forward," stated Jade.

"Yeah, Jade's going to finish law school to become a defense attorney. Chloe was telling us how she's going to become a victim-advocate worker, and our friend Trevor finally revealed to us that he is planning on becoming a private investigator."

"Oh, that's cool," stated Armando.

"It fits because you like sticking your nose in other people's business as it is," stated Payton as he decided to extend his middle finger and a smile as she walked over to pat him on the back. "You know, we still love you for it."

"Yeah, but what about you guys?" asked Trevor.

"Well, I'm planning on becoming a forensic psychologist," claimed Brice.

"You guys already know that I'm going for Crime Scene Investigator for the state department. I like forensics, but I'll have to keep going to school for a little longer," responded Payton.

"Nerd," I coughed, as she looked over at me with anger in her eyes.

"Hey, fuck you," she said as the two of us gazed at each other, before we all started laughing.

"What about you two?" asked Brice.

"Well, I've sent in my application for the police academy, but haven't heard back yet. Then I figured I'd later go into forensics and try to stay local as much as I can," I told them.

"Nerd," coughed Payton.

"You bet your ass I am," I told her, as we all began to laugh again.

"Well, after everything that's been going on with the Ozone epidemic, I've been thinking about going to work for the DEA," Armando stated.

"You had better run, Trevor," stated Jade, as he looked somewhat shocked.

"I've just been thinking about it, but…" continued Armando. "I actually am planning on moving back to Florida, where I sent my application to one of the police academies down there where my family is originally from."

"Ugh! I'm going to miss you guys, so much," Brice stated as he began to hug each one of us independently. I'm not entirely sure if he even really knew Trevor or Armando, but that really didn't stop him from getting emotional when saying goodbye to all of us.

"Love you," said Payton.

"We'll miss you, too," I told him as he walked away from us. I then saw that Jessica was over talking with Jacob. As much as it hurt, I knew that it was time to say goodbye to my criminal justice friends that I've come to know over the years. "As much as I hate to go, I got to go talk to some other people."

"See you soon, Mills," stated Payton.

"It's cool. We'll see you in line, buddy," stated Trevor as they all returned to their conversation. I then made my way over to my closer friends. I watched Krista approach the two of them, trying to fix her cap and giving Jessica a hug.

"Hey, buddy," Jacob said as he noticed me approaching. We also gave each other a loud slap on each other's back as I gave Krista a hug as well.

"It's good to see you guys," I told them as I took Jessica's hand to hold. She returned the courtesy by smiling as we turned back to our friends. "It's been a crazy last few weeks."

"Yeah, tell me about it," stated Jacob. Krista looked slightly irritated as both Jessica and I looked at him. "Sorry, but seriously, how's your dad…and your sister?"

"They're okay," answered Jessica, looking hopeful. "Well, dad is recovering alright from his ordeal and Nicky…she's going to spend this summer with some relatives in Indiana to…get some help."

There was a small awkward silence, for a brief moment, seeing as how none of us really knew what to say. I knew that Jessica had already been forced to suffer more than she or her family deserved, but the fact was that there was little that any of us could say or do that would have much of an effect. Krista then hugged Jessica again.

"It's going to be okay. She is going to be okay," Krista told her. Jacob and I looked over at each other, not really sure of what to say next.

"So, is Nicky, or your dad, here to see you walk across the stage?" asked Krista.

"Yeah, Nicky and Daddy are both here. They're inside with Logan's mom," Jessica stated.

"That's good," stated Jacob. I nodded as I thought about my mother and was glad that she wasn't in there sitting alone. I hated that my father wasn't there by her side, but I'd like to think he was still here with us in spirit.

"Alright, everyone. We're about to walk inside. Just like in rehearsal, this morning!" shouted a woman I assumed to be the dean of the college, but may very well have just been the graduation administrator. After several years, you'd think that I'd actually paid enough attention to know who the head of the school was, but alas, I had enough to think about instead of tedious titles like that. "Get in line!"

"I'm going to miss you guys," Jacob said as he hugged me. "Just to be clear, we are still going to hang out, right?"

"Of course, man," I told him. "Somebody has to kick your ass in air hockey."

"Hey, watch it," he said, as he began to look slightly mad. I knew it wasn't real anger from the stupid grin still on his face.

"Love you, too," I told him as they began to walk away towards the other childhood and early education majors.

"See you later?" I asked Jessica as she began to walk towards her fellow biology majors.

"I'll see you on the other side," she assured me with a smile as I let go of her hand. I then made my way back over to my criminal justice friends as we began to form the line. It was easy for us to get in line as I knew that I only had to find Payton and stand in front of her. I passed by Armando, who stood behind Chloe. I then passed Jade and Trevor and found Payton and squeezed in between her and a classmate whose name I honestly couldn't remember at the top of my head, but whose last name was likely between the letters H through M.

"You ready?" I asked Payton.

"Hell, no," she uttered quickly. I couldn't help but softly laugh as I knew exactly what she was feeling, as I was feeling the same. We then saw one of the professors whom I hadn't personally taken, was signaling for the line to start moving, and we went into the auditorium where hundreds of friends and family members sat all around the room.

As we made our way to our seats, I quickly glanced around the room to see if I could see anybody I recognized. After several steps, I quickly glanced over to see Jacob's family over by one of the staircases. I could see his brother trying to tend to his baby sitting next to him. I continued to glance around the many faces and finally saw Jessica's brother and sister, sitting next to their loved ones on the opposite side of the room from the stage.

I saw my own mother sitting next to Jessica's mother, both of whom were trying to wave and catch our attention among the cheering crowd. I briefly waved at them before making my way to my row and sitting down as Payton and another person whom I didn't really know sat next to me. It took several minutes for everyone else behind us to sit down. It took an extra minute or two for everyone in the audience to stop clapping and cheering for the actual dean to make his way to the microphone.

"Good evening, ladies and gentlemen. Tonight, we are here to celebrate the spring class of twenty twenty-one. Each student here has worked tirelessly over the last several years. We will bring everyone up by major of study, one at a time. We're going to ask that everyone stay seated and hold their applause to the end to ensure that everyone hears their name being called," the dean started to say. I must admit that I really didn't pay attention to the rest of what he had to say. I looked to see where the rest of my friends were sitting.

I looked around as the dean continued to prattle on to see that Armando and Jade were sitting close to right in front of me. I could see that both Jacob and Krista were also sitting next to each other in the second row on the other set of seats with the other students graduating with education degrees. I could only tell it was Jacob, who continued to look around. I'd like to think he was looking for me as I nodded to him. He decided to return my gesture with a smile as he began to scratch his face to quickly extend his middle finger to me one last time before we were official graduates. I smiled and decided to return the gesture and saw him laugh.

I looked over to see Jessica in the front row of my section of seats with the other biology majors. I only knew it was her because of the back of her hair and the way that she designed the top of her graduation cap. It was only a second after I found her among the crowd that she began to stand up. I realized that the dean had finished his speech. She made her way up the stage as she turned over to see me giving her a huge grin on my face. She looked back at me for a brief second with a smile as she made her way towards the stage.

Jessica quickly made her way to the stage. The other rows began to line-up, including Jacob and Krista. I knew it wouldn't be long before it was our turn, but I wanted to make sure that I paid attention when they called her name. Despite the dean's instructions for everyone in the audience to hold their applause until the end, I figured I could find a loophole since I wasn't technically in the audience, not that many people followed the dean's instructions anyway. The moment they called Jessica's name, I couldn't help but let out a whistle. It didn't take her long to figure out where it was coming from and she gave a slight blush as she shook the dean's hand. Payton then tapped my arm.

"Don't embarrass her," she suggested, looking slightly aggravated. I figured that she had a point that in my efforts to show pride in Jessica, I may have incidentally made her feel uncomfortable, but I'm sure she'll find it in her heart to forgive me. Besides, I was her boyfriend. Although I didn't have a specific rulebook, I knew such a book surely would include a section that required me to show support to the point of embarrassment.

As Jacob walked across the stage next, he couldn't help but deliver his own peace sign to the audience. After he had finished, Krista began to walk across the stage next. It was time for my row to stand up. This was it, the moment I had spent the last four years of my life preparing for. I stood up to see Jessica smiling as I walked past her on my way to the stage, I also saw Jacob and Krista both looking at me from their seats as I walked past them.

"Now, here are the graduates for a bachelor's degree in criminal justice," the announcer stated.

"Chloe Cassidy!" he said, as I saw Chloe make her way across the stage. Although I knew that she was excited to be graduating from college, I could tell that she seemed a bit nervous as she walked across the stage with so many people in the galleries watching her.

"Armando Diaz!" he announced again. I saw Armando smile as we walked up to grab his diploma, but I could see that he was nervous. I also knew that every name that was announced was a moment closer to being mine before it was my time to shine.

"Jade Foster, Magna Cum laude," announced the dean.

"What's that?" Payton asked, behind me. "I've been hearing it a couple times as people walk across the stage."

"It's like a special honor you get when you have a high enough grade point average at graduation," I informed her.

"I don't even know my grade point average," she stated.

"Well, I'll cross my fingers for you and hope you'll extend me the same courtesy," I told her as I saw Trevor make his way to the stage.

"Trevor Hatcher, cum laude!" announced the dean. I completely turned around to Payton as we both looked in shock over Trevor's success and figured that it would be a final fond memory of our friend. After the person in front of me walked across the stage, my feet approached the stage with the single thought of pride that this was truly it.

"I'll see you on the other side," I told Payton, as I knew she would be next after me.

"Logan Mills, cum laude," announced the dean as I made my way to the top of the stage. For a brief moment, I felt my heart begin to pound rapidly as I walked on stage and saw the hundreds of people, my friends, my family, and others that I cared about, watching as I left this part of my life behind as I shook the dean's hand and took my diploma from him.

"Payton Murphy, cum laude!" I heard as I stepped down from the stage, realizing that my moment of triumph was already over. I glanced around to see Payton walking behind me. I could tell that she was also a little nervous about walking in front of a large crowd like this one, but it was less than a moment later that she returned to her seat next to mine. As we both sat down, she sighed.

"Well, this is really it, isn't it?" she asked as we both continued to look at the other graduates continuing to walk across the stage.

"This is it," I stated as I nodded.

"We had some fun times," she stated.

"Yeah, we did," I agreed with half a smile, beginning to reminisce on all the wonderful memories I've shared with my friends over the past four years.

"I just thought it would feel different, you know," she stated, looking uneased.

"How so?" I asked.

"Well, this is supposed to be a happy day. One of the biggest accomplishments we will ever have. Back in high school, it felt different because we knew we were coming here, but now, I don't know, I'm kind of bittersweet," she claimed.

"I know you're not going to miss all the work, right? All the stress and the other bullshit, right?" I asked in the hopes of aggravating her one last time.

"No, I'm not going to miss the work," she said, as she let out a soft chuckle.

"Hmm, I'll miss you, too," I told her as I patted her leg next to mine. After a few more minutes, the last student walked across the stage as the dean stood in front of us one more time. After spending another roughly thirty minutes on the rest of the other majors, the ceremony began to come to its end.

"Graduates, you may move your tassels," announced the dean. Everyone did as they were instructed as the last act as students; we moved our tassels.

"Ladies and gentlemen, it is my honor to present to you the Spring Class of twenty twenty-one," he announced. For the next several minutes, everyone in the stands stood up and began clapping. I'm pretty sure everyone did the same thing that I did and looked around at all the applause that we had spent so long trying to earn. I looked over at my family, with Jessica's seeing everyone I cared about standing up, smiling and clapping.

After several minutes, music began to play, indicating it was the end of the ceremony, and I turned around to see that the graduates were beginning to stand up and leave the auditorium. For a moment, it was hard for me to stand. I realized that the moment I walked out the door, it was completely and truly over. I took a deep breath. I thought of all the everything that we had all been leading to this moment life. I knew that whatever life was about to throw at me, I would surely be able to handle it, especially after everything I've already been through lately. I then stood up and followed Payton out of the auditorium to begin my new life.

As the graduates began to leave the auditorium, those in the audience began to do the same. It was less than a minute before the entire lobby was crowded. Everyone began to look for their loved ones. With the blue graduation gowns and everyone in their nice clothes, ties, and dresses, the entire lobby became a literal ocean of people. It became difficult to breathe and damn near impossible to not bump into someone.

I knew that it was likely that everyone was in the exact same position that I was in, as we were all trying to find our close loved ones in this thick crowd of people. I decided to stand still for a minute, which by itself may not have been the brightest idea, since the area became even more crowded as everyone began taking pictures and talking with all their loved ones.

After a moment of searching, I finally saw Jessica standing in front of Krista as the two hugged each other. Krista began to walk away as I approached her. Jessica then gave me a hug as she jumped into my arms. I kissed her once on the cheek.

"We did it!" she exclaimed, with what may have been the largest smile I'd ever seen on her face.

"Yeah, we did," I told her as I kissed the side of her forehead. We began to look around for our families. I took her hand, and once again attempted to make our path through the large crowd.

"You see them?" I asked her as we tried to focus on, well, anyone that we knew.

"There!" she was forced to say loudly as hundreds of conversations began to fill the lobby. I must admit, I was having trouble seeing any of their faces.

"Where?" I shouted. She then pointed somewhere through the crowd as I tried to look. She ended up taking the lead and my hand as we walked through the crowd. After another minute of bumping into random strangers in the crowd, I could see her mother's blonde hair and soon everyone else around her, including my own mother.

"There they are!" shouted Doris Kennedy as she jumped and gave her daughter a huge hug, and proceeded to give me one. My mother then proceeded to give us each one next, as did everyone else in the family.

"Okay, everyone. Take a picture of the happy couple!" requested Mrs. Kennedy. "You two, get closer and smile."

Jessica and I smiled as we both got closer. I put my arm around her shoulder as she put her arm across my side. Nicky and both our mothers began to take many pictures, to the point where I was nearly blinded by all the flashes. By the time I looked back over to Jessica, I could tell she was having a similar issue as she began to squint her eyes before she let out a soft giggle.

"We're so proud of you!" my mom stated as she began to hug us again.

"Thank you," responded Jessica.

"We are really proud of you both," stated David, as he looked over to me and smiled. The truth was that I was just grateful to be able to be here, surrounded by the people who love and care about me. "Hang on, I'm going to borrow Logan for a minute."

"Okay. Hurry back," stated my mother as the two of us tried to make our way out of the crowd in order to speak privately.

"How do you feel?" I asked him.

"My oldest daughter just graduated from college. I'm here to celebrate the occasion with my family while knowing that Jordan Adam's Ozone operation is being dismantled as we speak. So, I can honestly say that I'm doing great, thanks to you," stated David as I looked down, not really sure if either one of us had any right to call what we did a win.

"What's wrong?" asked David.

"I just can't help but wonder if what we did was right or not," I responded.

"Logan, you have to remember that Jordan Adams was the bad guy. He was the ringleader of the Ozone epidemic that killed dozens of people, including a close friend of yours. Not to mention the fact that he nearly killed me and my daughter."

"I know what we did. I know that our actions are going to help save a lot of people in the large scheme of things, but we still killed several people to do it. I mean, Walker, Clark, and Adams. Do you not at least question whether our actions of late were right or wrong?"

"The way that I see it, every single one of them were murderers, one way or another. They weren't victims, they had victims. As much as you may not like it, you were right about what you told me the night Joe Walker died. Our actions were nothing short of a necessary evil," he stated. I nodded as I remembered that I told him that when he caught me standing over Joe Walker's body, but there was still a small part of me that wasn't sure anymore.

"I know. I'm just afraid that the more we get caught up in these…situations, the less humanity that either one of us will have left," I told him.

"Does that mean you want to stop?" he asked.

"There is a part of me that desperately wants to say yes. There is also another part of me that thinks about what you said and what would've happened if the police failed to stop them without help. What next? How many people will have suffered like both of our families have?"

"So, what are you saying?" asked David, as he crossed his arms, giving me a puzzled expression.

"I'm saying that criminals are getting smarter and should the smart ones like Arthur Phillips or Jordan Adams ever begin making trouble for us, again, then maybe, we'll be forced to do something about it," I told David. He started at me again, before nodding and accepting my terms, before shaking my hand. "You do still have that file on Harold Reeves, don't you?"

"Yeah, it's still in my car," he said.

"Okay, remind me in a couple of days and I'll have a look at it." I told him as I looked back over at our loved ones who were still talking. Jessica was taking selfies with her siblings.

"By the way, I've been meaning to give you something," David said as he pulled out an envelope from his jacket pocket.

"What's this?" I asked as he smiled.

"Open it," he suggested with a smile. I opened the letter to see that it was from the Rockgate police academy that I had applied to last month. It stated that my application had been accepted. I couldn't help but look shocked, "After everything that happened recently, I was contemplating whether or not I should give you that or not. But like you said, criminals are getting smarter. It's time we started hiring smarter officers, too. Training starts next month."

"Thank you," I told him, as I quickly found myself shaking his hand again. The two of us walked back over to our families as Andrea began to signal us.

"Here, family photo," stated Andrea, who took her phone and

asked all of us to stand close together. I stood next to Jessica and my mother as David walked behind all three of his children, standing next to his wife. We all stared at Andrea, who took our picture together, one that would end up being one of my favorite photos. Afterwards, I went to take off my cap and gown before we all headed out the door.

As we all went outside, I saw that the moonlight was once again shining upon all of us, and I once again found myself staring at a beautifully crescent moon. Even if I did end up breaking my goal of being involved in another killing, it was still for the right reasons. Despite all the darkness I knew that was still inside of me, I figured that the moonlight may have been the perfect metaphor for my situation. With the stars serving as many specs of light within the darkness, I liked to think that both David and I still had a positive light within us and only using our own personal darkness when it becomes an absolute necessity.

"Beautiful night, isn't it?" asked Jessica as she began to hold my hand. We both gazed into the night sky. I nodded as I looked back at her. By this point, she had already taken off her cap and gown and was showing off her dress.

"Yes, it is," I told her.

"We're going out to eat. You are still going to join us, right?" she asked.

"Yeah, mom and I will catch up," I told her, as we ended up kissing each other. With the cool spring wind softly blowing, I felt as if fate was truly giving me a win. The truth of the matter was that I wasn't entirely sure that I deserved her anymore. I wasn't sure if what David and I had done was truly good or evil, but was the idea of embracing the darkness for the light such a bad thought after all?

I gazed back into the night sky, hoping for some kind of answer, but realized that whether or not what David and I had done was right or wrong, it was effective. As much as I disliked it, I'm not delusional in thinking that taking a life isn't wrong, but when I began to think of how many people we saved by stopping Adams, it did make me feel better. So, maybe my questions on morality could afford to be put on hold for a while.

Although I think it is safe to say that we all have our issues on the matter to work out, we will still be around to support one another when it's all said and done. Now was not the time to worry, now was the time to celebrate. The fact of the matter was that both our families are once again back together. Everyone was safe, healthy, and happy. Jessica and I were now officially college graduates, and maybe, maybe this truly was enough.

I stood back and gazed upon the building one more time as I turned around and went back to my car, where my mother was waiting for me. As we followed the Kennedy's to dinner to celebrate our graduation, I realized that I was driving over to the next chapter of my life. Where I was sure that life was going to take us, I couldn't say for certain, but one thing was certain, though, it wasn't a question that I had to worry about tonight.

Grant Heming

Logans Lawful Limbs

Coming This Winter

Other works

School of Payback (2019)

High School is a place where you grow into the person that you're meant to be. As a student, the biggest stress' in life are supposed to come from the social drama like rumors and relationships, getting good grades in class, puberty. But when his school becomes the target of a dangerous conspiracy at work, sixteen-year-old Austin Murdock, will fight for not only his own life, but the lives of his closest friends. Murdock will be faced with impossible odds and forced into situations that not only make him question himself as a simple country boy, but as a decent human being.

War of Payback (2020)

One year after the shooting at Greenville High and having his story known nationwide, Austin Murdock has become a local town hero as he and his closest friends, try to get back to a sense of normalcy after their traumatic experiences. But as his home has come under siege of a massive increase in crime and death, Austin begins to believe that saving Damian Simmons life may not have been in the best interest of his home. Murdock will be forced to question everything he knows about Simmons and the criminal organization known as the Hellenes in this riveting sequel to "School of Payback."

City of Payback (2021)

Damaged and living only for revenge, Austin Murdock allies himself with his closest friends for a final confrontation with the sinister Hellenes organization. Secrets and lies will be revealed as Murdock attempts to keep the promise he made to his deceased lover, Sidney Moore, and finish his vendetta by murdering his former friend, Charles Taylor, and end the Hellenes and the corrupt Mayor of Stay Bay, Damian Simmons, once and for all. Murdock will be pushed to his limits as he is forced to decide who he really is and who he is meant to be in the final installment of the Payback trilogy.

Living Logans Life (2021)

Life is great for Logan Mills. He's in his final year of college while planning on a career in law enforcement. He has a great girlfriend, and a loving family. However, his perfect life is about to be turned upside down when he's begins to examine an active serial killer investigation and stumbles upon a group of killers terrorizing his hometown. With no evidence and a personal vendetta against the group, Mills may be forced to throw away his own personal ethics and take the law into his own hands in this thrilling tale of morality, revenge, and survival.

Made in the USA
Columbia, SC
11 March 2022